Copyright © 2011

by Anita Bartholomew
Published by Bartholomew & Co., Inc.

ISBN: 978-0-9839922-0-2

Cover design by Oscar Trugler

Cover photograph by Anita Bartholomew

Circus—Fiction. Ghost—Fiction. Supernatural—Fiction. Paranormal—Fiction. Historical—Fiction.

The Midget's House

A CIRCUS STORY...

A LOVE STORY...

A GHOST STORY

Anita Bartholomew

PROLOGUE

MARCH 2004

THE HEIGHT OF THE LAST FLORIDA REAL ESTATE BOOM

A faded gray Buick clunker idled in the winding drive. Palm trees whipped by the wind blowing off Sarasota Bay cast tentacle-like shadows across its chassis.

The plump young night nurse slipped out of the house by the side door. She hadn't dared leave until she was certain her patient was asleep but, having heard the deep, even snores, she felt confident that the amply medicated old lady would be unconscious at least until daybreak.

Enid Parker's bones had gone brittle and her muscles had atrophied, making it impossible for her to do much beyond lie in her bed if she did awaken. Her hair, long since leached of all color, had thinned to baby fine strands. As senile and infirm as she was though, Enid could still make a ruckus when she felt ignored. The nurse had earned several screeches of complaint over the past three evenings, which was how long she'd been employed as Enid Parker's caregiver. She was glad for the work and accustomed to difficult patients so she didn't consider turning down the assignment even after learning that an earlier nurse had walked off the job in the middle of the night, blithering incomprehensibly. Some other nurses simply couldn't hack it, she knew, but she didn't have much sympathy for them. Handling the job, where crotchety old folks were concerned, meant sucking it up when they heaved verbal abuse, not just parceling out the pills at the appropriate hours or cleaning up the messes from their saggy bottoms to their soiled linens.

But now that the old woman slept, she saw no reason to lurk in the creaky old house through the night.

She darted to the car, swung her wide hips onto the passenger seat, and quietly pulled the door closed behind her. The young man at the wheel put his sputtering vehicle in gear, drove it past the decorative iron gate and on toward the outside world. She'd be back in plenty of time with no one the wiser.

*

Despite enough medication to sedate a Clydesdale horse, Enid Parker did not rest easily. Moments after her nurse's departure, her creped eyelids fluttered open.

"Papa?" she murmured. "Are we going to the circus? Can I ride the elephant? You promised."

Not getting an answer, she reached out tentatively with one arthritic hand, as if attempting to see through her fingertips. Wispy white eyebrows bunched together as clouded pupils strained to focus.

Then anger sparked in those dull eyes.

"Lucinda!" she shrieked. "You get out of here. Get out. GET OUT OF MY HOUSE. My house ..." Her heart accelerated, pumping blood through tired veins and arteries, tingling her desiccated skin to an almost healthy pink.

Forgetting her infirmity, Enid forced herself upright, determined to eject the intruder.

The effort exhausted what little life was left in her.

1. MARISA DELANO

Marisa Delano turned her ancient white convertible west toward Indian Beach, an older section of Sarasota that had once been home to several of the circus kings.

An eight-foot high wall, stucco-coated, and painted the ubiquitous pale Florida pink, enclosed her Aunt Enid's estate. She drove through the wall's single gap, past the ornate wrought iron gate that Harry Scanlon had thoughtfully left open. When had she last been inside? She tried to remember. She couldn't have been more than seven years old.

The once manicured grounds had reverted to jungle. Massive banyans threatened to engulf the playful cherub statues that lined either side of the drive. Split leaf philodendrons that might dwell as polite little house plants in New York or Boston, here tangled into impossibly long tropical vines and intertwined with bougainvillea.

As her tires scattered the gravel, the dread that had been poking at the back of her consciousness pushed its way forward and clenched her chest.

She pulled into a space in front of the garage halfway down the drive, across from Enid's curious little house.

She and her mother had once lived in the apartment above the garage but Marisa felt no nostalgia for it; couldn't remember what it looked like inside. It was just the place where she and her mom had slept nights. Enid's house, where they spent the daylight hours — that felt like home.

For several long moments she stood outside, drinking in the details, determined to get the most from this last visit. The exterior badly needed painting, and some of the wood trim was rotted at the edges. Still, it exuded magic: the carved shutters, the medieval look of the scrolled black ironwork, the peaks and gables.

She rested her cheek against its heavy arched wooden door. Her fingers lightly grazed the wall. Her cousin Otto, Enid's apparent heir, had made no secret of his intention to tear down the house and sell off the land the moment Enid was in the ground. He already had a buyer.

She would have pleaded with him to preserve it but what could she say? It was already as good as gone.

*

Like an enchanted cottage in a Brothers Grimm tale, Enid's house belonged in the European countryside of a couple of centuries ago. Instead, here in Florida it incongruously sat, a half-mile south of the opulent mansion and museum built by John Ringling, the youngest of the legendary circus brothers, with a line of Longboat Key's high-rise condominiums staring at it from across the bay.

Sometime in the 1920s, Enid's father, Cyrus Parker, had moved the house to his sprawling 22-acre bay front estate. Nobody seemed to know where it came from, only that it originated elsewhere. It was designed in Norman revival style, but slightly scaled down. An average-sized person would find it comfortable enough but an especially tall man might need to duck to get through certain doorways.

Cyrus Parker had once owned a traveling circus and the local legend was that he had housed his circus midgets there. Unlikely as the legend was, people in the neighborhood still called it the midget house.

When Marisa was small, her mother had moved them to the estate so she could nurse the distant cousin who it was easier to call simply "Aunt" Enid. Marisa's mother had complained of strange sensations and refused to be in the house after dark. Marisa felt the magic too, but reacted in the opposite fashion. She would sneak up the stairs, despite being warned against it, trailing her fingers along the walls, wandering from room to room.

She'd been a lonely little girl but, in the midget house, it was easy to conjure up an imaginary playmate who she chased up the turret staircase and around the rooms until the friend disappeared.

As Marisa got older, she outgrew such fantasies but not the house. She wept for days when her mother told her that they were moving away. Enid had flown into a rage about some imagined transgression and refused to have anything more to do with them.

*

Marisa noticed movement at a second story window. Harry must be upstairs already, cataloguing Enid's belongings and impatient for her to come inside.

She composed herself, took hold of the heavy iron knocker, and banged it against the door.

Harry opened it quickly. The smile crinkling his blue eyes extended all the way to the edges of his grey brushcut hair. Marisa knew him slightly from when he and her mother dated, which they had on and off for a few years. With a mock-dramatic sweep of his arm, he welcomed her inside.

"Congratulations, Marisa," the old lawyer barked. "All this is now yours."

"Don't tease me, Harry. It's hard enough saying good-bye."

"No, I'm serious. Enid left the property to your mother. Your mother passed away before Enid. You're named as the contingent beneficiary."

"What about Otto?"

"He got a little something in the trust. Not what he wanted, of course —"

"But he's already sold it."

"I don't doubt Otto expected more," said Harry. "But he can't sell what he doesn't own."

The news jolted her, making her lightheaded. There's a catch, she thought. But she stopped herself from questioning Harry further. If it was all a mistake, she didn't want to know, not yet.

As she stepped over the threshold, the stink of mildew brought her elation down a notch. Even so, the charm of the place broke through.

The walls of the foyer and staircase were paneled in pecky cypress and led into a library with exposed beams. Off in one corner was the tiny stone fireplace with a tile hearth that Marisa remembered from years before.

The place was unkempt, the dark Victorian furniture dusty, its upholstery shredding, but she loved it all, could imagine it all, cleaned up, painted, and patched like new again. Harry stood silently by, just watching. She plopped herself down on the ceramic-tiled floor of the great room.

"It's really mine?"

Harry simply nodded.

Marisa climbed the narrow staircase to the second floor. A small chandelier, coated in cobwebs, dangled from its high ceiling; its bottom-most crystals hung low. Harry ducked as he moved under it.

An antique oval mirror, in an intricately carved gold leafed frame, greeted them at the top of the landing.

She wandered into a bedroom. Almost everything was white — or at least, had once been white. Although the ceilings were too high to touch with arms stretched upward, something about the room seemed child-sized. It took a moment to recognize what it was: the bottoms of the window frames behind the window seat were level with her knees, the tops about level with her chin. She hadn't remembered that. As a child, though, she wouldn't have noticed anything unusual. Now, she had to duck down to see out.

She used the old-fashioned crank to open one of the windows, then cranked it back to shut it again. It wouldn't close all the way. Harry laughed. Marisa shrugged. In the midst of such enchantment, what did it matter if an ancient window didn't quite behave the way it ought to?

The room was decorated with ancient lace and littered with antique dolls. Cobwebs and dust bunnies didn't diminish its allure. The sun streaming through the stained glass oval above the French doors on the west wall threw the softest of rainbows across the canopy bed, painting its yellowed coverlet in lavender, rose and blue.

Marisa stepped toward the glass-paned doors but Harry blocked her way with his arm before she could walk onto the balcony. She looked where he pointed. The balcony's rusted bolts were half unfastened from the wall and rot had opened wide gaps between the wooden floor boards.

"Guess I'll put that on my list of repairs."

"That could be a very long list, young lady," Harry replied dryly. "Before you get too excited about this little rat-trap, we should talk about practicalities."

"Oh, Harry, you can't tell me you don't secretly love this place. I saw you sitting in the upstairs window seat when I drove up."

"I promise you, I have never felt the urge to gaze out that window," said Harry. "I got here only minutes before you and hadn't had a chance to go upstairs yet."

"But I saw—"

Harry interrupted. "Not up there, you didn't. Not unless Enid made her way back after the funeral service."

*

"We can sit and talk down there," said Harry, as he led her outside, pointing to some old concrete benches overlooking the water. "The mildew is wreaking havoc on my sinuses."

Marisa gazed past him to where land met water, extending the backyard for liquid blue miles.

"Right over there is where Cyrus's mansion stood." He pointed to what was left: a crumbling stone foundation, cracked marble steps, an overgrown walkway to the boat dock, and little else. The breeze tossed a soothing mist back at them.

"Now that was a house," Harry said, admiring the ruins as if he could picture it whole. "A jilted lady friend set it afire, with Cyrus Parker still in it, back in the 1920s. She tripped and cracked her skull while running from the blaze and died the same night — or so the story goes."

Harry swept his arm back toward the midget house. "As for Enid, well, she wanted to live out her last years in her own home," said Harry. "We had to sell off everything else she had to make that happen. Sold all the acreage around it a decade ago. Couple of years back, with nothing left to sell, the estate fell behind on the taxes."

Harry explained that the county had sold the rights to collect the taxes to an investor, Nicholas Young. And Young had placed a lien on the property. To keep Enid in her house, Harry had worked out a deal with Young. The house would be sold upon Enid's death and the estate would pay the investor an extra ten percent interest on the money he was owed. So, Young had agreed not to foreclose while Enid was alive but, now that she was dead, he would be expecting his money.

"Young's a good guy. I'll tell him you need a few weeks to negotiate a sale and close the deal."

"How much would I have to pay this Nicholas Young to keep the house?"

"Forget it, Marisa. You're talking about two years worth of back taxes, plus interest, figure ten, maybe twelve thousand dollars."

"But if I could come up with the money—?"

"Last year's taxes are due now, too."

"I'll get a mortgage."

"Banks want to know you can pay. Not to pry, Marisa, I gather that you're unemployed."

"It's called freelancing. And I help out Kelly a few days a week at her store."

"If this goes to foreclosure auction, it'll sell for a fraction of its worth."

"I'm not selling, Harry."

"Marisa, you have no means of support. It's not just the taxes. There's upkeep. Otto's been doing that but, after today, I wouldn't expect any help from him."

She glanced back at the house. "From the looks of things, Otto hasn't held up his half of the bargain."

Harry reached into his breast pocket, pulled out a business card, tapped at it, then handed it to her. "That developer bought up the rest of what used to be the Parker estate. Enid's property sits in the middle of the parcel and he needs it to complete his plans. He'll pay a great deal for it—more than it's worth. You'll have enough to build yourself a bigger better house," he paused and smiled for effect, "with central air conditioning and windows that actually close."

"Harry, you don't understand. Getting the house — I feel like this is a sign that the long, slow bleeding away of everything I love is ending."

"A charming notion, Marisa, but one with no basis in reality. All you have here is a derelict building taking up space on otherwise valuable land."

"No, Harry, I believe I inherited it for a reason. I think I'm supposed to save it—"

Harry's expression of fatherly disapproval stopped her mid-sentence.

"As I said, I'll see if I can buy you a little time. But we're talking weeks, not months."

She looked at the business card Harry had pressed into her hand — John Guinness Construction & Development Corp. — then tried to give it back to him.

He gently pushed her hand away. "Keep the guy's number. At least he'll offer a fair price, which is more than I can say for the vultures who'll come sniffing around soon enough."

2. LUCINDA

OTHERNESS

Lucinda was vaguely aware that the people — they must have been people, right? — who were wandering through her house had left. They appeared blurred, translucent to her; their conversations hollow, like something heard underwater.

Since entering this existence that she could only describe to herself as otherness, Lucinda had, from time to time, heard and viewed other people.

Those that broke through to wherever it was that Lucinda now existed weren't quite real to her. They moved too quickly for her to be certain they were there.

And then, as if by magic, they weren't.

Lucinda faded in and out, not knowing who or what set the rhythm.

She accepted that this was her punishment for that last night, and Cyrus's death. Alone in this peculiar hell, she was condemned to dream of her past, only to wake into emptiness.

3. Lucinda

If you looked quickly when you saw us walking together down the road, you'd maybe guess my gangly brother Albert's age at sixteen. And, considering my height and the way I clung to his hand as if letting go of it was like letting go of life itself, you'd probably suspect I was seven or so. You'd be right about my big brother, but wrong about me.

I was fifteen at the time, a year younger than Albert.

I'd been a sickly baby, and an equally sickly child. The doctor came once when I was about three. He told Mama I was going to die and there was nothing to be done about it. But I didn't die, probably because my Mama wouldn't let me, no matter what the doctor said. She wrapped me in her arms when I shivered and wiped me with cool wet cloths when I had fever. She forced me to drink broth when I was too sick to eat. And she sang to me and read to me as she did her chores.

Mama had two more children after me, boys, each normal sized and healthy, the kind Daddy was glad to have, to help him farm the acreage we leased from Cal Hodgeson, who owned almost all the land north of the creek in Hodgeson County.

I didn't grow but I survived, though I'm not sure Daddy was happy about that. What good was a daughter so small and sick she couldn't hardly work in the fields?

It was clear by the time I was thirteen, I never would grow, not any more. My breasts budded. I sprouted hair in places that women were supposed to. But my smallest brother, Jacob, then eight, outgrew me.

Mama got pregnant with a fifth child, another girl, who died as she was being born. Then Mama died too. She bled until the life poured right out of her. She was well past thirty, too old to have more babies, but you can't stop them from coming, that's what Daddy said.

Daddy got bitter after Mama's death. The way he saw it, I suspect, was that girl babies were a curse, those that died and those that lived.

He cut himself off from neighbors and family. He almost never talked to us children except to yell orders. Still, you could see the difference between the way he looked at me and the way he looked at the boys. His sons were his hope, what he stayed alive for. I just reminded him of his loss.

He called me a good-for-nothing freak — too small to marry off to any man with sense. A burden to test his virtue, that's what he said I was, my only saving grace was that I took little to feed.

He hardly raised his hand against me when Mama was alive. After she was gone, he took every excuse he could find to whup me. Dinner was late. Dinner was early, too salty, too cold. His buttons were sewed on wrong. The chickens didn't lay the way they used to.

He'd drink corn whiskey, then grab me by the hair and drag me out behind the barn. I saw Albert once run out to the yard after us. He must have heard me crying. He must have heard Daddy tell me to drop my drawers so he could whup me with the belt. I imagine this hurt Albert almost as much as it would have hurt Mama. Albert knew not to interfere, though. Daddy wouldn't tolerate interference.

Then after, when Daddy was done, Albert might have heard our father, begging the Lord to forgive him, cursing the Lord for leaving him so alone and afflicting him so, telling the Lord he was sorry for taking out his sorrows on a child, and promising that this was the last time.

Except it wasn't.

One day, when Daddy was at the market and we were supposed to be picking beans in the north field, Albert took me by the hand and told me to gather up enough food for a few days. He said he was going to take me away where I would be safe. He told me to say good-bye to Jacob and our other brother, Frank, because I wasn't likely to see them anytime soon. I wasn't coming back here any more.

My brother and I walked barefoot along the dirt roads, hardly exchanging a word until we'd crossed over into the next county. Our overalls, handed down to us from the ladies in the church, hung loosely over ragged shirts that didn't fit any better. We didn't know enough to be ashamed. These were just our clothes, the only ones we owned. Shoes were for Sunday and we plumb forgot to take them with us. We hadn't worn any since Mama died the past April. We hadn't gone to Sunday service since then either, so it didn't enter our minds that we'd need them. I never liked them anyway. They pinched my toes and blistered my heels. Besides, the calluses on our feet were as thick and hard as leather so we didn't really need any, at least not in the summer, which it was.

Hardly anybody looks too closely at dirty children wandering down the road. The farmer might eye them a while, make sure they don't steal his tomatoes. Those are the only particulars that would interest him or anyone else, or so it seemed to me at the time.

We must have gone at least five miles before I got up the courage to ask:

"What do we do if Daddy comes after us?"

"Best not borrow trouble, sis."

I guessed that Albert didn't want me to be scared. I knew as well as he did that Daddy wouldn't take kindly to a daughter running off. Nevermind that Daddy didn't want me. His pride wouldn't allow it. Married or dead, those were the only two ways a girl-child would be leaving the family farm, if our father had the choice.

*

After we'd put a couple days distance between us and the farm, I started feeling lighter. Even the sun seemed shinier than I remembered it being since before Mama died.

Mama used to read fairy tales to me when I was sick so I imagined that Albert and I were characters in such a tale as we traveled the country roads. "What's that back there?" I teased, knowing Albert would have to look, even though there was nothing to see.

"Oh, lordy, Albert, it must be an ogre. No, it's Daddy. No, it's Daddy and he's the ogre." I told him to quick, sprinkle me with fairy dust so the ogre-Daddy wouldn't see us.

Albert laughed and pretended that the loose dirt on the road was fairy dust. He kicked it up all around us as he shuffled his feet.

Then he came at me with his arms hanging down and his back bent. I squealed and ran away from him, picked up some dirt from the road and threw it in the air over my head, and folded my arms like an invisible fairy, giggling as Albert loped around, pretending to look under the bushes and along the gutter without finding me.

We must have trekked across Tennessee for almost a week. I didn't know where we were going. As it turned out, neither did Albert. He had no plan, other than to get me away from Daddy.

We finished the food I packed by the third morning but it was harvest time so all the farms we passed needed help. We got day work picking beans. It was easy enough to sneak a few raw ones into our mouths every so often when our bellies made demands.

At night, we could have slept in the camps with the other pickers but Albert said he didn't like the way some of the hands looked at me. We took our helpings at the campfires then found a place to sleep at the edges of the fields.

We didn't talk directly about what might happen to us after the last harvest. I could tell it was on Albert's mind because he said we needed to get wherever we were going, though it was clear he didn't know where that would be.

One morning, we started walking again and didn't stop, passing by farms that needed pickers as if that was no concern of ours. I wasn't sure what we were looking for, but I looked around, just the same. After a while, the houses got bigger and closer together, and the fields looked better tended. A few miles later, the houses were right next to each other with no crops around them at all. And, off in front of us, down a freshly graded road, we could see a place where the buildings were so high and tightly packed together, it made our eyes pop.

We had bumped into a city. Lordy me, it sure looked big to us. We'd never been in one before.

The streets were crowded with buggies and automobiles, and even more people walking along the sides, in and out of the buildings and stores. Everyone looked like they were dressed for Sunday.

People on the streets in the city were talking about the circus coming. Somebody had tacked up signs all over the place, telling when the show would arrive.

Mama's people came from out near Knoxville and, when she was a little girl, she used to tell us, a circus would come through every year, sometimes two shows, one right after another. Nothing like that came within miles of Hodgeson County.

The pictures on the posters captivated me in the same way as Mama's fairy stories. Women wearing silver and gold balanced on wires in the air; men rode on the backs of wild animals from dark Africa.

I never saw Albert so excited before. "Every night, since we left, I've been talking to Mama, telling her how I didn't know if she could hear me up there in heaven but we sure did need her help. And here, we run right into this." He pointed to the poster with the beautiful circus lady balanced on the high wire. "If that isn't an answer, I don't know what is."

We ignored the rumblings in our stomachs and the

weariness in our legs. We ran to the railway track, hoping to catch up with something that, even with the memories of the posters imprinted in our minds, we couldn't begin to imagine: the circus train.

4. MARISA

Marisa dressed in the dark blue jacket and jeans she'd first worn when she met Harry at the house. In that outfit, her luck had changed and maybe, she thought, the clothes would act almost a talisman against having the house snatched away again.

Harry's secretary asked Marisa to wait while she buzzed her boss.

He came out almost immediately, flashed his bright smile and grabbed her hand in both of his in more of an avuncular embrace than a handshake.

"C'mon in here and we'll get started." He led her into a conference room.

Harry explained that, because Enid's house was passing to Marisa from her living trust, they could avoid the long, complicated probate process and he, as trustee, would sign over the property immediately.

"Just a little matter I want to bring up before we transfer the deed," he passed a couple of white sheets of paper across the varnished mahogany conference table. "I got this letter about the property from an environmental group that has a habit of harassing developers."

Marisa skimmed the letter. It said that the former Parker estate was one of the few remaining unspoiled habitats for threatened gopher tortoises on the west coast of Florida, and that Sarasota Green Coalition members had spotted endangered scrub jays there as well. The attorney signing it said the group had already filed for an injunction against the developer who owned the bulk of the property to prevent the habitat from being developed. The letter hinted that she would be sued, too, if she disturbed the land around her house.

The tension in her shoulders eased. The Sarasota Green Coalition couldn't know it, but the tortoises and birds had nothing to fear from her, which meant, it seemed, she had nothing to fear from them.

"I'd advise you to sell now, Marisa, before those granola crunchers bleed you dry."

"I think they're saying they'll sue if I do let some developer tear down my house. Which I won't."

Harry puffed his cheeks and let out an exasperated sigh. "Marisa, you're not protecting anything, least of all yourself. Don't wait until you get hit with a foreclosure notice. Sell now."

"I'm keeping it, Harry."

"Will you at least consider how your mother felt about that rat-trap? She hated it. Aren't you at least a little curious about why?"

She did need answers but she wouldn't get any straight ones from Harry, not when he was so set against her decision. She'd investigate after she left him and knew just where to begin.

Harry slid some papers across the glossy wood of the table, each page with a highlighted yellow line at the bottom, to show where Marisa should sign. His secretary acted as a witness.

Six or seven signatures later, she wasn't even certain she was scribbling her name correctly.

Not that it seemed to matter. The secretary notarized everything without a glance at Marisa's scrawl. Then they both congratulated her.

That was it.

She owned the house, the views, the trees — even, she supposed, the endangered gopher tortoises and scrub jays.

She walked out Harry's office door in a pleasant fog, colliding with a craggy-faced dark-haired man coming the other way. Apologizing, she scooted to her car, and just sat there with her hands clutching the wheel without turning the ignition key until she had come down enough from her endorphin high to safely drive.

*

The historical society was a plain concrete building wedged between the tourist information office and the city's art center on Sarasota's main thoroughfare, Tamiami Trail. Marisa wandered to the back and spotted the person she wanted. Myrtle Applegate once, long ago, had helped change Marisa's diapers and warm her baby bottles; she was now deputy chief historian for the society.

"Hey, Myrtle," Marisa called in a stage whisper to the plump woman bent over a file cabinet. The historian's steel-grey hair was styled in a straight bob, and she wore a pink sweater set.

Myrtle lifted her head and smiled in recognition. All her features congregated in the center of a soft, chinless face.

"You'll never guess what I just inherited," said Marisa.

"Let me think. The map to a pirate's treasure buried off Siesta Beach? No, that can't be it. I have the only copy," Myrtle joked, a sparkle in those tiny blue eyes. "I give up. What?"

"You're looking at the proud new owner of the midget house."

"Enid Parker's old house? How did you end up with that?"

"It seems that Enid left it to Mom. And Mom, well, you know."

"I was so sorry to hear about your mother," Myrtle cooed. "Such a loss, and so young. Everybody loved her."

"Just when I think I've accepted that she's gone, I pick up the phone to tell her something and — I can't."

"It's hard, I know," said Myrtle, patting Marisa on the shoulder. "But let's focus on your good news for now, shall we? Tell me about your new home."

"Actually, I hoped you could tell me something about it, like whether the stories about it are true."

"Well, there's one story I think it's safe to say is just silly superstition, about it being haunted. As for the rest, I'm afraid I don't have anything here about the house itself. It wasn't considered architecturally significant. And since it appears to have been built elsewhere, there are no building records on it. I have plenty of information on the rest of Cyrus Parker's estate though, if you're interested."

"If that's all you've got," Marisa said.

"A lot of the oldtime circus owners wintered in Sarasota. Years before John Ringling made Sarasota the circus's headquarters, he and several other big shots were already heavily investing here, thinking they could turn it into the next Miami Beach. Never mind that all they had to work with was this little bitty burg that hardly qualified as a city."

"And Cyrus Parker was one of these big shots?"

Myrtle nodded. "After he sold his circus, he took charge at his father's bank. Made a fortune for himself. Let me dig up some information for you."

Myrtle pointed down the hall. Marisa understood this meant she should follow, which she did, as the historian opened the door into a smaller room that looked like it was used mostly for storage. Metal shelves held books, maps, and photographs. The room was dimly lit, its walls painted a dull grey. An old, scratched up wooden desk was stuck between two sets of shelves. The green leather chair was cracked from wear.

"Have a seat, dear," Myrtle said, motioning to the desk and chair.

From a high shelf, Myrtle pulled down an old dark-blue clothbound photo album and laid it in front of Marisa.

"Here are some pictures of the Parker house," said Myrtle, opening the book to a page near the center. The photographs were held in place by tiny paper triangles, pasted to faded black paper pages that felt brittle under Marisa's fingers.

The first showed the mansion as it had looked before the fire. A magnificent structure, it had been less showy than John Ringling's Venetian-inspired mansion, but no less impressive.

The marble steps that were now all that was left of the home's ruins once led up to a semicircular columned portico. Tall arched and hooded windows lined the wide expanses of the first and second floors; shorter, dormered windows on a third floor under a mansard roof looked like they might have been for servants' quarters. Unlike anything Marisa could recall seeing in modern-day Florida, its façade appeared in the old photograph to have been marble or granite, its features ornamented by intricate stone carvings of mythic birds, flowers and gargoyles. To Marisa's architecturally uneducated eye, the house looked like an understated French palace, if such a structure weren't a contradiction in terms.

"If you flip through here, you'll get a good idea of what Sarasota used to look like," said the historian, turning the page to a photograph of John Ringling's waterfront home.

"This is all fascinating, Myrtle. But, I was hoping for something that might at least provide some clues about my new home. Like, whether anything odd ever happened there and if it was really built for midgets."

"I never believed that old midget story," Myrtle said. "Men like Cyrus Parker strived for respectability and circus ties weren't considered entirely respectable. No, Cyrus Parker would never have housed freak attractions on his own estate."

Marisa felt let down. "I don't suppose there are any old-timers around who remember that far back."

Myrtle made a show of concentrating, squinching her eyes into two thin dashes and pursing her small mouth. "You know who you could try? Dapper Dan Brogan."

"You're kidding. That's his name?"

"His stage name, yes. He's an amateur freak show historian but quite knowledgeable. Dan runs a traveling sideshow and still has a freak or two in the cast, the only one I know of who does. In the off-season, he lives about an hour north of here, in Gibsonton. Sells tickets to a little exhibit out back that he calls the Museum of the Macabre. If you can catch him before he goes back on the road, he's worth a try."

5. Otto

Sweat trickled off his pink scalp and into his monk-like salt-and-pepper fringe of hair. He stripped down to his boxers. Even in March, the Florida heat could drain him of energy.

Or maybe this heat was generated by rage.

All his adult life, he'd lived on the skimpy proceeds from the trust fund set up for him by his parents. He'd learned the wisdom of frugality and, indeed, he got satisfaction from it. What kept him going though was the inheritance Enid had promised and the knowledge that he wouldn't need to be frugal forever. But they'd stolen it from him. He still couldn't believe it. All those years, wiping the slobber from dear cousin Enid's chin and listening to her demented babbling. For what?

Somebody was banging on the door downstairs. He rummaged through the laundry piled at the foot of the bed for the golf shorts he'd peeled off earlier. As he zipped them, the banging became more insistent. He slipped his feet into green and white plastic flip-flops and toddled down the stairs.

"I'm coming," he called, opening the door when he reached the bottom. Marisa Delano stood on the other side.

She was imposing herself already, thought Otto, lording it over him that she'd inherited the house and even the small apartment that was his home. "How nice to see you, love," he said, smiling. "I'm sorry we didn't get a chance to chat at the funeral. I'd invite you up but the place is such a mess."

"I tried the bell."

"Oh goodness me, I'm so sorry," he answered. "The bell is broken. I probably should fix it but I get so few visitors here. What can I do for you, Marisa?"

"Well, I'd like to get an idea of what your plans are. I mean, now that Enid's gone, I'm sure you'll want a place of your own, and I just thought, you know."

Yes, he knew all right. And how, exactly, was he in her way?

"Marisa, whatever gave you the idea I was leaving?"

"I just assumed."

"You didn't read Enid's living trust."

"Harry told me what I inherited—"

"But not, apparently, what Enid left me. The life estate?"

He waited for a sign of recognition. Getting none, he continued. "It's the sum total of my inheritance: the right to live in that apartment up there 'til I'm dead, after which the property's heir — that would be you — can take possession. Ask Harry. He'll tell you. I got absolutely nothing, nothing, for all my years of devotion, except a rent-free dump above a rickety old garage."

"So, you intend to stay?"

"Even if I chose to leave, which I don't, I'd feel it's my responsibility to stick around, given the ugly business with the house."

"If you mean the tax lien, I'll figure that out myself."

He shook his head and gave her a sympathetic smile. "I'm talking about the house, Marisa. And what's in it. Even I wouldn't stay there alone. I certainly would never forgive myself if I left you all alone there with nobody within shouting distance."

Not so smug now, are you? Otto thought as he saw Marisa take a step back.

"You're sweet to be concerned Otto, but Enid lived in that house almost all her life. It doesn't seem to have hurt her any."

"Enid never tried to live there alone, Marisa. When she was younger, she had live-in servants, and then, the nurses. The house frightened each of them into leaving but she always managed to lure more, from out of town, mostly, where they hadn't heard about the disturbances. Every time one got spooked, the agency sent another. But they all ran away. All of them." He paused to let his speech sink in before continuing. "Enid always had me, of course, just across the drive, in case the presence in that old dump ever got too frisky."

The young woman backed up a step, looking uneasy.

"Remember, Marisa," he said. "If anything happens over there that upsets you, anything at all, don't hesitate. Come get me. I'll be right here."

6. Lucinda

Sounds lingered in the air, echoing long after their sources had moved on, a cross between a tinkling bell and a whisper – insubstantial, like herself.

All that seemed real to her was the dream. And so, she returned to it, falling backward in time, re-dreaming a life she had long since lost.

Parting – 1917

Albert and I waited at the tracks for the circus train to pull in, at the far end of the city. We couldn't even get close enough to the train to see what was inside. It didn't matter. Lordy, what a thrill it was, just to see the steam shoot up from the locomotive's chimney, to hear the brakes shriek as the iron monster came to a stop, and to listen for the roar of the animals.

Swarms of people pushed ahead of us. Some lifted up their children or sweethearts to help them see what was going on, which blocked our view of anything except the top of the train itself.

We stood there watching anyway, happy just to be near the excitement. Soon, above the heads of the people in front of us, we saw the most amazing sight — three elephants, taller than the rail cars themselves. Two full-sized men wouldn't reach such a height if one were balanced on the shoulders of the other. The trunks of these magical-looking beasts were long enough to sweep the ground. The elephants walked languidly past us, squirming those trunks around in front of them like fat saggy snakes.

Most of the onlookers followed the animals as their trainers led them up a slight hill over toward the field about a half-mile away that the circus would use as its fairgrounds.

A wagon filled with long poles that was pulled by a team of six brown horses got stuck climbing the hill. We heard the workers yelling back and forth. A couple of men tried to push from behind but it wouldn't budge. The man who was leading the team from the front yelled, "We need us one of them bulls." An elephant trainer steered his massive animal around and walked it over to the back of the wagon. The elephant seemed to know what was expected of it. Lowering its head, it pushed the back of the wagon while the horses pulled. Pretty soon, the vehicle had cleared whatever it was that got it stuck and moved along behind the others.

With the crowd by the tracks shrunk down to just a couple dozen youngsters, including us, we got our first glimpses of the circus people other than the workers. They appeared to be ordinary folks, for the most part. But some looked odd in more ways than I thought possible.

The tallest, ugliest person I'd ever seen came out from the back of a train car. His huge head and shoulders slumped down as if he was trying to make himself smaller. His eyes drooped too, like a hound's, with sickly dark gray semi-circles underneath them. He could have been an ogre from one of Mama's fairy stories, except that, when he glanced at us children, he flashed a sweet, almost shy smile. Then he turned to help a lady get down from the train. At least I thought she was a lady. She wore a skirt but her face was covered with black whiskers.

This pair was quickly followed by two more men. One wore a white turban on his head, like the pictures in the book about Ali Baba and Scheherazade, and had a fat live snake wound around his neck and back. The other man had colorful tattoos covering every part of his body, even across his bald head. The men waited by the door to help a lady who was so heavy, she had to turn a little to the right to fit through. They boosted the lady into a surrey hitched to a mule and driven by a laborer, then off they all slogged toward the fairgrounds.

From the other end of the same car tottered about ten tiny men and women, some even shorter than I was. A few looked perfectly normal except for their small size but some had arms and legs too short for their heads and the rest of their bodies.

These people seemed so easy together, going about their business like anyone else of any size. A trio of the small women giggled as they walked together, deep in gossip. They were about my height and yet they belonged, in a way that I never had and thought I never could. I called out to them inside my head. Look at me, I wanted to shout. Over here. I'm one of you. But my lips wouldn't move. My eyes puddled up, just watching as they marched along toward the field. I scrunched closer to Albert, and clung to his hand. I almost forgot to breathe.

He squeezed my fingers and smiled. None of the troupe paid any mind to the group of children in front of them.

I watched until they disappeared over a hill.

By now, the train had almost emptied itself; those spilling out of it dwindled to a trickle. People chattered and shouted back and forth, often in strange-sounding languages. Rough-looking laborers led white horses down planks from the freight cars. The roar of what might have been a lion or tiger echoed from somewhere beyond the tracks. Men hauled crates and trunks from the railcars, and loaded them on buggies.

The sights, smells, and sounds coming from the train made me almost dizzy. If anyone had described this caravan to me, I'd have said the person was spinning a tale. Except it all happened, right there in front of me and my big brother Albert.

A wiry old man in a red shirt and black vest called out to a bunch of us youngsters: "Free passes for any of y'all that helps set up the chairs in the big top."

Following the other children, we raced along behind the red-shirted man. He turned without breaking his stride, looked at Albert and held up his palm as if to say, stop. "Sorry boy, but you got to take your little sister home afore you come."

"Please, sir," Albert said, trotting after him with me a half-step behind. "She's older than she looks. And she's very strong. Please, can we both come?"

The man squinted, then let his eyes drop and travel down to the top of my overalls. His gray-bristled jaw gapped open and his lips tilted up into a wide, nearly toothless smile. "Why, lord a mercy, what've we got here? Guess I plain wasn't looking, huh? Sure, you both can come. I bet Mr. Cyrus'll be eager to meet this little one," he said, and patted me on the head.

*

Albert and I carried and unfolded the rows of circus chairs until it felt like our arms had stretched to twice their length and were set to fall off our bodies. Dozens of circus people worked alongside us and the other youngsters that the red-shirted man had recruited. And still it seemed to take forever. There must have been more than a thousand chairs to set up in this tent that was the size of ten barns.

By the time we were done setting up, I was more wrung out than after a day working the fields. I wanted to lie across a couple of the seats and just close my eyes a spell but the ticket takers started letting the audience come in. The noise the crowd made was like nothing I'd heard before — a mingled chorus of everyone talking, yelling and laughing at once that sounded almost like a shouted buzz.

One of the workers showed us where to sit, way up in the back, on some of the last seats we set up. The lights dimmed. The smells of the sweets that the people in the audience carried in with them filtered up to us, reminding me how hungry I was. A boy about Albert's age walked up the aisle calling, "Peanuts, popcorn, pink lemonade." Albert bought us one of each. After going the whole day without any food, we gulped it down without hardly tasting it. We were chewing away at the last morsels of popcorn when a blast from a horn down in the circus ring nearly scared me out of my seat.

Everything lit up at once. The orchestra that had somehow assembled on the edge of the ring, without my noticing, played a marching song that was so loud, my whole body vibrated with the clash of the cymbals. Into the big tent, a hundred or more performers strutted and pranced, their costumes glittering in the lights. White horses high-stepped, acrobats tumbled, and a caged lion roared. Jugglers, clowns and elephants followed — my eyes didn't know where to look first.

We grabbed each other's hands as aerialists swung way at the top of the tent from trapezes. We gasped along with a thousand others as one somersaulted through the air into the arms of another, then flew back again.

Lady equestriennes rode out into the ring, on the backs of beautiful horses. Performers twirled and leaped and balanced on wires and tumbled until it all became a big blur in my mind and I felt as exhausted as I was excited from watching them.

*

When it was over, I didn't want to leave. Albert looked as dumbstruck as I felt so we just sat there, content to wait while the other people filed out of the tent. The red-shirted man, who told us his name was Zack, came up the aisle looking for us afterwards. It was too loud to hear anything in the tent so he just motioned for us to follow, which we did. While we were inside watching the show, other circus folk had set up games of skill and chance, outside. It was almost as noisy out here as in the tent. Zack led us to a quieter spot, just beyond where all the circus attractions were set up.

"So I guess y'all is set to run away and join the circus, huh?" Zack asked. He looked straight at me, not Albert, which surprised me. Most people never talked to me at all, only my brother. I didn't know how to answer, or even if I should.

"You'd have a fine life with us, better'n any you could have out there." He tilted his head toward the buildings of the city.

Could a whole life change that easily? My only skills were

domestic: sewing, cooking, baking. That wouldn't get me very far with the acrobats, clowns, ballerinas and animal trainers.

Still, when Zack suggested it, I figured that maybe Albert was right about Mama. Maybe she'd pointed us here.

"I need to talk this over with my big brother," I said.

Albert's face was a jumble of emotion: hope, fear, sadness, happiness. He brushed away the hair that had stuck to his sweaty forehead, and looked at me intently. "You can stay with the circus if you want," he whispered as we moved a few feet away from Zack for privacy. "I think you'll be safe with them but I can't stay with you."

I knew that he couldn't. He'd been away from the farm too long already. Daddy needed him. Without the skill and strength of his oldest son, Daddy wouldn't be able to keep food on the table for himself or my two little brothers.

Albert had to go back. And I could not. So whatever other particulars there might be, it was settled.

I told Zack, yes.

He led us across a pasture back to the train station. We could hear squeals, shouts and laughter from the fairgrounds. "I think we need to get y'all straightened up a bit afore we introduce you to Mr. Cyrus. Make a good impression, if you know what I mean."

Zack took me to a rail car that had been uncoupled from the rest of the train and parked on a parallel track about twenty feet away from it. He said Mr. Cyrus, the circus owner, used it for his private quarters. Cyrus Parker would be at the big top, overseeing the show, Zack said, so it would be all right. Zack brought in a gray-haired lady who smiled and nodded a lot but who spoke no English. With gestures, Zack made it clear that he wanted her to give me a bath and some fresh clothes. Then he left us.

The woman filled a tub with buckets of steamy water as I looked around the private car. I'd never seen anything so rich. The walls were trimmed with dark wood and covered in carved red velvet. The furniture was made of the same dark wood, and was bolted to the rail car's floor. It gleamed with polish. A burnt, not unpleasant odor hung in the air, the scent of cigar smoke.

I peeled away my overalls and shirt and stepped into the tub. I hadn't had a bath in longer than I could remember. Albert and I had taken turns swimming wherever we found a private enough spot. Our feet had slipped along slimy creek and stream bottoms as we quickly dipped into icy water. This soak in warm, sweet-smelling suds was as far from those swims as we were from Hodgeson County.

The lady mumbled something I couldn't begin to guess the meaning of and stepped out of the rail car. I dunked myself all the way down into the warmth beneath the bubbles. She returned a several minutes later with a frilly ankle-length pink and white dress, shiny white buckled shoes, and clean white undergarments. She motioned to me that I should put these on.

At the same moment I rose to dry off, a man's voice shouted from the entrance to the car, "All right, Zack, what's this about?" as the owner of the voice stumbled in.

I had nothing to cover myself with. I stood there stunned for a second, then plopped myself back into the tub.

The man, his cheeks pinking up, looked more embarrassed than I felt. He grumbled something and quickly left through the same door.

The foreign lady helped me dry off and get dressed.

I found Albert and Zack waiting in a clearing near the tracks, talking to the man who had entered the car.

I knew this had to be Mr. Cyrus. His dark fedora, perfectly trimmed hair, long stiff mustache, and pressed black suit — everything about him said that he was important.

Zack grinned as he saw me approach. "Whaddya think, Mr. Cyrus? Ain't she perfect for the fairy princess routine?"

The important man peered at me up and down, nodding his head. I glanced at Albert. He looked so proud, I could have cried. And I saw relief in his face, too. My big brother had done what he'd set out to do. He had brought me to safety — and better.

"You look beautiful, Lucinda," said Albert. "I only wish Mama could see you now."

"I'll write you every week, Albert," was about all I could get out without risking a gusher of tears.

Albert swore he'd write me too, every chance he got, and tell me about what was going on at the farm. "Although now that you're going to be in show business, you probably won't care any more."

I'd care, I told him. I'd always care.

Albert shook Mr. Cyrus's hand, then Zack's, then hugged me. I could feel the dampness of tears on his cheek as he reached down to kiss me good-bye and I couldn't stop mine from falling. Before either of us could get any sadder, Albert started walking away, turning to wave every so often as he walked.

I waved back, and kept on smiling, determined not to let on to my big brother that I was no longer sure.

It wasn't just that I was alone for the first time. I had seen something in Mr. Cyrus's face that moment I stood in the tub. No one had ever looked at me that way before. I didn't quite understand.

7. Marisa

Against a background of calliope music, a baritone voice, eerie yet inviting, delivered the recorded phone message. "Thank you for calling the Museum of the Macabre, home of the most shocking, most titillating, most awe-inspiring sensations the world has ever known. Be forewarned, our attractions are not for the faint of heart. The images you see here will so haunt you, you may never be the same."

Marisa held the phone between her ear and shoulder as the voice, incongruously, went on to say, "We are currently closed for the season but will re-open on October 31st. Press one for schedules and pricing, press two for driving directions."

Back in character after blandly reciting the menu of options, the voice instructed, "Leave a message — if you dare."

"Mr. Brogan, my name is Marisa Delano. I'm a freelance journalist researching side show performers of the early twentieth century."

Her words were technically true. She hadn't actually claimed she was writing a story. But she knew people got back to reporters more quickly than they did the merely curious, especially people whose businesses thrived on publicity. She left her name and number, said that she'd heard he was an expert on the topic, and asked him to contact her as soon as possible. With any luck, he'd call from the road. October was months away. She needed some answers before she moved to the house. Not that she believed any of the spooky old stories. But there was still the question Harry raised that she couldn't quite banish from her mind: why had her mother hated it so?

*

She'd spent most of the morning packing the contents of the apartment that originally had been her mom's. She'd moved in just before Lisa Delano became ill and stayed on after she died. Sitting on the bare wood floor, she sifted the detritus from the valued possessions.

In the back of the hall closet, she found the family photo album. She flipped pages, past the prom scenes and the photographs of her long-dead grandparents, stopping when she found the snapshot of a man with dark longish hair, wearing a white t-shirt and jeans, holding a baby on his lap.

It had been taken right before Mario Delano returned to the carnie life. His head was inclined toward his daughter. At that angle his face was half-obscured but Marisa obsessively tilted the photo this way and that, trying to read his expression.

She assumed he was still alive somewhere. She hadn't attempted to find him though. What would she say to the man? Who knew how many other children he might have fathered and left in how many other bungalows in the years since?

Her mother never spoke about him at all except to call him a free spirit. Over time, from her grandparents and her mother's friends, Marisa had learned about her father. He'd been several years older than her mom. Her grandparents had tried to discourage the relationship. That probably had added to the sense of adventure for her mother, who had been in high school when they met. Marisa could just imagine a much younger Lisa Broadhurst, sneaking out the window of her ranch house after her parents fell asleep, and meeting her leather-clad bad boy at the corner where he waited, Harley revving.

At least for a time, Mario Delano had surprised everyone by settling down, marrying Marisa's mother, and getting a job at the local Ford dealership in the service department. When Lisa became pregnant, Mario chose the name for their baby:

Marisa, a combination of his name and his wife's.

But he was back on the road before Marisa began crawling and, by the time she could walk, her grandmother had told Marisa, everyone realized that he wouldn't be returning.

Marisa seemed fated to follow the same path as her mother. In high school, she didn't choose just one bad boy but dated a steady parade of sullen drop-outs. Even in college, surrounded by over-achievers, Marisa managed to hook up with only those young men who were sure to disappoint her.

She slowly figured out that she'd been searching that parade of alienated young men for a stand-in for the man in the photograph, someone who could reverse her father's abandonment. Realizing that she was, instead, only repeating the losses of her childhood, she swore off romantic entanglements and, after graduation, threw herself into her work, first as a reporter at a small daily paper in Buffalo, and then as a copywriter in a New York City ad agency.

That was where she met art director Dietrich Paulsen. Confident and brilliant, Dietrich seemed as different from her old loser boyfriends as possible..

He sent her funny cards, flowers, CDs of love songs, and eventually melted her resistance. She felt connected to him as she never had with anyone else. A moment before the phone rang, she'd know he was about to call. Without planning to, they'd run into each other, in a store, a museum, on the subway. Like magnets find metal. They seemed, at first, almost to be two halves of a whole, incomplete without each other.

When they married, she felt sure that the old cycle was broken.

He was moving up in the ad agency and she'd moved on to a demanding editorial job at a woman's magazine. But, despite her birth control, she became pregnant. It was inconvenient but there would never be a truly convenient moment to have a baby, not for two high-powered career people in New York City. She figured Dietrich would be as thrilled as she was.

He wasn't.

"Marisa, this is the worst possible time," he said.

He told her to get an abortion. He wasn't ready to be a father, he said. Maybe he never would be.

She stroked her belly. New life was growing there, part of her, part of him. She couldn't destroy it.

They fought for weeks, then each retreated into silence.

She could sense the ultimatum in his coolness toward her without his having to express it: him or the baby. The thought of losing him tore her up, until she accepted that she already had.

"Come home," her mom had said. "Come home, and we'll raise the baby together."

She left Dietrich, quit her job, and moved back to Sarasota.

Three weeks later, she miscarried. And while Marisa was still mourning the baby, and the end of her marriage, her mother was getting a confirmation from her doctor of stage four ovarian cancer.

The disease took her within months. Had Marisa's baby survived, her mom would not have lived to see it.

*

Marisa dropped the photo album. She reached up to touch her breast, imagining the lost baby who would never nuzzle there. She closed her eyes and saw Dietrich as clearly as if he were in the room beside her, his smile loving, as it once had been. As her hand grazed her nipple, she moaned from the memory of Dietrich's hands on her.

She tamped down the hurt.

She would not give in. She had packing to do.

But after a few minutes the compulsion overpowered common sense. She told herself she wanted to share her good news with him. Surely, she could allow herself that.

She reached for the handset, hit *67, to block her number from appearing on his Caller ID, and punched in ten digits from memory. Her heart pumped in her throat, in her temples; she could feel the beat in her ear as she paced.

If she could just hear his voice again — a recording of it

anyway; he'd be at lunch — she could let go and move forward. Where was the harm?

Two rings. Three. "Dietrich Paulsen," he answered on the fourth ring. She almost dropped the phone but quickly clicked off the connection instead, her heartbeat now tingling through her fingers.

Her knees threatened to fold. Letting go is a process. She'd read that somewhere. Nobody seemed able to tell her how long this process was going to take.

Her cat Murphy charged from across the room, scattering empty cartons; he jumped inside one half-filled with books, batted at some imaginary prey, then jumped up, doing a quarter-turn, mid-air, before he landed.

She reached over to pet the little guy and reminded herself that life was falling into place. She was going home to the midget house. One door closed, another opened.

She didn't need Dietrich. Didn't need him. Didn't need him. Sure.

*

The last carton packed, Marisa left for Kelly's store.

As she helped Kelly re-stock the shelves, she filled her in on her encounter with Otto.

"He gets to stay?" said Kelly, while ripping open a carton of incense burners. "No way. You've got to get him out of there."

"Harry says I can't."

Unpacking a crate from Brazil filled with amethyst crystals, Kelly arranged a few on a glass shelf between the rose quartz and the citrine, then gave Marisa a handful of the purple crystals. "Put these in my bag. We'll take them over to the midget house. They're good for protection — from midget ghosts and from Odd-o."

"I'm still trying to find out whether there were ever any live midgets in the house."

"Okay, but that still leaves old Odd-o over the garage." She got up and walked around the store, picking up stray talismans and grabbing a handful of the thick aromatic dried twig-and-leaf bundles called smudge sticks.

Back when they were in school together, Kelly Gallagher had been the straightest kid on the block. She'd since done a complete 180-degree turn to New Age goddess and her metaphysical gift shop and book store, Gaia, was Sarasota's New Age Central. If you wanted a Tarot card reading, aromatherapy oils, crystals, or a tambourine to take to Sunday's drumming circle at Siesta Beach, Gaia had it.

The jingling of the tiny brass bells hanging from the front door handles interrupted Kelly's scavenger hunt. Rena, Gaia's chief astrologer, Tarot reader and all-purpose spiritual counselor, swept in. With her multiple chins, flowing ethnic outfits and dramatic make-up, Rena bore a striking resemblance to a younger Liz Taylor. The flamboyance didn't come naturally, however. Rena had begun her adult life as a Catholic nun and, in her off-hours, reverted to the unglamorous style of the modern convent resident.

"Am I late?" Rena asked. She bent down to check her tomato-red lipstick in a mirror on the jewelry counter.

After about five years in one of the stricter orders, Rena had declared herself an atheist, if only briefly. She drifted for years, trying on and discarding different belief systems until she discovered the Church of Scientology in Clearwater, north of Sarasota. The Scientologists' teachings awakened her intuition, but Rena had bitter memories of her later years in the church's compound which, she claimed, was run by a bunch of money-grubbing crazies.

Marisa figured that Rena was the only genuine article in the store and the primary reason for Gaia's success. She also suspected that Rena had a crush on Kelly, to which Kelly, whose antennae seemed to be always out where men were concerned, appeared oblivious.

"Rena, I tried to reach you," Kelly said. "Your client has to re-schedule." She leaned in toward Marisa's ear, "How about we have Rena sweet talk those midget ghosts out of hiding."

"Actually," said Marisa. "I'd rather they stayed hidden."

*

With Kelly following in her Jeep, Marisa steered down the winding drive.

The estate felt different today, heavier somehow. The jungle of vines seemed now to darken the overgrown areas, throwing tangled shadows that seemed ominous. She felt a sense of wrongness, like a physical force, pushing at her ribcage.

Then she opened the door to the house — her house — and the weight on her chest lifted as if it hadn't been there at all.

The cleaning crew had done a thorough job. Ragged old curtains had been taken down. Gone were the dusty cobwebs that had hung in the corners. The rank odors were mostly dispelled too, replaced by a lemony soap smell. Only a faint mustiness still hung in the air.

Kelly marched in through the open door. "The house is magic," she said, looking around. "I love it."

Opening her big canvas purse, Kelly pulled out crystals, candles, the smudge sticks, a feather, a small brass statue of the elephant-headed Hindu god Ganesh, and a chime.

Kelly placed the tiny statue on an end table — to promote domestic harmony, she said — and a glass of water and the feather on the fireplace hearth. She lit a white candle, then hit the metal chime with a small black wooden mallet. The sound resonated for what seemed an impossibly long time.

"Ommmm," Kelly chanted, waving at Marisa to signal that she should join in. Marisa complied as Kelly again tapped the mallet against the chime.

She lit one of the smudge sticks. "Sage," said Kelly. "It'll cleanse away the old energies."

The fat bundle of burning leaves generated a surprising volume of sweet grey smoke. She waved the smudge stick over Marisa's head and along the length of her body, then handed it to Marisa to do the same to her. She "smudged" the front door. "Negative energies, wherever you're lurking, leave this house immediately," Kelly demanded.

"Yeah," Marisa ad libbed, as she followed behind with the white candle. "You've gotta move on so I can move in."

They filled the downstairs with a burnt sage fog, then climbed up the stairs inside the turret, stopping at each of the stained glass windows. Marisa, walking behind Kelly, tripped, almost dropping the candle.

"I'll take care of your house. I promise," Marisa blurted without thinking.

"Who are you talking to?"

"Damned if I know."

Scented smoke tickled their nostrils and formed a visible cloud above their heads. "Now we repeat the process with the cedar smudge," Kelly said.

They padded through the rooms, and up and down the stairs again, adding to the smoke that clung to the ceiling and extended a couple of feet down, almost touching the tops of their heads.

From her bag, Kelly pulled another dozen or so small uncut chunks of amethyst and handed them to Marisa. "Put one of these at or near each of the doors and by some of the larger windows."

Marisa obeyed, her head buzzing pleasantly.

She found a spot for the last amethyst on a table near the front door. She did feel that, just maybe, Kelly's charms were erecting an invisible protective barrier between her and whatever might be in the house.

How could she know that, instead, their little ceremony had the opposite effect? In whatever barrier had been in place, they'd hit a fault line. And, imperceptibly, it began to crack.

8. LUCINDA

OTHERNESS

Lucinda raced through the rooms, finding them clouded with smoke. Two indistinct forms, carrying a burning stick, waved it at her, trapping her in a corner on the landing.

She grasped for the window crank. It passed right through her. Yet the window held her back, a solid barrier to her less-than-solid self.

They were trying to drive her out. But there was no place for her to go.

Then, the forms retreated; the smoke dissolved into an array of tiny particles that sparkled in the moonlight as they rained onto the floors.

It was over, except, that something within her had shifted, become more real. Just for a moment.

Exhausted now, Lucinda slipped into dreamstate.

She was racing to the rail yard, thinking she was late and that the circus train would leave without her, stranding her in some unknown and hostile town—

She fought her way back from the dream, unsure that the forms had gone.

Yes. Alone now.

And she let go.

9. Lucinda

1917- The Circus

Three elephants, ears twitching and tails swishing, and a couple dozen hard-muscled men, hoisted the canvas up on massive poles, while the crew boss set the pace, hollering:

Heave it,
weave it,
shake it,
take it,
break it,
make it
move along.

The men and elephants tugged in time with the chantey. What began as a single slack, formless expanse of canvas covering a field, metamorphosed into the big top.

I think my mouth must have gaped open at the sight because two little children scooting past me pointed in my direction and giggled then chanted, "First of May, First of May," as if it was a nursery rhyme.

Racing along right behind them was a small brown and yellow monkey in a red jacket. The taller of the two boys called out, "Skippy, here," and the monkey jumped on his outstretched arm and climbed his shoulder.

"Coming through," yelled a voice behind me. I looked back and saw a team of large work horses pulling a long wagon with a tarp covering its contents. I moved out of the way.

The teamster pulled on the reins, jumped down from the driver's seat, and pulled back the cover. Under the tarp was a tiger in a cage. Her yellow eyes were rimmed in black. The stripes along her body seemed to undulate as she panted. Standing just a few feet away as I was, I almost jumped at the sight of the big cat. The way she stared back at me, you'd think she wanted to say something.

"I wouldn't get too close if I was you," said the driver. "To Sheba, a little thing like you could look like a mighty fine breakfast. And she'd still have room for seconds."

I thought of the barn cats on the farm and how they raced after each other, sprinting the distance from the henhouse to the outhouse faster than any living thing ought to be able to move. Mostly, I thought of the joy they took in their runs and leaps. It didn't seem right that this tiger, who might have everything in common with those cats except size, was stuck in a cage that barely let her turn around.

The driver was probably right though — Sheba could make a meal of me as easily as our barn cats would of a blue jay. It didn't stop me from feeling sad for her.

"There you are," someone hollered. "Lucinda, get on over here."

I saw Zack trotting toward me, as spry as the red-coated monkey, although he had to have some years on him.

"I went looking for you at the sleeping car," said Zack. "You finding your way around okay?"

I shrugged. I had no idea where anything was. I just didn't want to stay in the cramped space where he'd left me the night before. That railroad car had nothing but berths, two-deep, along each wall. The smaller child-sized berths lined either side of the front of the car. There were twelve of those for us midgets and dwarfs and a few were empty so I picked out a bottom one. Farther inside, other performers from the sideshow as well as non-starring acts of the big top, filled larger berths. Down a ways, in a lower berth on the left, I could hear voices joking and carrying on like they were playing a card game. Nobody was walking around and I understood why. The narrowest of aisles separated the bunks on either side.

Zack had said this car was where the single performers slept. The married ones traveled in the car behind ours although, if their berths were lined up the same way, I couldn't see how that was any more private.

The train had lurched forth sometime late at night. I figured I'd been lying there awake for a few hours by that time, kept awake by the snores and whispers that traveled the cabin all the way back to the other end of the car, and that the thin curtains did nothing to mute. Once the train got going though, it was like being rocked in a cradle. I slept until I was scared half witless by the squeal of the brakes, a sound not unlike a hawk as it swoops to the ground for its prey. The train rattled to a stop as the sky began to light up with the morning.

*

Zack pointed out the different parts of the lot — the menagerie, the concession stands, and the backyard, where circus people gathered, rehearsed and socialized and the townies weren't allowed.

The big top was already up and the men and elephants moved on to where another canvas was spread on the ground. I marveled at how quickly they worked.

Zack led me to the dressing area, in a part of the big top behind where the audience would be seated, but hidden from view by canvas. "This here's where y'all get ready for the show.

"Teeny, Tiny and Toy," he nodded to the three small women who were chattering to each other. "Meet Lucinda."

Zack told them that I was a First of May. "That just means you're new 'round here," he added for my benefit.

Two of the women were oddly proportioned, their limbs unusually short while their heads and torsos were about the size of a person of ordinary height. The third, who Zack called Toy, looked older. Her body was small but otherwise normal, like mine. She could have been mistaken for a child except for her full bosom and her metal-gray hair. Toy looked me up and down, then turned to her mirror as she talked to Zack without looking at him. "You really think this circus needs another midget, Zack?" she said through stretched lips as she applied a red lipstick first to the top lip, then the bottom.

"Well, Nettie's gonna be leaving soon," Zack replied.

"Not soon enough," answered Toy. The other two women giggled nervously. "And what's that got to do with her?" she motioned with her head in my direction. "I can take over Nettie's part in the spec."

"Why don't we leave that decision to Mr. Cyrus, okay Toy?" said Zack. "And, meanwhile, y'all could try to make the new gal feel welcome, dontcha think?"

"Why, so she can steal the bread right outta my mouth? We got enough midgets, Zack. You can tell Mr. Cyrus I says so." She looked into her mirror as she positioned a curly blonde wig on her head. Her gaze was directed, not at the wig but at me. I saw anger and maybe the hint of a threat in that look.

Toy's reaction hit me like a kick from a billy goat. I'd been so thrilled when I first saw these small people tumble out of the rail car. Why had I assumed that, just because they were my size, they would like me? I suddenly felt utterly alone, even more than I had the evening before, when Albert had left for home.

Behind Zack, a beautiful lady walked in to the dressing area. She was smaller than I was, and perfectly formed. Her eyes were huge and blue as cornflowers. Long wavy blonde hair bounced on her shoulders as she moved, shining so brightly, it looked golden.

"Hey, Nettie, we got us a First of May, here. Meet Lucinda," said Zack.

The lovely little woman smiled. "So pleased," she said and held out her hands to take mine in both of hers. She had an unusually high voice and a thick accent, so it took me a minute to understand what she said. The warmth of her greeting was easy to understand, even if her speech wasn't. The tension eased a bit. Maybe she would be my friend.

"Can't you find another dressing space for the Kraut?" Toy yelled over to Zack, jutting her chin in Nettie's direction. "In case you haven't heard, there's a war on."

"You wanna lay off, Toy," he answered. "They're going soon, okay? 'Til then, y'all are gonna have to learn to live with it."

Toy turned away as if she hadn't heard him and joined Teeny and Tiny in their whispered conversation.

Nettie looked as hurt as I'd felt a moment earlier.

Ignoring Toy and her friends, Zack went on with my orientation. "You'll get ready over there," he pointed to a chair just inches from where Toy was now sitting.

"Britta'll be in later to fit you with costumes. You met up with her earlier at Mr. Cyrus's car. She's the one that brung you the dress you're wearing. Don't expect another bath like the one Britta just gave you, 'cause it's your last for as long as you're on the road. Whatever washing y'all gotta do — sponge bath, laundry, anything else— you hafta make do with two buckets, like everyone else."

I nodded.

"Hey, I bet you're hungry, huh?" Zack said. "Nettie and me'll take you on over to the cook house. Then, I'll get y'all set up for your first sideshow."

*

Hans, Nettie's husband, a dashing German gentleman who was somewhat shorter than Nettie, met us on the way. Dressed in a dark suit and bow tie, with his slicked-back brown hair, and his thick, dark lashes, he had the looks of a matinee idol in miniature. He gave a slight bow at Zack's introduction, and saying a few words of greeting in thickly accented English, he took his wife's arm and walked with us toward the cookhouse. I pointed to a printed banner waving above the tent where the food was served.

"Why does the flag say 'hotel'?"

"Beats the hell outta me," said Zack. "But you see that flag go up, you best get in line, 'cause the good chow goes to the ones that are quick."

"The circus has its own language," Hans said. "But you will learn it all soon enough, do not worry." He, too, had a high-pitched voice which, coupled with his accent, forced me to strain to understand. I didn't think my own voice was any different than that of ordinary sized folk, at least it didn't seem so to my ears, but I wondered what I sounded like to others.

Someone up ahead of me grumbled that the brisket and ham were already gone, dished out to those who had gotten there earliest. I was dazzled by the great quantities of food. I couldn't imagine what else anyone could want as I heaped my plate with grits, biscuits, gravy and eggs, more than I could ever remember eating in one sitting. My eyes, as Mama used to say to my brothers, turned out to be bigger than my stomach. I forced myself to wipe my plate clean, reminding myself of another of Mama's sayings, that wasting food was a sin.

Nettie and Hans had roles in the big show so we said good-bye to them after the meal.

"The sideshow top's just yonder," Zack said, pointing to a smaller tent between the ticket office and the menagerie.

A big man in a sparkly coat and black top hat stood outside.

"Lucinda, this here is Marvin, the talker for the sideshow. Marvin, can we put Lucinda on the same stage as Teeny, Tiny and Toy?"

Marvin threw his head back and guffawed, almost losing his hat in the process.

"Sure, we can do that," said Marvin, "if you're keen on seeing the world war fought right here. I think we'd have a better time of it if we paired this little lady with Ivan. Whaddya think, Zack?"

Zack snapped his fingers in agreement and bounded over to a platform where a large man sat in a huge wooden chair.

I had seen this giant before, when Albert and I met the train. His head had seemed too big for his enormous body. I remembered his droopy hound dog eyes. I'd thought at the time he was the ugliest person ever, and now felt guilty for that.

"Ivan," Zack called as he ran. "I've got a new partner for you."

The giant smiled shyly as Zack introduced me and helped me up to the platform next to him. "Y'all are a made-to-order sideshow couple if ever I seen one," Zack said. "Just one thing. How 'bout we put Lucinda here in the big chair and Ivan, you stand beside her."

Ivan frowned a moment. "My legs, boss, they give me much ache," the large man replied, a slight accent in his deep voice. "I do for show, is good idea, but I must sit other times."

"Please, let me stand and Ivan can sit," I said.

Ivan broke out into a big smile that showed a mouth full of crooked grayish teeth. "No, no, little one," he said. "Mr. Zack makes right choice. Is best you sit. I make more money, you sit. I sits when the peoples leave to go to the big top, okay?"

Okay, I said. Ivan would rest in the chair until the first gawkers came through and at any time when there was a lull. Whenever there was an audience, he would lift me into the chair and stand beside it.

Zack pulled out a pocket watch. "It's getting close to show time."

I suddenly felt panicky. "What should I do?"

"Just sit there, smile and wave," said Zack, as he hurried out.

I heard the sounds of the people arriving. Just a few shouts and laughs and murmurs at first and then there were more voices, and the words blurred into the hum of a crowd. The steady buzz of townies grew louder and the candy butchers began hollering above it all, "Popcorn, peanuts, lemonade."

My heart thumped faster. Ivan lifted me into the large chair. He'd been smiling but now, he twisted his expression into a fierce scowl.

Marvin called out to the gathering crowd, "Here they are, ladies and gentlemen, freaks of nature you won't see anywhere else. Step right up to the freak show. Prepare to be dazzled and amazed."

It's surprising how a word can change the way you see things. It wasn't like I didn't know exactly what I was doing here or why they wanted me. I knew. It was the sound of that single word that made it all so awful, where before it had seemed exciting and fun. The word turned everything upside down: not sideshow. Freak show.

In the frenzy of running from my Daddy and finding what seemed to be a safe place in the circus, I hadn't thought things through. I hadn't realized until this moment what it would mean to be here, on display, next to a giant and across from a bearded lady and a snake charmer as hordes of normal-sized curiosity seekers stampeded past.

A crawly sensation tingled over my scalp and down my arms. My mouth dried up and my throat clutched like I had swallowed a cup of cotton balls.

I wanted to climb out of Ivan's chair and hide under the platform but it was too late. They had bought their tickets to the sideshow, these men and women, boys and girls, and now they were here, well-prepared to be amazed. They laughed and pointed and stared and covered their eyes. They shrieked in horror and screamed with glee at the freaks.

At me.

"I'd up and die of shame if I looked that way."

"Aren't the midgets precious?"

"If that ain't enough to give you nightmares—"

Oh my God, oh my God, oh my God. I want to go home.

I couldn't go home, of course. I didn't even know where home was any more.

I tried not to whimper out loud. I sat on my hands so no one would see them trembling.

10. MARISA

BEACHBUM'S HIDEAWAY

Marisa and Kelly settled at a table shaded by a palm-frond-covered overhang at Beachbum's Hideaway, Sarasota's last remaining beachfront tiki bar. Jah Glory, a local reggae group, pumped the volume. A half-dozen women, one in a black bikini top and flowered sarong skirt, the others in shorts, danced suggestively to the sensual beat. No one seemed to be dancing with any particular partner.

The two friends ordered a pitcher of Margueritas from a waitress in tight black short-shorts with brass-yellow hair bleached so dry, it resembled straw.

Marisa thanked the waitress; Kelly scanned the crowd.

"Toddler alert," whispered Kelly, her eye on a college-aged sunburnt blond guy, most likely there on spring break. He walked in behind a couple of other boys whose pink faces and forearms spoke of underestimating the power of Florida's sun. As the trio passed their table. Kelly flashed her trademark look — chin dropped, lips pouty, sideways glance. Marisa, accustomed to her friend's style, was unsurprised when, a moment later, the toddler-du-jour was hanging over their table whispering in Kelly's ear. In less than two minutes, the sunburnt dude was writing Kelly's number on a matchbook. He left to rejoin his friends at the bar. Marisa watched briefly, curious whether his ID would pass inspection by the bartender.

"Someday you'll have to tell me what you see in a kid so young he probably thinks The Beatles are garden bugs."

"Not much," said Kelly. "It's just fun to get reassured every now and then that the toddlers of the world still see something in me."

Marisa laughed. The straw-haired waitress returned, impatient for their order.

"Is the grouper fresh?" asked Marisa.

"Honey, that fish is so fresh, I'm not sure they're done reeling it in yet."

"I'll have that."

"Veggie pasta, please," said Kelly, handing her menu up to the waitress.

At the band's break, Claude, the dreadlocked lead singer, and the only actual Jamaican in Jah Glory, sauntered to their table. With a smile that lit his green eyes, he dumped out the contents of Kelly's water glass onto the pool deck and poured himself a hefty helping from the Marguerita pitcher. He took a slug before saying anything, then sat down next to Kelly, giving her shoulder an affectionate squeeze.

"Hey, mon," he said as he turned his attention to Marisa. Claude's voice would sound musical and sexy even if all he did was count to ten. "I hear you getting the house with all the tiny duppies."

"Duppies?" Marisa repeated.

"You know, duppies. Ghosts, mon, spirits. An old girlfriend of mine, she worked for that old lady, Enid. Mon, those duppies cause an awful lot of trouble. An awful lot."

He told an elaborate tale of tiny ghosts kicking over books and pottery in the middle of the night, waking up his ex-girlfriend, and generally causing a ruckus. "They 'bout half the size of Birdie, mon, 'bout half the size of Birdie."

"Who's Birdie?" Marisa asked.

"Birdie, mon, she the sweetest little old lady. And I do mean little. She the volunteer lady over by the Circus Museum. Stand about this high." He held his hand to a height of maybe three feet. "She know all about the circus. She could prob'ly tell you who put a curse on that house."

"C'mon, Claude, there is no such thing as a curse."

"Hmmph," he snorted. "You try telling that to my old girlfriend. She see them duppies, running all around like that, mon, she couldn't wait to get out of that place."

He made it sound as if the house was positively infested.

"It's an old house. The stairs creak. The wind coming in from the bay can make an eerie sound at times," Marisa said. "People sometimes confuse perfectly ordinary noises with sinister manifestations."

If she was not quite convinced by her own blanket dismissal, she felt a reflexive need to defend her little castle.

"I wouldn't talk like that if I was you," he answered. "You gotta show the proper respect for the spirits. Yah, mon, the proper respect."

Having just finished trying to cleanse the house of unseen energies, Marisa let him have the last word.

"So, didja hear what they going to do to Beachbum's?" He scooted his chair closer and pointed with his chin at a bartender. "Timmy tell me they gonna come in here with the bulldozers and tear the whole place down. Yah, mon. Gonna build condominiums soon as the county says okay. You know the last thing this town needs is another big stack of ugly condominiums."

Timmy, the bartender, was chatting animatedly with a couple of guys in neat-looking jeans and starched blue Oxford shirts. For Beachbum's, where faded Budweiser t-shirts, swim trunks and flip-flops were the uniform of choice, theirs was an unusual display of sartorial sophistication. One fellow turned around for a moment. Marisa knew she'd seen him before but couldn't quite place him.

He had a slightly hooked nose. His deeply lined face indicated someone who spent plenty of time outdoors, but his grooming and body language said golf course, not laborer.

He wore his dark hair on the longish side. Laughing at some comment Timmy made, he seemed friendly and relaxed. She guessed his age at about forty.

"Who's the guy talking to Timmy," she asked. "He looks familiar."

"I wouldn't mind getting familiar with him," Kelly said.

"Down, girl," teased Marisa. "He got that beer without being carded — way old for you."

Claude frowned at the banter, apparently having other ideas about who Kelly should be getting familiar with.

The guy at the bar looked at Marisa and gave a slight wave. He started walking toward their table.

"Hi," he said, all smiles. "Don't I know you from somewhere?"

She remembered then: the craggy-faced man she'd plowed into after signing the legal papers. "Marisa Delano," she answered. "I think I saw you at Harry Scanlon's."

"You inherited the house that's smack in the middle of my property." He reached into his wallet, pulled out a business card, and offered it. "John Guinness. I'd like to talk to you about that."

Son of a bitch. He was the one who wanted to tear down her house. It took will power to hold in her temper. He'd have no reason to understand how much that idea upset her. For him, it was just a real estate transaction.

She answered him as blandly as she could. "Thanks but the house isn't for sale."

Claude excused himself, explaining that he had to get back for his next set. As he left, he gave Kelly's shoulder another affectionate squeeze, then glared for a beat at John Guinness — who refused to notice.

"I can see why you'd want to keep the place. It's beautiful out there."

Kelly smiled up at him. "Yeah, it's great, isn't it? Sit." She patted Claude's now-empty chair.

"I'm here with a business associate. And he's ready to leave. I would," he said, turning back again to Marisa, "like to call you sometime. Maybe we could get together for lunch or something. You have a number where I can reach you?"

"I don't date. And I don't give out my number. But Harry gave me your card if I need to reach you."

His smile faded a bit as he backed up a couple of steps. "Please – call any time."

11. Lucinda

1917— The Circus

I didn't want to ever get back on the stage again but I had nowhere else to go. So I appeared for the second show, just like the first. And the one the day after that. I felt calmer in the long moments when people weren't staring and pointing at me. The mostly empty hours ticked by. I started easing up a little about being where I was.

By the second day, I began to study the acts around me. One thing I noticed right off: I was the only one just sitting around doing nothing. The other performers danced, sold souvenirs, and told the audience sad (and unlikely) tales of how they got to be members of the circus freak show.

Teeny, Tiny and Toy waltzed together as a threesome and sold post cards of themselves to the onlookers.

Annabelle, the fat lady, appeared in a frilly pink camisole and petticoat, her baby fine honey-colored hair tied into little girl pigtails. She danced too, hoochey-koochey style, a way that made her fat jiggle, front and back, and made the people laugh and slap their knees. Annabelle sold bibles with her autograph on the inside cover. The more she shimmied, the more bibles she sold.

Like the trio of Teeny, Tiny and Toy, and several other attractions, the bearded lady, Stephania, sold post cards of herself. For a dollar more, she would step outside and pose with the townies. Peter, a photographer who traveled with the show, took the pictures. She also sold postcards of Ivan (and took a cut of the sales) so that Ivan could play the ferocious giant part, the playacting making it difficult for him to switch to selling and such like.

None of them seemed to mind being freaks, or even to mind the way the townies laughed and made fun of them.

"Did you see the way that old farmer's jaw dropped when Ivan growled," Stephania said between giggles as we sat around a fire that evening. "I swear he was gonna piss his pants."

The others laughed as Ivan repeated his earlier performance, pulling his lips back, baring his teeth and letting his tongue loll out like a mad dog. Stephania, pretending she was terrified, held up her arms and ran backwards like the old farmer did. Watching her, Ivan started laughing and sat back down.

"Doesn't it bother you," I asked later, when Ivan and I were alone, "that the people hate you so much?"

"Hate me? Lucinda, the peoples don't hate me. Nobody comes to circus to see what they hate. They love me. They love I frighten them. If I do not, they feel cheated."

I marveled at his answer. He happily played his part in the game with the crowds of townies, giving them what they wanted, and he got a kind of love in return.

Maybe it was all a matter of how you looked at it. The townies were laughing at us but Ivan and the others were poking fun right back at them.

Over the next few days, as I got used to my role in the sideshow, I had to admit, it wasn't so bad to sit in a big chair on a small stage all afternoon and wave to the people who came by. Sometimes, they jeered, and that hurt something awful. Mostly though, the audience was real nice, with people saying things like, "Isn't she cute," and, "Look, a living doll." So, no denying it, I was a freak in their eyes. Ivan was right, too. They loved us.

*

"Miss—?"

I didn't have to turn to know who was calling me although I'd heard him speak just once before. The handsomest man I'd ever laid eyes on had a voice to match his appearance — deep and soft, yet it carried, setting off strange vibrations in my belly.

"It's Lucinda, Mr. Parker," I said. "Lucinda Lacey."

"Lucinda," he said it like he was trying out the sound and enjoying what he heard. "How are you finding life in the circus so far, Lucinda?"

I thanked him for his interest and told him that Zack and Ivan were explaining how everything worked.

"I want to be certain you do well with us."

I wanted to answer but my mind was aflutter and words didn't come. I stood there next to him, grinning like a fool, and couldn't get my lips to turn down even after he'd tipped his hat and walked on.

He did favor me, didn't he, nevermind if he couldn't show it? Or was I reading too much into a few words of courtesy?

Doing well in the sideshow, as Cyrus had put it, meant making money. I had talked to Peter about having him print up some postcards with a picture of me on the front. Peter wouldn't shoot the photographs until I could pay him, so I planned to save up what I got from the paymaster come Monday. It would take me about three weeks before I had the full amount.

When I told Ivan, he said to forget the postcards. He had a better plan, one that would we could start on right away.

"You sell peoples the chance to take picture with us," he said. "We both make money."

His idea was to tempt the townies into paying us to pose with them while making them believe it was their idea.

"I growl at them," said Ivan, "then you sing song and I stop."

Once he went from beastly to acting gentle, Ivan said I should start talking about how I was the only one who could tame him. Then, just casually, Ivan said, I should mention that some men who came to the circus were so brave, they had the photographer take pictures of themselves with him and me while he was all peaceful like that.

I couldn't see anyone being foolish enough to fall for that, I said.

"Ah, Lucinda, I would bet you money but is too easy to win."

Ivan held up a thick black leather collar he'd gotten on loan from the menagerie manager, the one the manager used around the neck of Kingsley, an ancient male lion, when he walked the big cat around the back lot.

Kingsley was mostly well behaved, either too old or too well fed or both, to hurt anyone. But he had this awful habit. During his strolls, he liked to stop to spray the sidewalls of the menagerie to mark his territory. The menagerie manager figured this was preferable to Kingsley spraying the onlookers who came to see him, which is what he would do if kept cooped up all day. So, Kingsley got to claim a wider territory and menagerie visitors didn't go home covered in lion pee.

This seemed to satisfy everyone, until the day before yesterday. Kingsley was out on his leash, doing what he always did, when Rebecca Bradley, a star aerialist, walked by in a new blue satin costume that had probably cost a week's pay even at her star-high salary. The foul yellow splatter hit the sidewall and ricocheted onto the star and her satin. The costume was ruined.

So, for now, Kingsley was being punished by confinement to his cage. As long as he wasn't using the cat's collar, the menagerie manager didn't mind Ivan borrowing it for a couple of days.

Ivan tied a length of thick hemp rope to the collar's metal ring, placed the leather band around his own neck, and handed me the rope's other end. He grinned so broadly, I could practically see his tonsils. Lordy, how did he expect me to pull off my part in this act when I couldn't stop giggling?

*

Off the train, into the sideshow top, back on the train, I was on an endless journey from here to there. I didn't always know where either here or there was or even what state we were in, the way the stops blurred into one another. The circus wrapped itself up into a tight package late at night, small enough to fit in a couple dozen rail cars, then hurled itself across the country to a different town. The next day, that package unfolded itself in that new place, rolling out its contents into fancy wagons with wheels painted red and yellow like sunbursts, spilling itself over grass or dirt or clay — any ground large enough to contain it — turning bare land into acres of magic.

We never stayed more than a day or two except in the bigger cities. The circus was always in a hurry, with the razorbacks clearing out the menagerie while Nicolai the Great still balanced on the high wire, not paying any mind as the big cats howled their discontent as they got loaded on the train. Pretty soon, the canvasmen toppled the big top, the teamsters hitched up their horses and hauled every pole, pulley, tent peg, and bail ring back to the tracks where all were crammed into boxcars and onto flats.

And off we rolled again.

My place in all this went from seeming impossible to natural. I didn't notice the change in myself until I strolled toward the cookhouse one morning and passed a group of acrobats practicing a human pyramid. And I kept on going without slowing down to watch. It had all begun to feel as ordinary as watching chickens scratching for corn.

*

"Hush, dear giant," I cooed as Ivan growled. "La-la-la. La-la-la."

Ivan slumped a bit as I sang and let his face go slack into an almost drunken stare.

"No need to worry now," I told the people in front of our stage. "As long as I serenade him, he's as gentle as a lamb."

I talked about how this young man had gone outside the tent with Ivan and me and ordered the photographer to take a picture of him between the two of us. One of the young men in front of us raised his hand.

"I might like to take a picture with you," he said.

For the next minute or two, he and his girlfriend had a whispered argument about this, her pulling him toward the next stage in the sideshow, where Kumar was playing with his snakes, and the young man not budging. The more she yanked at him, the more determined he got to stay put and do it.

I made a show of coaxing Ivan outside by the long hemp leash. And by the time we got to where Peter had his equipment set up, three more young men were waiting in line, to show they were just as brave.

Cyrus walked by, saw me fiddling with the collar around Ivan's neck, shook his head and laughed so hard his hat almost fell off. With the noise of the midway, our line of customers didn't seem to notice. He gave me the OK sign and kept walking, which was just as well, because if he stayed another second, I'd have caught a case of the giggles too, and I needed to stay serious so the rubes wouldn't think we were cheating them.

*

The last few stragglers from the sideshow audience hustled out as the blare from the trombones and tuba alerted them that they were going to be late for the main attraction. The spec parade was starting. As soon as the townies were good and gone, I followed behind. I'd hoped to catch Nettie's act but had missed most of the spec again. I got there in time to see the jugglers, the last ones in the parade.

From my spot behind a tent flap, I could guess the elephants were coming through even if I didn't turn to see them. The ground trembled as their feet hit the packed dirt and one made a sound that could have come from a horn in the orchestra.

They marched by me, trunks swaying, tails swishing, spangled showgirls astride them. I recognized two of the girls, Wanda and Pattie, because Nettie had pointed them out as members of the dance troupe who performed with her in the spec. The man who trained the beasts walked alongside shouting commands and sometimes flicking a switch at them when they didn't obey right away.

I wondered what it would feel like to be up there in the saddle, high enough to look down on the world, running my hand over the bristly hair that stuck up on the top of the elephants' heads and getting fanned by those wing-like ears.

Wanda didn't seem to think she was lucky to be riding up there. I'd heard her complaining the day before that the biggest of the beasts, Gerta, played tricks on her all the time, especially in the finale where the trainer made the elephants walk around the hippodrome track, each with a showgirl in its mouth.

"I can feel that damned bull poking at me with her tongue," Wanda said as they exited the ring. "It's like she's taking a taste and deciding if she wants more."

Wanda demanded to be allowed to quit the act but the trainer said no. Gerta, it seemed, would only let certain people ride her. And for whatever reason, Gerta liked Wanda.

We'd had a mule on the farm with a temperamental streak like that. Mama wouldn't let any of us on its back, for fear it might have one of its ornery spells and throw a child onto the ground. It would be bad enough getting tossed from a mule but an elephant was a good ten times the size.

The elephants got to the part of the act where they laid their front feet on small platforms and sort of danced around with their back feet while the orchestra played a Strauss waltz. I noticed I wasn't the only one standing near the exit flap. A young man about Albert's age stood several feet behind me. He seemed to be trying to hide back there in the shadows, but he poked his head out every so often to get a look before ducking out of sight again. He wore a tie but no jacket and from his sweat-soaked shirt and the mud that caked his shoes and splattered his trousers, I could tell he was a laborer.

I heard another man behind us calling out in a voice that was whispery but carried across the yard:

"Hey, you. Leroy. Ain't you got work to do?"

The younger man named Leroy said no, they'd long ago

unloaded the train and he was off until it was time to pack up again.

"If you don't wanna be off for good, you'd best stay far away from them dancing girls," the older man said. "Bosses catch you, they gonna ditch you faster than a gimpy horse."

Leroy just waved to the man, as if he hadn't understood or maybe didn't care. The older man walked off, looking peeved. Leroy started sneaking peeks again, not at the elephants but at Wanda, sitting up high on Gerta's thick neck, the lights catching the spangles on her costume and making her glimmer like she was covered in starlight.

The act left the ring as the next performers entered, and the elephants with their riders exited past us. Leroy smiled at Wanda with a hopeful look. She stared ahead as she passed him, like she didn't notice anyone was there. Still, she didn't have that sour frown from the night before, the one she'd let show as soon as she was offstage. With her chin jutting out and her shoulders back, it seemed to me like she was still playing to an audience, only now, it was an audience of a single smitten razorback.

Moments later, the girls had climbed off their "bulls" and headed to their dressing areas to change costumes. The trainer and an assistant led the elephants back to the holding pens.

The Fabulous Alexander Family, mother, father and three children, were already riding around the ring on their horses, performing tricks as they rode.

The footsteps behind me made me think that Leroy had come back, but when I turned to look, I saw Cyrus Parker, his blue eyes catching a spark of light from the spots. He smiled at me and I felt myself blush as I always seemed to do when near him. He gestured toward the family on their high-stepping horses.

"Barnum brought them over from Russia," said Cyrus. "And I stole them from him. They're great, aren't they?"

Yes, I said, feeling awkward but thrilled that he was speaking to me so casually.

"The ringmaster couldn't pronounce their family name, so we just call them by the father's first name, Alexander."

I don't know what I answered, surely nothing intelligent, but he didn't seem to notice.

We stood watching for a long moment, not looking at each other, not talking, not touching, but Lordy me, there was something tingling between us like electricity. Maybe I was crazy to believe he experienced it too but I couldn't imagine anything that powerful happening and him not noticing.

"I very much look forward to seeing you join our big top performers," he said, with a tip from his hat. "Good night, Lucinda."

He walked in through the opening and began talking to the ringmaster. I stared after him for a few moments, more interested in watching the back of his head and the gestures he made with his hands when he spoke than in seeing the Alexanders somersaulting and juggling on the bare backs of their animals.

I headed back to the sleeping car, feeling my heart do its own little somersaults. I knew I was being a fool, but I was a happy fool.

12. Marisa

Three tattooed movers jumped out of the van's cab and unloaded Marisa's boxes, emptying their truck more quickly than they had packed it.

Marisa trotted up the staircase, opened the door to the smaller bedroom, where she had closed in her cat, Murphy, to keep him from running through the open front door. Murphy huddled under the bed in the farthest corner. She cooed at him for a few moments, trying to coax him out. He slunk further back and out of reach.

Closing the door again, she ran down to the kitchen where she had already stashed a quarter-pound of his usual bribe in the refrigerator: thinly sliced turkey coldcuts.

"Murphy!" she called as she walked back in. "Goodies."

The small striped feline slunk halfway out, eyes wide. Though confused about where he was, Murphy stayed true to his pragmatic disposition. He nibbled daintily on the turkey and after a moment, seemed to relax. He blinked up at her contentedly but refused to come all the way out of his new hiding place.

Leaving the cat to decide for himself when to explore his new digs, she walked back downstairs to the kitchen and sliced open a carton. All of Enid's belongings still crowded the cupboards. She moved Enid's gold-trimmed floral china to the back and stacked her heavier pottery in front.

She poured herself a glass of Cabernet, then pulled Enid's old clothes off the hangers in the downstairs closet, dropping them into large black lawn bags. She hung her own shirts, skirts and jeans in their place.

Exhausted after a few hours of unpacking, Marisa stopped to rest on Enid's ornate mahogany settee.

She didn't remember dozing off but was startled awake by a dream, the details of which evaporated as she opened her eyes. Uneasy in the now-dark house, she took a moment to orient herself.

Something felt strange. Maybe it was simply that she had awakened in the still new to her surroundings. She could swear it was more than that, but—

Out of the corner of her eye, she imagined she saw movement. A loud gust blowing inland from the bay made her jump. She got up and flicked on a light switch. There. Nothing. A moment later, a windblown branch or errant raccoon tripped the motion sensor and the outside lights blazed on, illuminating the back of the house.

She quickmarched around the downstairs, turning on every light. She struggled to close a reluctant window. She chain-locked the front door. The gusts kept whistling up from the bay, adding to her edginess.

It's the house, Marisa ... Enid never tried to live there alone.

"No," she said out loud. She would not let Otto's scare tactics get to her.

Walking back toward the great room, she heard something behind her, like fingernails striking the wood of the front door. Not knocking or tapping. Scraping. Before she could focus enough to make sense of the sound, it stopped. All she heard was the ka-thump, ka-thump of her heart, as if it had climbed up her throat to hammer against her eardrums. Seconds later, the scraping sound was back, a little to the left of where she'd heard it before.

Somebody was trying to get in.

She thought of Enid, who had died in the house just

two weeks before, whose clothes and possessions she had carelessly shunted aside for the better part of the afternoon to replace with her own.

Marisa's fear formed an image of Enid coming at her with impossibly long blood-red fingernails. She shook the picture from her head — stop being ridiculous — and forced herself to calm down and listen.

The scratching sound originated, not from the front door, but nearer the stairs.

It was already inside the house.

She froze.

From within the wall where she'd heard the scratching, now there was a new sound. A chirpy twitter.

A squirrel?

Jeez. She laughed out loud.

Murphy, taking the noise more seriously, sat by the staircase, transfixed by what his senses told him was on the other side.

She tried to relax after that, but the uneasiness wouldn't leave her. Well past two o'clock, wiped out from the move and her roller coaster emotions, Marisa walked upstairs to lie down in the bedroom that Kelly had nicknamed the playroom. It barely mattered that the bed sagged and that, even with fresh new linen on it, it smelled of mildew. She was too tired to care.

*

Sunlight slanting in through the child-sized windows woke her too early. She crinkled her nose at the moldy scent of the mattress that now clung to the t-shirt she slept in.

An antique doll caught Marisa's eye; she picked it up to get a better look. Its chiffon dress was filthy from decades of neglect but she could see that under the grey of ancient dust it was meant to be a soft rose color. Its tiny chiffon wings were beginning to shred. Marisa carefully placed her back on the vanity among the other dolls.

Out toward the bay, a tall, slender white egret stood on the grass just to the left of the old mansion's ruins. The bird posed in such utter stillness, it appeared to be a lawn ornament. Then it took a few running steps on black stick-like legs, finally lifting off, slowly flapping its wide wings over the water. Wisps of cloud feathered the otherwise unbroken turquoise of the sky.

The serenity of the scene soothed away any residual fears of the night before.

Remembering that squirrels can eat through wiring, she got dressed and knocked on Otto's door to ask if Enid had kept any Havahart traps around.

He stared at her blankly. "What sort of traps?"

"Havahart, you know, as in have-a-heart. The squirrel goes inside to get a snack and the door locks behind him. Then we take it to some far corner of the woods and set it free."

"They're rats with fuzzy tails, Marisa. Poison the filthy things and be done with it."

"Never mind, Otto. I'll check the Yellow Pages."

*

She found a pest control company that took Mastercard. Amazing how far plastic could take the broke and under-employed; she'd worry about the bill later. Roy of Bugging Out Pests arrived within the hour. After telling him to place Havahart traps wherever animals might be gaining entry, she asked him to close up the holes so they couldn't get back in.

Roy crawled under the house. He came up a few minutes later, shaking his head and carrying a chunk of rotted wood, about the size of a baseball bat, which he held out for Marisa to see. "I pulled this off of one of your joists," he said, then crumbled it between his hands into sawdust.

"Squirrels are the least of your problems," said Roy. "Termites are eating this house from the inside out. You did know you had termites, right?"

"I suspected."

He gave her a look that seemed almost accusing.

"You'd better get a structural engineer out here to assess the damage."

"How bad do you think it is?"

He snorted in a way that she took to mean he was blown away by his own estimate. "You could be looking at maybe ten thousand dollars to repair all this." He swept his arm across the air for emphasis.

"Can't this wait awhile?"

He snorted again, shook his head ominously and threw up his hands.

*

Roy agreed to do the termite treatment after the squirrel had been rescued and said he'd be back to check the traps in a couple of days.

Heavy grey clouds filled the sky to the west over the bay and appeared to be headed for shore.

A loud boom, followed by a crack of lightning signaled a thunderstorm's beginnings. Murphy dashed into the downstairs bedroom to hide.

Moments later, she heard the patter of raindrops on the great room roof. The sound soothed her rattled nerves. The cloudburst seemed symbolic, a good drenching to scrub clean the remnants of sadness that had for so long lingered around her. She'd arrived at the beginning again, back to the one place where she might have a chance to heal. And, problems be damned, she would not let anyone force her from this spot.

She opened the back door to watch the rain pour down. It came in sheets but under the overhang above the door, only a few tiny droplets touched her face. The rain felt fresh and cool.

It took her a few minutes to realize that she could hear water coming down, not just in front of her, but behind her as well.

There, in the center of the great room above the ceiling fan, and over in the corner where the newer addition had been attached to the older part of the house, water splattered through the ceiling, making puddles on the floor.

13. Lucinda

Dust floated lightly above the doll on the vanity and around Lucinda's other possessions, sometimes dancing almost prettily, a mist of tiny, lacey particles. It was the doll that the souvenir sellers had hawked to circus-goers, meant to resemble Lucinda's fairy princess character in the spec.

There it always had been, a constant that greeted her each time she returned from dreamstate to the almost-reality of her existence.

Then suddenly, the doll was gone, as a form swept through Lucinda's bedroom — a blur, really—but Lucinda sensed it was a woman.

The doll reappeared a moment later but its pose was all wrong; its fairy wings, askew.

Lucinda tried to move it back to the way it should be. She seemed to over-reach, then under-reach, never quite touching it.

Why did this small change in the toy's position alarm her? That this part of her world had stayed the same until now didn't mean she could count on its constancy. Yet, she had counted on it, had taken comfort in this single point of sameness.

She felt a queer, quiet kind of panic. She controlled nothing. Her entire world could collapse around her. Would she then ... still ... even ... be?

She reached for it again. The doll eluded her, never quite there when her almost-real hand arrived at that place where her almost-real eyes told her to aim.

The bay swallowed the last bite of orange sun. Still, she grasped for it, growing more distraught at her inability to connect.

Time, in its strangeness, passed — quickly, slowly, she couldn't say which.

Morning brightened the room.

And, she felt it, the chiffon of a fairy wing. Awkwardly, she poked at it, thrilled at the sensation of something physical, something real, making contact with her almost-real self. She prodded it again, mostly to assure herself that she could.

She could not coax the doll back into the pose she remembered. That mattered less now. Simply experiencing this sense overrode her need for a specific result.

Feeling joy in her own power, Lucinda reached out again. The force of her exertion sent the little souvenir mannequin flying off the vanity in a wide upward arc.

It landed with a bounce on the wooden floor.

14. Marisa

Adjustments

Drips hit the buckets she'd placed under the leaks. Plink. Plink-a-plunk. The toilet, not to be upstaged, provided accompaniment. The serenade of cascading water urged Marisa out of bed.

She jiggled the chrome handle. The cascade stopped. She crawled back under the covers in the downstairs bedroom that had been Enid's. It lacked the charm of the playroom but also lacked the mildew. The toilet started running again.

Somehow, she fell asleep again, lost in dreams until a thud from above startled her awake just as dawn began to lighten the sky.

Murphy, her groggy mind assumed. He must have knocked over something in the bedroom upstairs.

She got up to check. The little winged doll she had admired the day before lay on the floor, halfway across the room.

She placed the doll against a yellowed decorative pillow on the child-sized rocking chair in the corner. She stopped and puzzled briefly at the initial "L" monogrammed at the pillow's center. Why not "E" for Enid or "P" for Parker?

Taking a quick inventory of the room for other fragile items she moved a stained glass box and a small framed mirror, then started back downstairs.

Murphy sat at the bottom of the steps, blinking at her as if nothing were wrong. Or maybe he meant to charm Marisa into forgetting about his mischief.

Except, the cat's attention was focused on the staircase to the left of Marisa.

He was blinking at something or someone else

She looked all around her and almost thought she saw a hint of movement as she turned her head. No. Nothing there. Nothing could have moved.

She forced herself to walk slowly down the stairs, while her imagination galloped as fast as her pulse. She shuffled through stored memories of the past few days and pulled up the worst, the fantasy image of Aunt Enid's bloody-nailed ghost.

Never mind that Enid was gone, not on the premises — and not coming back.

Determined to read the morning's email and ignore her qualms, she sat in front of her computer. From her desk, at the edges of her peripheral vision, she could still glimpse Murphy, utterly still, muscles tensed, staring at empty space at mid-staircase.

The cat's eyes followed whoever or whatever he seemed to see descending the stairs.

Suddenly, Murphy jumped straight up in the air, like a Jack-in-the-box.

He rushed to the door, stretching his body as high as he could reach, and batted at the doorknob with his left front paw — the same way he would bat at a bug or a lizard, only with greater energy. He stretched up further and leaned in for a tentative sniff at the knob.

If she didn't know better, she'd think that whatever/whoever he'd been watching just walked through the door — literally, through the door, since it hadn't opened.

Getting up, she gently shooed Murphy out of the way, and peeked outside.

Nothing there.

Feeling bolder, she stepped out and scouted around the perimeter of the house. No one there, either. She walked a few feet down the long driveway, gravel digging into her bare feet, mindful that she had nothing on but the oversized t-shirt she'd slept in. There, past the palms, banyans, and vines, a little girl in ankle length pale skirt stood framed by the entryway arch on the other side of the gate. She was too distant for Marisa to make out her features, but she looked about the size of one of the cherub statues that lined the driveway.

Something about the girl struck Marisa as odd; she couldn't say what.

The child was curious about the house, Marisa told herself, that's all. How many times had children looked through that gate over the years at this miniature fairy tale manor?

She turned back to inspect the immediate vicinity one more time.

Nothing seemed out of the ordinary.

Nor did anything appear unusual when she stepped back inside. Murphy sat in the kitchen window seat grooming himself, looked contented enough. If he'd been frightened a moment before, he didn't show it now.

*

After finishing the last of her coffee, Marisa showered, pulled on jeans and a blue knit cowl neck top. She walked across the drive to knock at Otto's door.

"Coming," Otto called down from his apartment.

He beamed a gap-toothed smile when he answered, one she found particularly irritating this morning. Why, she thought, shouldn't he smile? He didn't have a care in the world. The leaks and termites were all Marisa's. The ghost — if there was one? That was hers, too. Meanwhile, Otto was living rent-free above her garage.

"Good morning, Marisa darling," he said. "What can I do for you?"

"Well, I'm hoping you know something about fixing roofs. And toilets." Looking at the overgrown yard, she added, "And do you think you could mow the lawn, please?"

"The lawn?" he crinkled his brow as if he were pondering

something far weightier. "Quite impossible, I'm afraid. There's no gas for the mower. But let me get my toolbox and I'll take a look at the rest."

*

An hour or so later, after he had peered into the gurgling toilet tank and shuffled around on the flat roof over the great room, Otto walked into Marisa's kitchen wearing a bigger smile than the one he'd greeted her with earlier.

"I might be able to fix the toilet," he said, "but that roof is so old, you'll have to call a professional roofer."

"Damn, I don't need this expense right now."

"Hold on just a minute, love," Otto said as he turned toward his own place. "There's something I want to show you."

He disappeared into the garage apartment, returning a moment later with a large sheaf of papers under his arm.

"You know it's impossible for you to keep up this place, don't you Marisa?" he said, dropping what she now saw was a thick legal document onto the kitchen table.

She ignored the comment and the papers.

"Consider yourself fortunate, dear cousin, because I'm going to help you in spite of yourself," he said. "In fact, we'll both make a bundle."

He began flipping pages, his smile broadening as he found what he wanted. "Look at all those zeroes after the dollar sign. And that's just the opening offer."

"So, Enid's bequest to you was valuable after all. I'm happy for you, Otto."

"You have to sell, too, of course. My stake is worthless without yours."

"I'm sorry Otto but Guinness wants my house so he can demolish it, and I won't let him do that."

"So, you'll do what, instead? Sit here and watch this old dump crumble around you while you destroy both our chances? This is the way out, Marisa."

"Otto. I'm late for work."

"Marisa, you need to face reality. Lucky for you, with me

86

as a partner, reality looks better than it otherwise would. Now listen carefully," his eyes growing wider, he pointed to another section of the document. "We have Guinness over a barrel. He needs that deep water dock by the ruins or he can't get the sailboat crowd to buy in. And the dock is part of this lot — our lot, Marisa. All right, technically yours, but we both have squatting rights."

"Otto, I'm sorry your rights are so tangled with mine, but —"

"No need to apologize, dear, it will all work out for the best. Just leave the negotiations to me." He moved in closer.

"No, damn it. No negotiations," she said, backing away from him. "No one is tearing down this house. Got it?"

Otto flushed purple.

"You are stupid, stupid, STUPID!" he yelled. "You ought to jump at this opportunity. Hell, you ought to kiss my feet."

"Okay, this is not going to work."

"Enid promised me this property."

"She must have changed her mind."

"I don't buy that," he snapped. "Not for an instant."

"Think what you like."

"Well, don't expect me to come running every time you have some new little repair crisis."

"Fine. I'll get somebody else to fix the toilet. You probably would have done a lousy job anyway.

*

Reaching for her purse and keys on the small table by the door, she noticed the red light on her answering machine blinking. She pushed the "play" button.

"Hello, this is Daniel Brogan, returning Marisa Delano's call," said a smooth southern baritone. Dan Brogan – the freak show expert that Myrtle recommended. He was calling back. "You can reach me at this number for the next hour or so. If I don't hear from you, I'll try you again later today or tomorrow."

She jotted Brogan's phone number on the pad next to the phone then dialed and let it ring about ten times. Neither Brogan nor his voice mail picked up.

Damn. If only she hadn't wasted time with Otto. She stuffed the paper with Brogan's number into her purse, and dashed outside and into her car. As she sped out of the gate, in the rearview mirror, she could see Otto standing by the garage, glaring after her, the papers clenched under his right arm.

*

Gaia occupied the northeast corner of an otherwise undistinguished strip mall. Marisa pulled into the parking lot; instead of heading straight for the store, she walked to the other end to the Third Bank of Sarasota.

She filled out a mortgage application, crossed her fingers, dropped off the papers with the receptionist, then crossed the parking lot to Gaia. She unlocked the front door, and hung the "Open" sign on the window and chalked in Petrika's name on the blackboard that told customers which psychic was working today.

*

At five o'clock, Kelly pulled into the parking lot in her Jeep. Claude, the reggae singer, was in the passenger seat.

The bells jingled as she opened the door. "Hey, Marisa, how'd it go today?"

"Slow in the store, but Petrika got plenty of readings."

"Well, it's official," said Kelly. "Guinness is demolishing Beachbum's. He's just waiting for his permits to come through. Claude is going to start doing readings here next week, just to tide him over until the band gets another gig, right Claude?" They smiled at each other in that way new lovers do.

Marisa didn't bother to mention that she'd never before heard a word about Claude possessing psychic powers.

15. LUCINDA

1917 — THE CIRCUS

As we sat together on the stage during the slow times, or for meals at the cookhouse, Ivan told me all the gossip. He pointed out the acrobat who regularly sneaked into an animal trainers' berth in the middle of the night, although during the day, they both acted like they hardly knew each other. The pickpocket who got caught by a sheriff in a town in Kentucky? Zack had made a show of running him off the lot but Ivan said it was just that, a show. The pickpocket paid eighteen-percent of his take to Zack, said Ivan. Sure enough, I saw that same grifter mingling with the circus crowds again at our next stop.

Ivan also explained why the men in the circus were all either past thirty or not yet twenty-one, something I hadn't noticed until he mentioned it. The draft board dogged the train at every major stop, making sure all the able-bodied young men signed up for the army. Even the freaks had to get draft cards although the army didn't want them to actually join.

And it wasn't just American men who were in short supply. Before the Great War, Ivan said, the circus bosses had actively scouted Europe for exotic attractions like himself.

"They mostly gone now," Ivan said as he sliced an apple in two with his pocket knife and handed half of it to me.

"This war, it divide circus like it do to the world outside."

Dozens of European performers had gone back to fight in

the armies on either side.

It was the war that had given me the chance to play a plum role in the circus spectacular.

In a small southern town, about a month ago, the Secret Service came to the circus and questioned everyone who knew Nettie and Hans, including Ivan. The government men didn't arrest the Schmidts but did suggest that they leave the United States (for their own good and the good of the circus). Ivan asked one of the government men if the Schmidts were suspected of anything. The Secret Service man answered, "Yeah, they're suspected of being German. Isn't that enough?"

Ivan didn't think so, but others in the circus did, especially Ruben, the dwarf, one the stars of the clown act.

"To hear Ruben talk, Hans must telegraph the Kaiser from every town," said Ivan, referring to the gossip the dwarf spread. "So much nonsense. What Hans is going to tell the German generals? How many bags of peanuts the peoples feed to the elephants?"

Nettie and Hans would leave for Germany at the next major city.

*

On my way back from the cookhouse, I stopped at the big top. Workmen scurried all around us, tying in the bail rings, block-and-tackle pulleys, ropes, ladders, and other trappings that attached to the apparatus the different acts used.

Nettie wasn't large enough or strong enough to put together her own gear, so Nicolai the Great laid out her equipment at the same time he worked on his own rigging.

"You ready for your big top debut?" he asked as he yanked on a diagonal wire. Looking displeased, he gave another half-turn to the thick metal implement that anchored it to the ground.

"Nettie needs this tight," he explained, "or the trick will not work right."

"Nettie doesn't walk on that thing, does she?" I asked.

"This? No, no, no," he laughed. "You have not yet seen

Nettie's act?"

I said I hadn't.

"Do not worry, Lucinda. It is a very easy trick. No walking on the wire. Nettie attaches her wrist harness to this and slides, that is all. A child could do it."

*

That evening, I hopped off the sideshow stage I shared with Ivan and raced to the big top before the last stragglers of our audience had moved along to the big tent. Marvin gave me a harsh look as I darted past him but I'd missed every chance to see Nettie perform during my first week.

The only time I'd seen the full spec was with Albert that first day. The memory was already a blur. I didn't recall anything about a fairy princess. I told myself that meant it must have been an insignificant part. Cyrus Parker and Zack thought I could do it and they understood that I'd never performed before. Still, there was that wire, and whatever she did on it that they expected me to do, too. It worried me, despite Nicolai's assurances about how easy it would be.

As I hurried along, I passed Leroy, standing at the side of the menagerie tent.

Bright lights still shone on the aisles, helping people find their way as they wriggled and pushed by one another to get to their seats, while the sawdust-covered arena was unlit. Above the hippodrome, ropes and equipment for at least a dozen different acts threw shadows that criss-crossed the circus top, making it look like a tangle left over from a giant game of cat's cradle gone wrong.

Just then, the house lights dimmed. The band began with a big boom and clang of cymbals, horns and drums. The spotlights glared on the entrance to the ring and on the center where the ringmaster stood. He blew hard on his whistle. Raucous, glittering performers began streaming in through the main entrance in time to the band. The clutter of trappings above them seemed to disappear.

First came the Littleville clown troupe, dressed in striped

red, black, yellow, and white costumes with oversized shoes. The five men (four midgets and dwarfs plus one tall, ex-acrobat, Zelenko) painted their faces white, then colored in the features with red and black. They painted their noses red, too, except for Ruben, who stuck a red rubber ball-shaped fake nose on his face with spirit gum. Each clown's face borrowed from the others but each was unique in its particulars. Hans streaked red sunbursts next to his eyes that made him look like he was always smiling. Ruben gave himself large red triangular eyebrows.

The crowd broke out in giggles and applause at the sight of them, even before they began chasing after each other and playing outrageous tricks. I'd seen the clown troupe perform between acts in several shows and still laughed as hard as anyone in the stands.

Zelenko wore the rags of a hobo. He had a big black frown painted around his mouth and, as he marched along, feigning seriousness, he juggled three colorful balls. The smaller clowns pulled on his coattails then ran around behind him so they were out of sight when he tried to catch them at it.

At last, Zelenko grabbed Hans by the scruff and held him in the air as Hans kicked his feet. The bigger clown pantomimed wagging his finger and scolding Hans while the trombone played a series of notes timed to his pretend tirade.

Behind the Littleville clowns came the Torellenos and their trained dogs: seven white-and-black spotted mongrels who danced and pranced on command. Their mistress and master, in matching white sequined tuxedoes, raised their arms as if to gather in the adoration of the circus audience.

Six white horses, their saddles draped in red satin, followed the Torellenos, carrying the six riders from The Fabulous Alexander Family — Mr. and Mrs. Vladeczesko, their three boys, ages 12, 13 and 15, and their daughter, 18. They sat in the saddles and waved to the crowds as their mounts high-stepped around the ring.

The beautiful aerialist, Rebecca Bradley, riding in an open

red carriage pulled by two large brown horses, followed behind them. She was dressed all in glittery gold and blew kisses at the crowds.

The orchestra switched from the blaring march that began the spec to "The Dance of the Sugarplum Fairy."

A light swept up from the sawdust and illuminated a spot about fifty feet above, where Nettie stood on a tiny platform. She must have been waiting there in the dark, as the others marched by. The spotlight concentrated on her face and picked up the sparkle of the fairy wings she wore on her back. Grasping a loop attached to a diagonal wire, she shoved off the little platform, gracefully gliding down, fast as can be, and landing at the front of a group of about a dozen dancers who had paraded into the big top behind Rebecca Bradley.

The dancers, in gauzy pink dresses like Nettie's, pirouetted around her as she bowed. Next, Nettie did a little dance while the normal-sized dancers bowed. Then they all moved along as the ringmaster whistled for the next acts to file in and join the spec parade.

My throat clutched up as I watched. Lordy me, Cyrus Parker expected me to do what she did? Impossible.

I wasn't graceful. I didn't know how to dance. And, if I tried to fly down that wire like Nettie, I would surely fall and kill myself. I could see myself now, dropping down, splat, in front of the beautiful carriage pulled by the great horses and being trampled to death while Rebecca Bradley kept on waving to her adoring fans.

*

Midway through the show, Hans found me by the tent flap and told me to meet Nettie under the big top, after the audience cleared out. She was going to teach me the "slide-for-life," he said. It was the first time I'd heard the term that described her hurtle down the wire to the sawdust. After watching the spec, I figured it was accurate description.

I waited inside the ring while the workers folded up the chairs in the big top.

Wanda was there, too. I said hello. She smiled and gave me the slightest nod then turned away. A minute or so after I arrived, Nicolai walked through the flap, waved to me, and walked to Wanda who stood a few feet beyond.

"You have an audience for your trapeze lesson," Nicolai said as he approached her, gesturing back toward the flap with his head.

I turned and saw Leroy outside, about fifty feet back.

"I don't talk to razorbacks," said Wanda, straightening her shoulders and looking haughty. "He ought to learn his place."

Even from that distance, I could see Leroy cringe as if someone had punched him in the gut. He backed off and slunk away. Poor lovesick soul. I felt almost as bad for him as if she'd said it to me.

Nicolai looked sympathetic but then turned back to Wanda. "It is safer for the boy if you discourage him," he said. "You do not want to make him lose his job. Come now, let us see what you remember of what I teach you last."

He led her into the center of the ring, held the trapeze for her then, using a pulley, raised it once she'd grasped the rung.

*

Nettie arrived about two minutes later and pointed me to the other end of the ring where she set about teaching me her routine. She coaxed me up a scratchy rope ladder that wiggled and twisted as I climbed, threatening to hurl me right back down on the ground. Already, I had trouble and I hadn't gotten anywhere yet. The ladder went straight to the tiny platform that she called a pedestal. Nettie followed after me, ascending with no more trouble than if it were a solid set of stairs, and began explaining the "slide-for-life."

Unlike the trap or the wire, Nettie said, her trick didn't require much skill.

"You were farm girl, yes?" she said. "If you can do that hard work, you are very strong. You can do this."

Her English was choppy but she had such a warm, encouraging way of talking, I didn't need to get every word to understand the meaning. Listening to her, I started to feel it might be possible.

The pedestal was hardly wide enough for one of us, nevermind two. I got dizzy looking down. She touched under my chin with her hand and waved her finger at me, "No, no. Don't look there," she chirped. She pushed up at my chin again. It did no good. Now that I'd seen how high up we were, I wasn't about to forget that picture of the long way down.

"Watch me. See?" She placed her hand through a small leather band, looped into a noose shape, that was attached with a metal connector to a small wheel. The wheel ran underneath the thick braided diagonal wire, and allowed it to move freely. The wire was tied to a pole behind us at the top and secured on the ground below with more complicated metal connectors.

Nettie moved the leather loop back and forth on the diagonal wire a few inches each way to show me, "Here, see?"

All I could think of was that I didn't want to fall. I figured it wouldn't do any good to let on how scared I was. So, I smiled and nodded, and clutched the pole.

Nettie slid the loop back and forth a few inches each way on the wire again, coaxing me to pay attention. She wrapped a white-gloved hand around the loop once, grasped that hand with her other and pushed off the pedestal, her back straight, one knee bent slightly into the crook of the other.

I almost lost my balance watching her, and had to grab the top of the rope ladder to steady myself.

Nettie ascended the ladder again. She took off the white leather gloves that kept her from getting friction blisters. She handed them to me.

"You try," she said.

One way or another, I'd have to get back down on the ground again. I put on the gloves and grabbed the loop. Nettie stopped me and shook her head. She re-positioned my hand. It seemed so awkward that I shifted it again. She shook her head in alarm.

It seemed hopeless. Nettie patted my hand, cooed at me

in German and moved my arm, wrist and hands until I had everything positioned as she wanted. Then she urged me with gestures to stand as she had, holding onto the hand in the loop with my free hand.

I don't know why or how I did it, but I lifted off the pedestal and flew down that wire. The tug on the inside of my arm made it feel like it had caught fire but I couldn't let go.

I swung around like a kite in a windstorm. The trip down was so much faster than it looked when Nettie did it. I hit the sawdust hard, skinning my knee, then twisted around to thump my bottom as well.

Nettie climbed down to where I sat in the dirt, and gave me a little clap of encouragement.

I had actually done it. I had flown down the wire, without breaking any bones.

And my graceless thumping had not attracted the notice of Nicolai and Wanda who were busy with their own rehearsal.

To my way of thinking, I'd done enough for one night, but not to Nettie's. She coaxed me up the wiggly ladder and onto the pedestal to try again.

The second time, I was no more graceful but I felt a little less scared. Nettie, ever patient, gave me more pointers.

We kept on long after Nicolai finished up with Wanda, only leaving when the canvas boss said it was time to pull the tops and load them on the train.

*

I practiced with Nettie a few minutes each night after the audience left the last show and before the canvas came down, and whenever else we could find the time. Sometimes we sneaked in a moment or two while most of the circus folks were at the cookhouse. Once, on a rainy day, we managed to practice for a couple of hours between the matinee and evening show because the sideshow was slow. By the second week, I made it to the bottom without twisting around all the way down.

The ringmaster, who peeked in on us to check my progress,

looked relieved that I ended up on my feet more often than on my knees, back and bottom. I was bruised in every place it was possible to be bruised and some places where it didn't seem possible. But I could do it.

Once on the ground, I was supposed to dance Nettie's magical fairy ballet. I had never danced in my life and probably looked more like I was throwing a fit. Nettie never laughed, despite my clumsiness, and clapped for me no matter how little I deserved it.

When we were both exhausted, she looped her arm through mine and we walked back to the rail car together. Some nights, Hans would wait until we were done with my lessons and walk with us but most often, he would already be back in his berth by the time we finished. Although we couldn't communicate well in words, Nettie and I became friends, spending more time in each other's company. I guess that's why Ruben, who was the unofficial leader of the little people, began treating me more coolly, like I was under suspicion, too.

"What're you up to," Ruben asked after we returned one night to the train car, "consorting with the enemy?"

I laughed at first as I passed him to walk inside, thinking he was making a joke. The look on his face and the way that the three other little people outside the railcar turned and suddenly found other things to do made me realize he meant it.

That wasn't the only thing that put distance between me and my fellow midgets. Sideshow acts who didn't perform under the big top made almost all their money by selling whatever souvenirs they could. I had come out of nowhere, had no talents, no experience, and yet had been given a choice role in the spec. It meant I got paid an extra five dollars a week and had the greater prestige of being in the big show. Toy took every chance to remind me that, to her way of thinking, the honor, and the money, should have gone to her.

Still, I had my hopes. I saw how happy Hans and Nettie were together. I secretly imagined that here among others who lived outside the everyday world, I would find a man to love me, even if my fantasies weren't focused on somebody my own size.

I couldn't let on even to Nettie that it was Cyrus Parker I daydreamed about. I saw him watch me from the shadows behind the tent flaps as Nettie trained me, or while we unloaded for the trip to the fairgrounds, or in the evenings as he talked with Zack or the equestrian director. I watched him, too, naturally, but from a distance. Any time our eyes met, I'd feel this powerful sensation, almost like I was hurt and happy at the same time. I told myself, don't be getting any wild ideas. For all I knew, he was keeping an eye on me because Ruben told him I was "consorting with the enemy."

We rarely spent any time talking. But he came to watch me rehearse one day and, when we were done, asked if I thought I was ready to take on the role.

"I don't know. I'm scared I'll seem more like a chicken running around with its head cut off than a fairy princess."

The way he looked at me, I almost expected him to put his arms around me. "Nonsense, Lucinda," he said. He reached down and lightly caressed my hair, just for the tiniest moment. "You are lovely in every respect. Every respect. The crowds will adore you." He smiled at me, tipped his hat to Nettie, and left.

Like my big brother Albert would say, I was plum goshbustified.

I re-lived that moment a thousand times in the next few days. What had he said, other than that he, my boss, was pleased with the job I was doing? That was all. I would be a fool to read more into it. Yet, I captured that moment in my memory like a photograph and took it out to look at it, every chance I got.

This tiny incident made me feel closer to him but it also made me even more shy around him. He was Cyrus Parker, the circus owner, and I was a midget. I had about as much chance with him as a one-legged man had at an ass-kicking.

Lordy, wouldn't Ruben just laugh from here to Judgment Day if he guessed how I felt? Everyone would. I thought about poor Leroy and how Wanda had put him in his place, and how bad that must have felt.

I was determined not to let on. So, if Cyrus Parker smiled at me or tipped his hat when he caught my eye, I'd pretend I hadn't seen him even though, in his dashing black suit, he was difficult to miss.

Then came the night I took over for Nettie. I wasn't ready but delay was impossible. Nettie and Hans were leaving the circus in the morning.

Wearing Nettie's costume with the chiffon fairy wings for the first time, I climbed the ladder to the pedestal before the audience streamed into the big top for the last show of the day. I waited for what seemed like forever. From my perch, I could see everyone and everything — the tops of the heads of the people in the audience, the open tent flaps where performers shuffled, getting ready for their entrance. Cyrus stood at another open tent flap, looking directly at me, the only person in this crowd of hundreds who seemed to realize I was there. I knew he had a good business reason to watch but I allowed myself to pretend that he was there just to see me. I imagined giving a perfect performance, taking bow after bow. And, at the end, I imagined Cyrus leading me away from the cheering crowd, taking me into his arms and kissing me.

Unfortunately, that was nothing like what actually happened.

I glanced down again a few minutes later and saw Ivan, fresh from the sideshow, and Nettie and Hans, now in street clothes, crowded around another tent opening, the one the performers used to exit after parading around the hippodrome.

I had to stop looking down. It was making me dizzy. I got to my feet and stood as comfortably as I could on the pedestal. I listened through the opening number for my cue. At last, I heard it, the first few notes of "The Dance of the Sugarplum Fairy." The spotlight shined on my face. I stared straight into it, not understanding that it could temporarily bore a dark hole through the center of my vision.

I flew down the wire in my first big top performance, half-blind from the spotlight. For an instant after I touched the ground, I stood completely still, forgetting to bow, and forgetting my dance. The larger dancers twirled around me. After a couple of seconds, I snapped out of it, and finished up my steps.

The next act, a stilt walker and a unicyclist, were only a few yards back. Then the elephants marched in behind them. I hoped that my mistakes would be missed by the audience as each new act delighted them. Clumsily, I followed the promenade. The blind spot began to melt away and was gone by the time we paraded through the exit, a short way from where the rest of the parade was still making its entrance.

Nettie, Hans and Ivan were there to congratulate me as, once beyond the big top, I fell out of the formation. They all insisted that I'd done just fine but I knew it wasn't true. The only thing good I could say about it was that I hadn't panicked while still up on the platform or I would have killed myself coming down.

Across the fairgrounds, I saw Cyrus Parker by the pathway near the other side of the big top. He was waving at me, hurrying my way. He looked anxious to get my attention.

I'd failed so miserably, my first performance would probably be my last. Maybe he was going to cut me from the spec. That had to be it. He'd made a mistake handing this spec act to a "First of May" and would give it, instead, to Toy.

I wouldn't mind so much if I lost it, but I couldn't bear to be fired by Cyrus. Let Zack tell me in the morning.

I pretended not to understand that he wanted me to stop and talk. I waved back as if nothing was wrong, then turned to join my friends. When I looked behind me a minute or two later, he was gone.

*

Nettie and Hans Schmidt left the show the next morning, catching a train from Philadelphia that would take them north to New York City, where they would board a ship to carry them across the Atlantic Ocean.

I didn't get fired in the morning. I heard nothing at all about my performance from anyone and again, that afternoon, as the audience shuffled in, I climbed the rope ladder to wait for my cue, and looked down slightly when the spotlight hit my face.

This time, nobody stood inside the tent flap to watch. And I remembered all the steps.

I saw Zack on my way to the cookhouse for breakfast the following day.

"Hey, Lucinda. Mr. Cyrus said to tell you he was sorry he missed y'all," Zack said. "You must've made an impression. He hardly said good-bye to anybody."

"Why was he saying good-bye?"

"I thought you knew," Zack answered. "Mr. Cyrus went and sold out to the Ringling Brothers. He left yesterday, same as Hans and Nettie. Only they went north to catch a boat. Mr. Cyrus headed down south, back home to Sarasota, Florida."

Zack explained that Mr. Cyrus's wife was gravely ill and was not expected to live out the year. Cyrus had gone back to be at her side and to take over the upbringing of their child. His circus days were over. He was taking a position at his father's bank.

I had to force myself to keep walking to the cookhouse. I sat with the other sideshow performers but felt lost and alone. I shoved the food from one end of my plate to the other, my head buzzing, my heart as heavy as a bucket of bird-shot.

For weeks afterward, I carried the heaviness with me.

The only times when the gloom lifted were when I'd see someone on the lot wearing a black suit like Cyrus's. My whole body would get warm and light and tingly, even though I knew it couldn't be him. It never was.

16. Marisa

She checked her phone messages before leaving Gaia. The bank's loan officer had phoned; he had a question about her current employment. At least he hadn't flat out rejected her application. She called back, got his voice mail, and left a message, then headed home.

From the bend at Indian Beach and Bay Shore Road, she could see the sun, half-settled into the water, like a slice of lemon peeking over the edge of a cocktail. A flock of squawking green Quaker parrots flew overhead, lighting on the tops of the wind-bent palm trees.

About a block ahead, she spotted the little girl she'd seen early this morning. She was pedaling a tricycle, the type of oversized three-wheeler that members of Sarasota's small local Mennonite population used in place of cars.

The trike seemed too big for the girl. Her body, lower than the seat, tilted left and right with each pump on the pedals. From this distance, Marisa might not have realized it was the same child except for the long, pale skirt, the one she wore that morning. As the girl turned the corner up a side street, Marisa again sensed that there was something different about her, about the way she moved. Or, maybe it was simply the surprise of seeing someone so small unaccompanied by an adult.

Before she could think too much about her, another cyclist,

this one in padded black bike shorts and white helmet, drove toward her from the opposite direction on a jazzy-looking red mountain bike. He pulled up next to Marisa's car. She slowed to a stop as she recognized the smiling face under the helmet.

"Hey, Marisa, I wondered if you'd be around," John Guinness called.

"I'm around," she said warily.

"You settling into your new house?" he asked, one lean leg resting lazily on a pedal.

"It's an old house," she corrected, "a very old house with a lot of problems."

"Uh-oh, I smell trouble."

"That still doesn't mean it's for sale."

"I know, I know."

"I wonder, considering your showing up just now," she said.

"I just felt we got off on the wrong foot. I don't want you to think I'm nothing more than a greedy land grabber."

"You're tearing down Beachbum's, I hear."

"Would it make me a better person to let some other developer do it? Either way, it's coming down."

They sat looking at each other for a long moment. He was right, of course. Sarasota was filled with real estate vultures. But that didn't absolve him for being a member of the flock. She could have said as much but why antagonize him?

John Guinness broke the silence. "Okay, so how about I concede that maybe I deserve the ice-maiden treatment. Is there some way I can make up for creating such a lousy first impression?"

Fat chance, buddy, she thought. Then she reminded herself that he was a contractor. After hesitating a moment she decided she had nothing to lose.

"What do you know about toilets?" she asked.

"Toilets?"

"Yes, toilets — the kind that run all night."

"Have you tried jiggling the handle?"

She said yes.

"No luck?"

She said no.

"Let me come inside and see what I can do."

*

She parked in front of the garage, relieved that Otto's car was gone. She turned toward her house.

The front door hung wide open.

She turned back to look for John. He had followed her car through the gate and was pedaling down the drive.

She stood by her car until John pulled up and then walked across the drive, through her open front door. The house had dimmed with the dusk; she pulled on the light cord of the stained glass hanging lamp to the left of the door. When it didn't light, she moved a few feet further into the house and flicked the switch on the floor lamp to the right. It didn't light either.

She could see now all the way into the great room. The back door hung wide open too.

She looked behind her at John and saw concern on his face. "You didn't leave the house like this, did you?" he asked.

Before she could answer, he grabbed Marisa's arm, pulled her out of the house and marched her to her car. "Drive to the gate and wait there until the police arrive."

He took a cell phone from under his bike seat and dialed 9-1-1.

*

Two cops, one male, one female, pulled up to the gate in a black and white police car.

The male, squat and unyielding, wrote notes on a small pad as Marisa spoke. His short black hair was slicked back with gel. His dark blue uniform fit snugly. His name tag said Sergeant Velasquez. The woman officer, a redhead until you got to the darker roots, stayed next to the driver's side of the squad car and spoke into the radio receiver. A male voice on the other end responded with staccato bursts of unintelligible conversation layered with static.

105

The stern faced Velasquez tucked his pad back in his pocket. Both officers got back into their squad car and drove down to the house.

*

"Ma'am, we've checked inside," said Sergeant Velasquez. "Nobody is in there now. There's no sign of a broken lock or window."

Marisa could tell by the cops' more relaxed demeanor that they didn't see this as a burglary.

She was willing to concede the possibility that she'd left the house unlocked. That didn't explain the lights.

As if reading her mind, the female officer said, "Your circuit breaker was switched off. Did you have a lot of appliances running? The air conditioner, maybe?"

"I don't think my toaster would blow the circuits. That's about as major an appliance as the house has."

"Well, you can't trust the wiring in these old places," the cop said, smiling slightly. "You want to walk through with me, see if anything's missing?"

*

Marisa followed the cop upstairs. She walked around the playroom. Nothing looked disturbed. Nothing else seemed out of place. Same for the smaller bedroom. Nothing, so far as she could tell, had been taken.

She felt embarrassed. The place looked just as she'd left it.

The redheaded officer wrote something on a business card and handed it to Marisa. "This is the case number for the incident," she said. "If you notice anything missing, call that extension and refer to that number."

"Sorry to have bothered you."

"No problem, ma'am. We'd rather come out and find nothing than have you second-guess things and walk in on an intruder," the cop said. She joined her partner in the squad car and they drove off the estate.

John stood in the kitchen, looking awkward. "Can I get you something?" Marisa asked. "A glass of wine, maybe?"

She reached for the bottle, then realized that, in her search through the house with the officer, she hadn't seen what mattered most to her.

"Murphy!"

"Murphy?" John repeated.

"My cat."

Leaving John standing alone in the kitchen, she darted into the other rooms, looking under the chairs, the sofa, and in all the dark corners. She raced upstairs and looked under the beds, under the night-table, in the bath tub.

Downstairs again, she walked past a bewildered John Guinness and got a flashlight from the kitchen drawer. Searching the downstairs more methodically this time, she shined the light into the closets, under the furniture, inside the cabinets, all the while feeling a sense of dread. Her eyes went to the back door that had been hanging open when she got home. She opened it again and stared at the dense brush, vines and woods.

"He's probably out chasing field mice," John said.

"He's a housecat. If he got outside, he wouldn't know where he was."

"I'll help you find him," John volunteered.

"Stay here," she snapped, more harshly than she meant to. "He doesn't know you." She ran down the drive, flashlight beam jittering along the ground.

*

Dietrich, when they were still married, had surprised her with the beige and gray kitten after she complained that he was working late too often. She'd been annoyed at the time that he would think a cat could substitute for human company but Murphy's antics were surprisingly entertaining. He could keep her distracted for hours. Soon after, as her marriage began to crumble, Murphy took to cuddling beside her on the bed at night. She found solace in his warmth as Dietrich grew cool.

When she lost the baby, she buried her face in his fur and sobbed. He lay perfectly still, seeming to understand how much she needed to connect with another soul.

And during the weeks after her mother died, when she didn't know what she'd do with all the empty hours, alone in an apartment where everything reminded her of her mom, Murphy kept her from sinking more deeply into depression. He needed her and that gave her a reason to get out of bed in the morning. Sometimes, when she tried to read a book, he'd sit on top of it and knead his paws on the pages. If she tried to write, he'd walk across the computer keyboard, adding cat-composed gibberish to her carefully constructed prose. He was a complete clown but she loved him.

He had given her what no human could — or would. Having lost almost everyone else, her bond with him was the most important one in her life right now.

She had to find him.

"Murphy, where are you?"

She was hoarse from calling him and scratched up from the thorny vines she'd stumbled through in her search. If Murphy was out there, he was either too afraid to show himself or he was already too far away to hear.

She gave up and walked into the back door.

"No luck?" asked John Guinness.

She shook her head.

"Well," he said with forced cheeriness, "if it's any consolation, while you were out looking, I fixed your toilet."

She gave him a weak thanks.

"Let me stay in the guest room tonight. You shouldn't be here by yourself. What if whoever broke in comes back?"

"No, I was in a rush this morning. I must have left the doors unlocked."

"It's not going to put me out."

"John, I appreciate the gesture but I need to be alone."

That wasn't quite true. She needed someone to hold her, stroke her hair, and tell her it would be all right. But Dietrich was gone, and this virtual stranger, no matter how kind he was acting now, was neither lover nor friend. John Guinness only wanted one thing: her house. Just thinking about that threatened to shatter what was left of her composure. With him standing in her kitchen, she felt more vulnerable and alone.

Otto's car spit gravel from his tires as he came down the drive.

"You expecting company?"

"That's only Otto."

"What if I ask him if he'll come in and stay with you?"

"NO." she yelled, surprising them both. "Sorry. My nerves are jangled but I'll be fine. I don't want him in here."

Otto probably still had a key to the house. She wondered if maybe this was his retaliation for their spat this morning. Another thought bumped into that one: for all she knew, if Otto did it, John Guinness put him up to it.

"I don't like leaving you alone like this," said John.

"I'll ask my friend Kelly to come over." John handed Marisa his cell phone.

"Kelly is on her way," she told John after hanging up. "Now, go. I'm okay."

*

For all his protesting, John seemed relieved to go.

Marisa stood at the window, eyes on the shadows she saw shifting through the shades as Otto moved around the upstairs apartment. She wondered if she should confront him.

Burglars and teenaged pranksters didn't make sense. Something would have been missing or messed with.

But she couldn't quite convince herself that it was Otto, either. He was a creep but not a fool. If he wanted to get back at her, he'd do something that couldn't be traced to him. That left one possibility, the one she didn't want to consider because it was completely illogical: that whatever Otto's motives, he had told the truth about the house.

Murphy had sensed it, maybe even seen it, on the stairs. Household servants and nurses had run from it. No matter how she tried to dismiss it, she had felt its presence. Several times.

"WHO ARE YOU?" she shouted in frustration. "Leave me alone, damn you."

Leave me alone.

She walked outside, into the brush again. "Murphy?" The sky was black. The woods melted into a single blurred shadow. If Murphy was out there, she wasn't going to find him.

*

A banged-up antique of a yellow Volkswagen bug came chugging down the drive with Claude at the wheel and Kelly in the passenger seat. The muffler, or what was left of it, had announced its arrival before it had come into view. Each of its fenders had at least one dent. As Claude pulled partway into the space next to Otto's car, Marisa noticed that a broken lens on the left tail light was covered in transparent red tape. Kelly got out and ran over to hug her.

"Thanks, I needed that."

"Didn't I tell you them duppies was gonna be a problem?" Claude shouted; though he was just a few feet away, the unmuffled engine made a normal conversational level impractical.

Kelly shook her head and laughed. "Here," she reached into her pocket, pulled out a set of keys, and handed them to Claude as she kissed him good-bye. "Pick me up in the morning about nine o'clock. And this time, take my Jeep."

As she turned back to Marisa, she explained, "There's a hole the size of a toaster oven in the floor of his Beetle. I kept worrying I'd put my foot through it."

"That's the air conditioning, mon," Claude called out, his dreadlocks bouncing as he laughed at his own joke.

*

Kelly held the flashlight as Marisa searched around the exterior of the house. A 'possum quick-waddled out of the light and disappeared into the brush. They saw no sign of Murphy.

"How much you want to bet he's still inside?" Kelly asked, and led her back inside.

"I'll take the downstairs," said Kelly. "You take the upstairs."

Opening the refrigerator, Marisa grabbed what she realized she should have gotten the moment she'd discovered him missing.

"He may not come to you without a little incentive," she said, handing Kelly three thin slices of turkey cold cuts. "Just call out, 'goodies,' as you look around."

A force pushed back against her chest as Marisa climbed the steps. She tried to tell herself she imagined it but, when she put her foot on the second floor landing, it got stronger.

Ignoring the odd sensation, she searched the smaller bedroom, got down on her knees and looked under the bed. "Goodies, Murphy," she said to no one.

She squeezed her face to the floor to look underneath the dresser.

That sense of something she couldn't name felt strongest at the playroom doorway. On her forearms, the tiny fine hairs stuck straight up.

She stepped over the threshold. The sensation passed. But ...

That was odd.

The right side of the wall under the vanity looked crooked, as if it had been pushed out from the inside. "Murphy?" she called as she crawled under it. The beaded wood panel was hinged at an odd angle where it met the other wall, leaving a gap of a few inches. She looked around for something she could use to pry the wood further back.

Kelly's voice stopped her. "Marisa, I found your cat."

She ran down the stairs. There he was, struggling to get free from Kelly's arms.

"Murphy!" Relief rushed through her like a drug. She took him from Kelly and snuggled her face in his fur.

"I was checking under the bed," said Kelly, "when I heard someone meowing behind me for this," she held up the remnants of a turkey slice.

As she put him down on the floor, Marisa noticed a dusty bit of cobweb clinging to his left ear. He wound himself back and forth around their ankles, begging for more of his goodies.

Marisa took the bits in Kelly's hand, bent down, and fed them to the kitty. "First thing tomorrow, I'm buying you a collar and an identification tag."

"There's a charge in the air that wasn't here the last time. Do you feel it?" Kelly asked. "We need to get Rena over here."

"Kelly, it's after nine o'clock."

"Rena won't mind," Kelly said as she flipped open her cell phone and punched a number in her speed dial. "She lives for this sort of thing."

17. LUCINDA

OTHERNESS

Lucinda hovered at the edge of the dream, exhausted by her exertions. Yet she resisted tipping over into that state again. She had touched the physical — the doll and the doors — had felt them. She had not simply filtered through reality as she always had before but had made it respond to her will.

The sensations thrilled her.

Time, which had raced by her, thwarting her attempts to connect with the physical world, had slowed enough for her to sense it again, and for it to respond to her.

She pushed against a closet door, trying to repeat her earlier successes, but it dissolved in her grasp. Or maybe, she was the one dissolving, back into dreamstate.

18. Lucinda

1917 – 1918

Circus season ended with the onset of winter. Everyone was either going home, or working in burlesque or vaudeville shows.

Stephania, who had joined the Parker Circus only a few months before I arrived, shaved for the trip back home. She had been a sideshow attraction twenty years before, when she and her bronco-riding husband first met at a Wild West show. Last year, her husband got thrown from a horse and couldn't work the shows any more, so Stephania let her whiskers grow out again and became the family's breadwinner.

Until next March, when the circus season began again, she would be just another housewife.

Ivan got us booked on weekends on the vaudeville circuit in the bigger cities through the south. With money in our pockets and most of the week free, we went to the picture show whenever we wanted and saw Charlie Chaplin in "Shoulder Arms" twice. My favorites were the cartoons, especially Mutt & Jeff which, I told Ivan, made me think of him and me.

About a month before we were set to go back to Kentucky to begin rehearsals for the next circus season, we got two full working weeks. Olympia Booking needed us to fill in for several performers who had come down with bad cases of influenza. We dashed from city to city, spending more time on rail cars than anywhere else.

By then, I was happy for the distraction. In those long evenings, in strange hotel rooms, waiting for sleep to come, my memory replayed the night that Cyrus Parker waved to get my attention, and I ran in the other direction. I missed him, damned fool that I was, and I knew it was crazy to imagine he felt anything for me. I had even less chance than poor Leroy, mooning over Wanda the dancing girl. Cyrus was back home with his family and, by now, he probably forgot I existed.

*

It was even stranger returning and not seeing Cyrus on the lot. Plenty else had changed over the winter with more boys having passed their twenty-first birthday, getting their draft cards, and either shipping out to France or getting set to go. Those men who still traveled with the show often got viewed with suspicion by the townies.

Our first day back, an angry older woman who came to the sideshow yelled at Danny, the tattooed man, "Why aren't you in uniform?"

He didn't answer her but I could see that it made him feel bad.

After a while, to keep the heckling down, Marvin took to weaving into his spiel about how all the freaks were in Class 5 — people who the army didn't want.

*

Most of the freaks couldn't read very well and some of the ones who could, like Stephania, needed glasses to see the small letters. In the slow times between shows, I'd read the news out loud to the rest of the sideshow performers.

If I hadn't thought too much about the war before, I couldn't think of much else now. The papers were full of news about the Germans and our brave soldiers. One story in a Kentucky newspaper was all about a German plot to invade America by sneaking across the border from Mexico. It said that the Kaiser's men were under orders to ravage all American women. Another news story, about an incident in Indiana, scared us even more:

Girls Escape Teuton Poison

When Tri Delta sorority girls at De Pauw University opened a bag of dried beans in their sorority house, and discovered blue spots on the beans, they took them to the head of the chemistry department, who found the coloring matter was poison. The beans were shipped from Chicago and the bag had been opened in transit. The girls believe Germans poisoned the beans on the theory that they would probably find their way to an army camp.

"So that's how they been making our doughboys sick," said Stephania. "All we been hearing about is this Spanish influenza when it's really German poison."

Ivan interrupted her, saying that there was no reason to make such a leap just because some school girls had a scare. Kumar seemed to think Stephania was onto something though.

"How much of that poison is in our foods right now?" said Kumar. "You cannot say no. You are not a chemistry professor. We must watch for the blue dots or we will all die, like the poisoned soldiers."

Ivan shrugged and shook his head, like he knew there was no point arguing with people who had their minds made up. I wanted to agree with him but I couldn't help it: I plumb lost my appetite. I don't think I ate more than hard-boiled eggs for the next few days, figuring that the Germans wouldn't be able to get their poison past the shells. People in the cookhouse passed their plates back and forth for group inspection, unable to agree on whether some fleck or other was a poison blue dot.

After a while, when nobody keeled over at the cookhouse — or anywhere else, as far as I was able to tell — I figured that Ivan was right, as usual. The Germans weren't poisoning us and weren't likely to. People kept warning against blue-speckled food around the back lot and on the line to the cookhouse though, making the danger sound worse with each telling.

Still, I didn't feel the full sting of the war until I read that the government planned to start taking farmers for the army. The newspaper said they could draft them as long as the army paid more money than farmers could earn working on the land.

"That's got to be a mistake," I said.

"Government does what it wants, Lucinda," said Ivan. "Is much better in America than under tsar but government is government. You cannot argue with it."

"But farming's got nothing to do with money. My family doesn't make money. They make food."

*

I stayed up nights fretting about what I would do if my Daddy had to go to war. Worse, what if they started calling up the younger men, too, like Albert? I'd have to go back home but I couldn't run that farm with just myself and my two little brothers. We couldn't make it produce enough.

Daddy paid Cal Hodgeson one-quarter of all the crops he grew for the use of the land. If Mr. Hodgeson didn't get enough from our family, he would take away our acreage and give it to another tenant farmer, along with our house and everything else the family had.

In the last letter I got from Albert, my big brother didn't seem to consider any of that. He would be eighteen in January. The army would be calling up eighteen-year-olds for the draft any time now, he said.

"I can't wait to fight, sis. I'll make those rotten Germans sorry they ever threatened our country."

Albert had never met Nettie or Hans or he'd know that not all Germans were bad. In certain ways, I realized, traveling with the circus had made me older than my big brother. I didn't know exactly why the war started or why President Wilson decided to get us in it but I was learning not to believe everything I read.

Then again, if Albert was going to have to fight, maybe it was better if he didn't share my doubts.

*

Federal investigators came snooping around more often, searching for dodgers or deserters they believed might be hiding out with the show. I suppose we hid more than a few without meaning to. The circus ran on transient labor. It was normal for drifters to show up, work for a few days or a few weeks, then disappear. If they were ducking the draft or the law, they didn't advertise it.

Even those who would never buck the government acted wary. Leroy was the only exception I knew. He didn't appear to care who might not take kindly to hearing his thoughts about the war.

"If them Germans invaded, we'd plow them down like Sherman going through Georgia," he said. "But we ain't got nobody invading us. And how're we supposed to defend our homes if they do, what with the government shipping half the country boys 'cross the ocean?"

"I've had about enough of your lies," said someone behind me. I recognized the voice as Ruben's. "Our soldiers are over there fighting right now. What'd you ever do, besides spread sedition?"

"Why, you little hornswoggler — you calling me a traitor?" Leroy looked ready to kill the dwarf. A couple of other men stood up and put their hands on his shoulders.

He shrugged off the hands that restrained him.

"I ain't gonna waste a whupping on the likes of you. You don't like what I got to say, don't listen. It's a free country."

It wasn't more than a few weeks after that when the Bureau of Investigation came, and people had all the proof they needed that it wasn't quite as free a country as Leroy believed, least not for anybody who said what the government didn't want him to.

Stephania saw them coming first. She half-strolled, half-trotted toward the backyard where the razorbacks were resting after unloading the train. Ivan and I had just reached the fairgrounds after leaving the train when we saw her rushing past. She stage-whispered, "Hey Rube," and kept on going, a big fake smile on her whiskered face. We understood. Trouble was coming and it was watching, too. We tried to catch up without looking like we were in any hurry.

As we followed along behind, Stephania marched up to a group of the laborers, grabbed Leroy by the arm and pulled him along like a mother with a misbehaving child.

"Get your behind in gear, boy, the government men are coming for you."

"I didn't do nothing wrong," he protested, trying to shake her grip.

"Nothing but shoot off your damned fool mouth," said Stephania.

"If you think I'm such a fool, why don't you let me be?"

"Because it ain't no crime being an idiot," Stephania answered, "leastways, it shouldn't be. I'm sorely tempted to take you behind the barn and beat your bottom red, but I can't abide them federal cops hauling a boy off to jail, not just for talking."

Something she said must have stuck because he stopped resisting her and starting trotting along by her side.

The other laborers closed ranks and gave them cover as Stephania and Leroy retreated. She led him around the side of the yard and doubled back toward where the circus tops were going up. Ivan and I kept a few paces behind until we were sure we were out of sight of the train. Stephania was pulling Leroy along toward where canvasmen were raising the menagerie top.

The circus's advance man always got to the stops along the show's route about a week before the circus itself. He put up the signs and posters telling everyone where the show would be, rented the fields, bought the feed and other supplies that the animals would need, saw to the deliveries, and generally smoothed the way. Evidence that the advance man had done his job was in the mountain of hay bales just beyond where the menagerie was going up. The tent's sidewalls blocked the view of the area from the eyes of anyone still near the rails.

Ivan pointed to the hay. There was a small wagon next to it.

"We put him underneath and pile hay around so it look like all bales."

Leroy shimmied under the wagon and we shifted a few of the bales from the front of the pile to disguise it. If anyone searched carefully, he'd be spotted but the circus was a huge enterprise, and it didn't seem likely that the government men would go digging in the hay.

With the help of the local sheriff, the federal officers, meanwhile, had been searching the trains. They wore suits instead of uniforms but their ruler-straight posture and stern expressions made them easy to spot among the people who had come for a carefree day at the circus. Trailing behind them when they got to the circus lot, was Ruben. I could see that he was talking excitedly but couldn't hear what he said. He pointed to the crew of razorbacks. One of the investigators strolled over to talk to them, trying to look casual, while two others began walking around the lot, looking hard at every man they passed, occasionally pulling out their badges as they stopped one here and there. From where I stood, it didn't look like the Bureau of Investigation was getting any help but Ivan, Stephania and I didn't dare say a word to each other about it the whole time. We got in line at the cookhouse and ate breakfast like any other morning, then headed to the sideshow top.

I saw one of the investigators station himself at the entrance to the sideshow for a while, trying to look like an ordinary townie but staring at every man who came in or out.

We didn't go back to check on Leroy until after the evening show. The investigators had long since gone. We moved the hay bales away and he crawled out from under the wagon, covered with bits of straw. Stephania and I had bundled up a couple of days' worth of provisions in some napkins and Ivan had picked up his belongings from one of the other laborers. That was about all anybody could do other than wish him well.

*

I worried that the war would put us out of business but we limped along and survived.

Then Ivan collapsed on stage one night, sick with the Spanish influenza, and looked to be near death for about a week. By the time his fever broke, the train master and the engineer complained of feeling ghastly. With nobody to run the trains, we got stuck in Virginia.

The engineer said he was ready to get rolling after four days, even hacking as he still was but by then, cities and towns along our route had begun to set up influenza quarantines, closing down schools, pool halls, churches, and any place else where people gathered. Nobody was going to the circus. And the circus had no place to go.

The tuba player, Zelenko the clown, and three laborers all got sick the same day. The next, about a dozen more took ill. Zack had the canvasmen set up an old tent as an infirmary so the sick wouldn't spread their illness in the close quarters of the sleeping cars. Three weeks after Ivan first fainted off the stage, the first person had died, one of the razorbacks, as strong and fit a man as you could find, the kind who looked like he should have lived to be 100.

Like a gasoline fire, nothing stopped the Spanish influenza and nobody was safe.

I counted 48 cots full of very sick people in the tent set up as a temporary infirmary. And men were hauling in more cots. It was like we had our own war here, without the guns and poison gas, but against an enemy just as intent on destroying us.

A Red Cross nurse came around to train those who were still healthy how to help the people in the hospital tent. She handed out masks made from gauze, with four strings at the sides to tie around the back of the head. With our faces covered like that, we looked like a bunch of train robbers. She wanted us to wear the gauze all the time so we wouldn't breathe in the germs. I understood the reasoning, but it got impossible to keep the mask on and do normal things like eating and talking.

Each of the sick needed somebody beside them, to hold their hands, at least, or whisper comforting words. There just weren't enough of us. When I went to one bedside, it meant leaving another. My insides felt hollowed out. No matter what I tried to do, I was mostly useless to these people.

I went to check on a sick candy butcher. The sound he made when he tried to breathe was like wind blowing through a baby's rattle. I wiped him down with a towel, pulled the covers back over him that he'd tossed on the ground, and sat at the edge of his cot, holding his hand.

"I need to come home, Mama," he rasped. "Don't let die here alone."

I wanted him to know I was there but he seemed to be looking somewhere beyond where I could see. Maybe he was dreaming that his Mama was beside him. I hoped that it gave him some comfort.

I laid my cheek against his, the only thing I could think to do for him. "You're not alone," I whispered.

For a second the room seemed to swim. I could hardly keep my eyes open. I hadn't gotten much rest in days. There was a sudden chill in the air that made me shiver. Or maybe it was the man's skin that had drained of warmth. I picked up my head and looked at him for a long moment, not sure if he was still breathing.

"Lucinda, get me a bucket of water, will ya?" Stephania called from the other end of the row of cots. Fluttering around like a mother hen, she was either soothing the ones lying down, or cackling orders at whoever was still standing.

I got up and reached for a pail, and the ground under my feet slipped away.

*

I felt so cold. My body trembled. Something covered me. A scratchy wool blanket. I pulled it up to my chin and clenched myself into a ball, trying to get warm.

A face, covered in a white gauze mask appeared inches from mine. Stephania? I could see movement under the mask where her lips would be.

What are you saying? I wanted to ask. Words wouldn't come. My mouth had disconnected from my brain.

I closed my eyes. The world spun me on a crazy midway ride, up, down, all around.

The chill passed. Heat washed over me and kept rising. I threw off the blanket and tried to pull off the clothes that seemed to want to smother me.

Stephania's masked face again. More hollow sounds. A wet cloth on my face. Its coolness almost burned. I tried to push away the hand with the cloth but she persisted.

Oh, Lordy, was I ever hurting. I'd have to feel better to die. I looked to my left and saw Mrs. Torelleno. I wondered for a second how that could be. Wasn't there supposed to be a dancer in the bed next to hers? Where did Pattie go?

My mind didn't want to figure it out. And my eyes wouldn't stay open.

*

I don't know how long I lay there in a fever. The first thing I remember after getting sick was someone bending me up so I was sitting, and pounding on my back. I coughed so long and so hard, I thought my ribs would break.

"She's coming around."

I couldn't tell who said it and didn't believe I was coming around. I felt worse than I could ever remember feeling. Everything hurt. I had to stop coughing so I could breathe but I couldn't stop coughing.

Somebody wet my lips with a damp cloth. The coolness of it brought me fully awake. So dry, so hot, so achy. I sensed though, that I had passed by a door that I wasn't going through.

I wasn't going to die.

I sank back to sleep, too worn out to dream.

*

I didn't quite feel human for another couple of weeks.

I must have dozed most of the way to the winters quarters in Kentucky. Ivan got me a room at a hotel that catered to showfolk. Days and nights swept by. I was bone-weary, like I hadn't slept in a hundred years, although I'd done almost nothing but for a month.

One early morning, I heard shouting in the streets. It sounded happy, not alarmed. I looked out the window of my room. People were laughing and crying and hugging each other. I couldn't tell what the commotion was about for the longest time until finally, I heard someone yell from down below:

"The war is over!"

I fell back on my pillow and drifted off again, tired still, yet getting stronger each day.

Ivan told me that at least thirty circus people died of the Spanish influenza. Mr. and Mrs. Torelleno had come through but Blanche was gone. Zack was fit and fine as ever, and so was Kumar. Wanda was recovering. Pattie and another dancer were dead.

My brother Albert wrote to say that the influenza had come to Hodgeson County, too. They had buried my little brother Frank, just fourteen years old, out next to Mama. They almost lost my youngest brother, Jacob, but he had pulled through.

*

One day, as I sat in my hotel room, looking out my window on a street dotted with the first cottony patches of snow, I realized that I had healed in more than just my body. Something had changed inside of me. I didn't know when exactly, or how or why. I just had this certainty in my heart: everything would be all right, even if the worst I could think of happened. I had stepped one toe over to the other side, taken a look around, and come back.

I couldn't ever understand why I'd lived when so many had died, any more than I could know why I was what I was.

What I did know was that I was safe in this warm room on a cold day.

I wasn't going to worry what my Daddy might do if he found me.

I wasn't going to fret when the townies pointed and hooted

and called me names.

And if I ever saw Cyrus Parker again, I wasn't going to run away like a damned fool. I'd grab hold of him and not let go.

I was alive. And I wasn't much afraid of anything any more.

19. MARISA

Marisa expected Rena to show up in her tie-dye regalia, with enough make-up to rival an aging Hollywood star. Instead, Gaia's favorite psychic appeared in gray sweatpants that bagged at the knees and an oversized gray sweatshirt that read, "Nitty-Gritty Dirt Band – Since 1966." Except for a slash of persimmon lipstick, her face was scrubbed clean. She hauled a frayed straw satchel almost large enough to be a suitcase. Marisa wouldn't have recognized her if they passed on the street.

"This better be good, darling girl," Rena told Kelly. "I'm missing Titanic."

"Rena, you've seen that movie a dozen times."

"And it gets better with each viewing."

"I'll buy you the DVD. C'mon, we need your help."

Rena held her palms up and out as she paced slowly around the room, all business now, Titanic forgotten, at least for the moment. She made slight squeezing motions with her hands, as if massaging the air.

Rena turned to Marisa for the first time. "Have you seen anything unusual in the house?"

"Me?" Marisa shook her head.

"You've felt something though?"

"Yes."

Heading toward the front door, Rena squeezed at the air

some more, seeming in deep thought.

"She sees you as an intruder," she said emphatically.

"Who does?"

"I can't get a clear signal but she died here. Weren't you and your aunt estranged?"

Marisa felt twinges of the old guilt, just for a moment, but whatever was in the house didn't feel like Enid to her.

"I get an even stronger sense of energy on the other side of this door," Rena continued as she walked back to the entrance.

"The ghost is outside?" Kelly asked.

Rena walked the room and paused again at the front door, frowning. "Danger is. Come with me."

*

Opening her car's trunk, Rena handed Kelly a ten-pound bag of bird seed, a dark blue beach towel, a quart of grain alcohol, two sealed vials of red powder, rubber gloves, and a pair of finger cymbals.

"Kelly darling, take these to the front of the house and set them on the lawn. Marisa, I'll need a big mixing bowl — the larger the better — and five kitchen knives."

"Knives?"

"Sharp and shiny. And give me ones that you can spare. You won't be getting them back."

Marisa grabbed an old set of steak knives from the silverware drawer, pulled down her Aunt Enid's big glass punch bowl from the cabinet above the refrigerator, and brought them out to the front of the house. Rena had laid out the beach towel on the grass and knelt there in the dark. She mumbled an invocation, and clanged the finger cymbals. Still mumbling, the large woman motioned to Kelly to pour the seed into the bowl Marisa held.

Rena removed her finger cymbals and pulled on a pair of rubber gloves. On top of the bird seed she sprinkled the colored powder from the vials. She mumbled something more, her eyes half-closed. She poured the alcohol over the powder and stirred the mixture with a rubber-gloved hand.

Louder now, she chanted:

"Gatta, gatta, peragatta, perasatgatta, bodiswava."

Rena repeated it several times then held her hand up for silence.

"Follow me, repeat what I say and do as I do." The nun-turned-psychic grabbed a handful of seed from the bowl. Marisa and Kelly each did the same. Scattering a few seeds in front of her, Rena intoned, "Feed the hungry ghosts … feed the hungry ghosts."

They continued all around the perimeter of the house.

"All right, you two, back inside now. The rest, I do alone."

Marisa and Kelly watched from the kitchen window. Under the night sky, her actions illuminated by the security lights, Rena chanted and gesticulated with one of the knives then plunged it into the ground. She used her hands to claw away the sandy soil around it, then pushed it down, parallel to the surface, and buried it, pointing outward. She did the same with each of the other knives all around the outside of the house.

Rejoining them in the kitchen, Rena pulled a compact mirror out of her satchel and fussed with her hair.

"Call me if anything else happens," Rena called flirtatiously over her shoulder as she left. "But make it after the movie."

*

Kelly insisted on sleeping in the playroom, despite the mildew.

Downstairs, Murphy jumped into bed with Marisa and rested his head on her foot. Cat and person warmly cuddled, and fell asleep almost immediately.

*

Marisa dreamed that something woke her — the smell of smoke.

In the dream, she opened her eyes and saw a gray-black cloud, perhaps four feet in diameter, floating near the window. For some reason she was in the playroom, although she'd gone to bed downstairs. She didn't know whether she was more frightened by the possibility that the house had caught fire or by the way the cloud metamorphosed. It trailed tendrils at its upper edges, which quickly coalesced into the image of a woman's long hair. A face formed, heart-shaped, with a frightened expression. Then the rest of a slender young body took shape, covered by the faint outlines of a frilly old-fashioned night-dress.

Fully transformed now into a transparent miniature of a person, the cloud-like apparition drifted toward the hallway. She seemed to be calling out to someone, becoming more and more agitated. Marisa could see the woman's mouth form words but heard nothing.

As the cloud/woman drifted from the room, Marisa knew that she had seen her face before. The burnt odor cleared, replaced by a scent of jasmine.

*

The ringing phone roused her from the dream. She let the answering machine take it. Someone from Third Bank of Sarasota asked her to call; the mortgage she'd applied for. A glance at the clock told her it wasn't as early as she'd thought. Past nine o'clock. She'd overslept.

From the kitchen, the music of Jamaican-accented laughter poured down the hallway. She closed her eyes another moment and tried to recall the face in the smoke cloud. Vivid as it had been, now it was lost.

*

Her comfortably ratty purple terry cloth robe wrapped around herself, she went out to greet her house guests.

"Hey mon," Claude beamed a bright smile as Marisa walked into the kitchen. Kelly's Jeep was parked by the garage. Claude had, as Kelly had requested, left the rusting VW at home.

Kelly, hair still wet from the shower, dressed in knit white v-neck and well-worn jeans, handed Marisa a steaming mug of black coffee. "Here, sleepyhead. You coming to Gaia with us this morning?"

"Can't. I want to go to the Ringling to see if anyone knows the real story behind this house. I won't have any peace until I find out what's in here and what it's trying to do — other than to force me out, that is."

"Want us to come back and check on you later?"

"I'll be fine. I have an editing assignment. The manuscript's supposed to come via FedEx this afternoon and my agent wants me to get right on it."

Marisa walked them out to the car. That same little girl stood framed in the gateway, next to her too-large tricycle. Marisa was about to tell Kelly and Claude that she'd seen the child before when Claude called out, "Yo, Birdie."

He loped up the drive toward the child. She stood there without moving, except to limply wave back to him.

After a moment, Claude began walking back toward the house again, the little girl following alongside on her oversized trike, her body leaning first left, then right, as her short legs struggled to push the pedals. Marisa got that same sense that something about her was strange but couldn't say what. As she got closer, Marisa noticed that her hair didn't catch the sun the way a healthy youngster's would. Her back wasn't as straight. She lacked the vitality of other children.

When they were about halfway down the drive, chatting to each other, Marisa could see crevices etched from the girl's nose to the corners of her down-turned mouth, making her appear stern. Lines striped her forehead and between her eyebrows. Finer wrinkles circled her lips. Her long hair, which had looked dusty blonde from a distance wasn't blonde at all. It had probably once been brown, but now it was lightened by streaks of white.

"You're a midget," said Marisa, immediately embarrassed for blurting it out.

"I can't be the first you've encountered. Not in the city that was practically built by the Ringling Brothers." The small woman extended her hand in greeting. "Alberta Lacey-Pruitt. Birdie for short — no pun intended."

Claude smiled from behind her. "Didn't I tell you about Birdie? She's the lady docent from the museum up the street.

She knows all about the circus, right Birdie? Maybe them duppies come from the circus."

"Duppies?" Alberta looked startled.

"Yah mon, you know, duppies, ghosts. Marisa got them in her house."

She waved his comment away. "Claude, really. There are no such things."

"You work at the Circus Museum?" Marisa said, hopefully. "Then you must know about the old sideshows."

"Volunteer, actually," answered Birdie. "And they only trained us docents about the big top. The sideshows were an entirely separate world, one they prefer to ignore, I'm afraid. Sorry I can't help."

"Anybody you know there who knows more?"

The midget shrugged and shook her head. "Not a one, to my knowledge. I do have some concerns about your neighbor above the garage, Otto Hinkle, which is why I've been, admittedly, snooping around a bit."

"What about him?"

"That lawyer didn't tell you anything?"

"Only that I'm stuck with him. I'm still a little surprised Enid didn't make him the owner of the estate. Harry said that Otto watched out for her like a son."

"He said that, did he? It makes me wonder which of them is more deranged, Harry or Otto."

"Alberta, what the hell are you talking about?"

"Call me Birdie," she said. "Everybody does."

"All right, Birdie. What the hell are you talking about?"

"Maybe 'deranged' is too strong," the small woman answered. "Let's just say that I believe Otto is disturbed. He certainly was as a child. I suspect he still is. You should take care not to be alone around him."

"You have some evidence to back that up?"

"You're not going to simply take the word of a stranger," said Birdie. "Fair enough. I can tell you that I've known Otto since he was eight or nine years old. His sister was my best friend. I do not make these statements lightly."

"I never knew he had a sister," said Marisa, "and he's some sort of distant cousin."

"Sharon died when she was just a girl," Birdie said.

"Why don't we go back inside and sit down, Birdie," Kelly said, wrapping her arm around the shoulder of the small older woman. "There's still some coffee in the pot, isn't there Marisa?"

"I thought you and Claude had to get to Gaia," Marisa answered.

"Petrika can open up. I wouldn't miss this for the world."

Back in the house, Marisa started a fresh pot of Cuban coffee. And Birdie told her tale.

20. BIRDIE

It was, I think, about 1952. I had just entered high school and was already battling with my parents about what I would do when I graduated. They wanted me to go to college or, at the very least, secretarial school.

The movie, "The Greatest Show on Earth," had just come out. It had been filmed in Sarasota. Sharon and I had gone to see it a half dozen times: four kiddie matinees, once in the evening with her parents and once with mine. We had both fallen in love with Cornell Wilde, who played a trapeze daredevil. We wanted to fly on the trapeze and swing into Cornell's arms. Never mind that we knew he didn't really do any of the stunts; the trapeze artist who actually did them was a neighbor. We were in love.

And we wanted to join the circus.

It was the most natural career choice in the world for us Sarasota adolescents. All the circus people have left Sarasota now but back then, almost every family on our street had some sort of circus connection. Our city was the Ringling Brothers' winter headquarters. Lots of the kids we went to school with traveled with their families in the spring on the circus train. Either they were already acrobats, animal trainers, or trapeze artists, or their parents were training them to join the act.

As a midget, I knew that I could join up any time and be welcomed in the sideshow but that held no interest for me.

Like my best friend, Sharon, my dreams centered on the glitter and glamour.

I had my own circus connections. My aunt had been a performer. But my father and mother were leery of all circus people, especially the Parkers, because my aunt had briefly lived on the Parker estate and had ... come to harm. Sharon's mother had been a Parker before marrying, so there was some added tension concerning our next-door neighbors, the Hinkles.

Still, my parents adored Sharon and knew that she and I were as close as sisters. Although I think they worried I'd run away on the Ringling train at the first opportunity, they gave me the leeway to play out my fantasies.

Mr. and Mrs. Hinkle set up a trampoline in their backyard and got a circus hostler to string a low wire a few feet away, just a foot or so above the grass so that we couldn't fall far.

We spent afternoons in the back yard practicing behind the Hinkles' huge pink-stuccoed house, just around the corner from here. Sharon's mother cheered and encouraged us. She made us tall glasses of lemonade when we came in drenched in perspiration from a workout.

The only cloud hanging over our sunny backyard practice was Sharon's younger brother, Otto. He could have joined us, if he'd wanted. Instead, he just stood around and stared.

He had always been troubled, the kind of boy who pulls the wings off butterflies.

Two years earlier, he'd killed Sharon's pet parrot, crushed it to death under his plump body and then plucked out its feathers. Her parents insisted he hadn't meant it, but they didn't bring home any other pets after that.

It's strange, isn't it, how you never know you're living the best time of your life at the moment you're living it? If you could appreciate, at that instant, that this is it, maybe you'd make certain your mind imprinted every detail of the sights, smells, sounds and sensations.

Then again, maybe knowing that life will only get duller,

sadder, less hopeful afterward would inject melancholy into that moment. You'd miss life's peak experience by mourning it before it passes.

So perhaps it's best not to know.

Sharon and I had the time of our life, bouncing and somersaulting on her trampoline, and then, with a six-foot length of bamboo for balance, taking turns walking the tightwire.

One day, Sharon's mother surprised us with new leotards she'd ordered for us from a catalog. Mine was a powder pink, a child's size six. Sharon's leotard was a soft baby blue. Mrs. Hinkle gave us sequins to sew on the bodices so we would sparkle like the circus stars we idolized.

The following day, when I saw Sharon at school, she seemed quite upset. I couldn't get her to tell me what was wrong. Finally, after extracting a promise that I would keep the secret, she told me what had happened.

She had caught Otto prancing and posing in front of her parents' full-length mirror, wearing her new blue leotard. She told him to take it off and threatened to tell on him to their mother.

He jumped on her in a rage, pummeling her like he wanted to kill her, and squeezing her throat as if to strangle her. Sharon managed to wriggle out of his grasp and scream for her mother. The incident shook her up badly.

By the following week though, everything seemed back to normal.

My father used to drive me to school on his way to the office so I was always the last one there, running in just before the bell.

One day, when I got to school, Sharon wasn't there. I didn't think much of it, assuming she was out sick for the day. Lots of girls were starting their monthlies around that time and it was fairly typical for girls to miss school the first time.

About an hour into the school day, the principal had me come to the office. I had no idea why. He wouldn't tell me anything, just made me sit on one of the big wooden chairs, to wait, he said. Pretty soon, my father walked through the door, looking teary-eyed.

I had never seen him like that. It positively terrified me. Had something happened at home? He wouldn't tell me anything either but said that we would go home and talk with my mother.

There, in my kitchen, my mother sat at the white Formica table. Her eyes were red and swollen. When we walked through the back door, she rushed over to hug me.

Sharon is dead, she told me.

I stood there, hearing but not hearing what she'd said. Time stopped.

As I'd given no indication that I understood, my mother repeated it: Sharon is dead.

She had been waiting on the corner for the school bus with her little brother, Otto. She had stumbled off the curb and into the street just as a delivery truck sped around the turn, cutting the corner. It hit her with such force that it threw her up into the air. She fell to the street again, broken and bleeding. She died on the way to the hospital.

That afternoon, I saw Otto out in the backyard, bouncing on the trampoline. I was certain it was the first time he had ever gone near it and now he was jumping — literally — for joy. I could hear him singing and laughing and babbling to himself. This child whose most prominent characteristic was his perpetual sullenness appeared positively gleeful.

Gleeful, on the afternoon that his only sister fell in front of a speeding truck!

After the funeral, the Hinkle family moved up north for a while. And when they came back, Otto didn't come with them. The story they told was that Otto had grieved so profoundly, he'd required hospitalization.

Whatever the reason they had institutionalized him, it wasn't because he was grief stricken. The little monster had been overjoyed.

21. Lucinda

Between worlds

Time ran like a manic movie: fast forward, slow motion, and back again, as Lucinda watched from her window.

What would have appeared to her as blurs at any other moment since she first passed into otherness now had some definition. Shapes briefly became recognizable as people.

She herself seemed to have more distinctness. Not a body, nothing that substantial, but a sense of energy that held together more in space.

Still, the people confounded her limited senses. She recognized that one might have been, like her, a midget.

She pounded on the window. "Who are you?" she tried to yell but lacked the voice. She rushed to the next window, pounded again, soundlessly called out. "Are you with a circus? A ten-in-one?"

The longing she experienced stunned her. She had been alone so long, but only at that moment did she feel the depth of her loneliness.

22. LUCINDA

THE TEN-IN-ONE SHOW

In the summer of 1919, word got back to us that Cyrus's wife had died. Lord forgive me, all I could think was, now he's free. I didn't have much time for romantic fantasies though. Just about two weeks after that, we learned that the Ringling Brothers were closing our circus down.

The influenza epidemic had mostly passed but it still whittled the crowds down well into the spring.

Everyone knew it was the end, even before Zack came around and made the announcement. The Ringlings had combined the two big circuses — Ringling Brothers and Barnum & Bailey — into one. They had already disbanded most of the other smaller circuses they bought.

We all felt uneasy, stranded out there in Kentucky farm country, not far from the circus's winter quarters. Most of us understood the Ringlings' thinking. Our show didn't draw the crowds of the big combined circus that they were calling, "the greatest show on earth." We still could siphon off some of the audiences though if we pulled into a town first.

The best performers and all the animal acts got offered new contracts with the combined Ringling and Barnum show. The menagerie went too. Skilled laborers and even the nimbler pickpockets joined up with the big show. The rest of us picked up our final pay from the paymaster, then packed up to look for any employment we could find to finish out the season before winter's cold shut everything down.

Prospects were scarce in the rural south for a midget and a giant with limited skills. We agreed that, whatever we faced next, we would face together.

A crate of little fairy doll souvenirs that the circus concessionaires had been selling had been dumped with the rest of the trash after our last show. Ivan retrieved the crate, figuring we could support ourselves for a while by performing on the streets and selling the dolls on the side.

We sneaked into barns to sleep at night, and poached vegetables from the fields along the way.

Lordy, things didn't look promising at all, but somehow we got lucky. It couldn't have been much more than a week when we saw posters saying that a county fair was coming to a nearby town. We walked the fifteen or so miles, Ivan dragging a makeshift cart with the crate of dolls and our other possessions behind us, his poor legs paining him, as they always did.

We knew we were close when we saw a canvas-covered wagon up ahead with a big sign peeking out the open back: "Toss a ring — win a prize."

A Confederate flag hung off to the side on a crooked pole.

The wagon jiggled along the dirt road. Fifty yards down, a half dozen other food and game concession wagons were scattered at the back of a pasture. Farm wagons came down the dusty road every couple of minutes, carting their best crops and livestock, some probably hoping to win a prize, and others, I imagined, just hoping to sell.

Two men strung a banner above the ticket seller's window to welcome everyone to the county fair, which opened officially the following morning. A man in a white straw hat waved at us and we waved back, like we were already part of the show. We headed for the bare patch where a bunch of carnies were setting up their canvas tops. Off a little further, some men were putting together a merry-go-round and beyond, that, a rickety-looking ferris wheel.

Ivan approached a man sitting outside a tent that advertised weird wonders and amazing sights but his show turned out to be a dime museum filled with gaffes: dragons' teeth, witches' fingers, and other objects fashioned from plaster and putty to frighten and delight the rubes.

"The fellow y'all want to see is named Casper. He should be pulling in by tonight," he said. "Meanwhile, head on over to the cookhouse. Tell them Lloyd Embry sent you. They'll treat you right."

*

So there I was, pretending to be a real fairy princess instead of just playing the role in a circus spec.

"Don't be shy, ladies and gentlemen. Come in, come closer. Take a peek. For just four bits, one half of a dollar, you can witness for yourself the most amazing living oddities ever displayed in America."

The people of the town stepped right up, as Casper ordered, and on command, they handed over their change.

Casper's Cavalcade of Living Curiosities was the kind of tent show called a ten-in-one by show folk, but ordinary people knew it as a freak show.

My transformation from Tennessee farm-girl midget to Nibelungland fairy princess came about thanks to the dolls that Ivan had hauled out of the trash. Just like in the circus sideshow, all the ten-in-one acts sold something. Casper looked at the toys and immediately saw the possibilities. Any show could have a midget. Casper's Cavalcade of Living Curiosities was going to have a genuine fairy.

This was show business. Nobody came to see the sad or the ordinary. They came to witness the stupendous, the fantastic, that which is beyond belief.

*

"Beyond belief and yet, here they stand, before you, in the flesh. Step right up! Don't be shy," Casper called out from the bally platform. "Ten attractions for the price of one." He had a way of making people feel comfortable with their fascination for the grotesque, this large tuxedoed man with his small, sparkling blue eyes, thinning white hair, and prosperous belly. When he called out to the marks, it was in the manner of an old friend, seeing them on the street, and bringing their attention to something he knew they wouldn't want to miss.

"Witness with your own eyes, my friends, Drago, the amazing Hindu fire eater." On the bally platform, Drago stood bare-chested (a precaution he had taken ever since his vest caught fire during his act a few years before) wearing only his deep red pantaloons and tightly wound red turban. His arms stretched wide, he held a flaming torch in each hand. As Casper ballyhooed the crowd, Drago spread his legs apart and bent his head backward so that his lips paralleled the top of the sky. He dipped first one, then the other torch into his mouth, extinguishing their flames as he drew his teeth around them. Gasps from the crowd were followed by polite applause. Drago threw the now unlit torches down on the stage, bowed, then stepped back, his arms folded, his expression severe.

"That's just a taste, ladies and gentlemen, if you'll excuse the pun, of what you will witness inside. Just a taste, my friends, ha-hah! Step right through this doorway and let Drago amaze you as he plunges a three-foot long razor-sharp blade through his lips and down his gullet. This ancient Hindu weapon is so long, you'll wonder how he does it without poking his pants right through to the other side." Casper paused for the nervous laughter from the crowd, as Drago dramatically swept inside under the canvas.

The people in the crowds were picturing it all right. Several stepped up to buy their tickets, but others shooed their children, wives and husbands along, away from this frightening image. Casper had something for everyone though. Before the marks could get very far, I stepped from behind the flap into the space Drago had just vacated on the bally platform.

"Where are you going, folks? Don't turn away now, or you'll miss the best, the most astounding part of the show. Come here, come closer. C'mon, it's all right. You'll kick yourselves here to Sunday if you miss what's coming up next. None other than her Royal Highness Lucinda Darling, Princess of Nibelungland, the first and only genuine fairy princess ever exhibited anywhere in the world." Townies who had begun to wander turned back as Casper commanded.

I danced around a bit, not as much as I had in the circus spec, since there was little space on the bally platform. While I twirled, Casper continued to spin his tale.

"Snatched from her fairy nest when just a child, the kidnappers clipped Lucinda's fairy wings to keep her from escaping her cru-el captivity." Casper's eyes turned inward, seeming to picture this imagined scene. "These pale gossamer replicas you see her wearing today are a mere shadow of the phantasmagorical wings of the Nibelungland royalty."

The wings he was talking about were left over from my circus spec costume. They were made of pale pink organza wrapped around shaped wires and trimmed with sequins. In the beginning, Casper had tried to pass them off as real wings, but not even the most gullible suckers fell for that, so he was forced to refine his spiel, spinning only slightly more believable versions of the tale. I never knew in advance what flourishes Casper might add to get the tip to turn (show folk talk for getting the crowd gathering outside to spend four bits to see the show inside). He always seemed to know what would tempt them.

The seduction began long before the show, with the bright painted banners, eight feet high by eight feet across, that drew the curious close enough to hear his pitch. The artist made our differences and deformities appear more grotesque (and therefore, more alluring) than they were. With splashes of bright paint, Horace, an otherwise ordinary boy of fourteen with a violently itchy, scale-like skin disorder that afflicted his arms, legs and chest, became the "Reptilian Wonder — Snake Boy," complete with a forked tongue and a shiny black slithery tale. Who could pass by that picture without wanting to see the hissing half-human, half-reptile monster in the flesh?

From the sensational images, you might think I was 12 inches high and could fly with my wings like a butterfly or that Ivan, advertised as my consort, was as tall as two houses.

Even the two-headed chicken had been painted to appear lively and ferocious. Never mind that the poor fowl had been dead so long, Casper glued clumps of new feathers on it every few days to replace those that disintegrated. He told me once that the bird had been preserved and stuffed by a taxidermist in Missouri (who, I suspect, had stitched on one of its heads from another source). The bright enormous pictures of impossible monstrosities baited the hook. And Casper reeled them in.

Under the canvas, illuminated by smoky carbide lights, the kind that miners used to find their way through caves, instead of the bright white spotlights of the circus, everyone looked a little eerier. And who could say, after leaving through the back door flaps what they'd really seen?

"Amazing, mystifying, unbelievable, ladies and gentlemen. But true," announced Bud, Casper's assistant and younger brother, who shepherded the farmers and townies from exhibit to exhibit under the sideshow top, picking up the story where Casper had left off. "Rescued from a life of slavery by one of her captors, a member of the ferocious tribe of giants from the isle of Gordia, witness for yourselves, the tiny fairy princess, side-by-side with her devoted giant consort. Ladies and gentlemen, Casper's Cavalcade of Living Curiosities presents for your amusement and amazement, tiny Lucinda Darling and ten-foot-tall Ivan the Gordian Giant, the world's most unusual couple."

*

One day, I saw Ivan staring into the crowds. He dropped the playacting, just for a moment. A hungry look took the place of the make-believe scowl. I followed his gaze to the young man in the audience who gaped back with a mixture of curiosity, shame and, the only word that I could think to describe it, that same hunger. I understood immediately, even if I was a little surprised. Ivan couldn't be called handsome, not on the darkest night after a long lonely spell. The young man wasn't much to look at either, come to think of it, although, next to Ivan, I suppose he would be. They saw something in each other, though, and it didn't matter how either of them looked to anybody else. You could almost slice the tension in the air between them.

We were playing a carnival that weekend, in a tiny town in Alabama just over the border from Mississippi. Casper usually closed the show an hour or so before the last of the concessions and games shut down for the night.

After watching the way the games of chance operated, Horace the snake boy joked that they should be re-named the games of no-chance-at-all.

The guy in the cowboy hat, for instance, who set up his sharp-shooter game next to the strong-man, adjusted his rifles' sites to be just a wee bit off. So, when a young man picked up one of the guns to impress his sweetheart with his marksmanship, and win her a kewpie doll, he was lucky to hit the bullseye one out of three times. To keep the townies happy, the cowboy gave out tiny prizes, like a whistle, if a man hit even once, telling him that, if he could get the next nine out of ten shots, he could trade up to the biggest prize on the shelf. With those rifles, a sharp-shooter would be lucky to hit the bullseye half that often. So, the cowboy would give him another, slightly bigger but still disappointing prize and make him another offer.

This could go on until the mark had laid down ten or fifteen dollars, and shot dozens of rounds. The cowboy always paid off with a "big prize" if the mark stayed around long enough and shot enough rounds. The prize probably cost the cowboy less than a dollar but it made the shooters happy. And sending one young couple down the midway with a fancy-looking prize was like chumming the waters.

A few yards down the midway, the skinny old man who ran the wheel-of-fortune had a different ruse. His daughter, a pretty girl who wore a scanty red costume, spun the wheel. The skinny man knew all eyes would be on her or the game. He sat on a three-legged stool next to the counter, and swept up the coins after each spin. The foot pedal he used to control the speed of the wheel and where it stopped, was kept under the counter, out of sight.

The man who ran the ring-toss and the fellow who had people guess where he'd placed the Queen of Hearts in the three-card-shuffle had their own ways of guaranteeing that none of their customers got too lucky.

After Casper closed down that night, I saw Ivan standing near the sharpshooter game, talking to the young man he'd locked eyes with earlier.

"Come on, fellow, win that pretty lady a pretty prize," the cowboy called to a couple walking past. He paid no more attention to Ivan and the young man than they gave him.

I bought a bag of peanuts and watched the last few stragglers wander off the fairgrounds. The carousel and wonder wheel stopped taking riders. The strong man dropped the sidewalls of his exhibition. Lloyd Embry snored in a chair outside his tent, oblivious to the needle skipping over his Victrola's black disk; a toppled jug of moonshine by his feet. Even the dancing girls had shimmied out of their spangled costumes and covered up as modestly as church ladies.

Ivan still hadn't gotten back by the time we all settled down into our sleeping tents.

The next morning, the young man was back, driving a large farm wagon pulled by two big brown mules. The wagon was empty except for a bundle of clothes slung in its bed.

"This here is Perry," Casper said, when he introduced him around later. "He'll be traveling with us for a bit and helping out."

I looked up at Ivan. His mouth stretched into such a wide smile, I'd swear his face was going to crack.

23. MARISA

In her car alone, after Birdie, Kelly, and Claude had left, Marisa mulled Birdie's warnings about Otto. She could almost picture him, a miniature of the man he now was, bouncing maniacally on a trampoline, celebrating the accident that eliminated his only rival for his parents' attention. And yet, another image of him, tucking a blanket around the useless legs of senile old Enid, competed with the first.

He had done what she hadn't, made certain Enid's needs were met when she could no longer do anything for herself. That counted for more than a second-hand tale about his childhood.

About a half-mile up Bay Shore Road, Marisa turned left onto the sprawling campus of the Ringling Museum. The 66-acre compound, with its opulent pseudo-Venetian bay front house named Cà d'Zan, and an art museum filled with baroque and rococo European art treasures, had once been the home of John Ringling. Marisa bypassed both mansion and art museum, heading instead for the smaller, less showy building that housed the Museum of the Circus.

She walked quickly past exhibits of circus clown make-up, performers' costumes, and antique animal cage wagons, to the curator's offices at the back. The door, slightly ajar, had a small sign at eye-level that read, "Private — No Admittance." She knocked softly. Nobody answered. She pushed it open a bit.

"Hello? Anybody in here?"

A man in a stained blue jumpsuit with "Walter" embroidered on the pocket walked in from another office.

"They're all gone today," he said. "Air conditioner problems."

"I'm looking for information —"

"I'm sorry, lady. The office is closed."

Realizing she would get nowhere here, she wandered down to the gift store.

"Do you have any books on circus midgets?" she asked the clerk.

"What little there is, you'll find on the top shelf," she pointed to a bookcase across the room. "Our books are mostly donations, some quite old."

Marisa checked her watch. It was past ten. She had to be back home by noon to meet the FedEx deliveryman.

She flipped through a musty-smelling old book called "Human Oddities," that appeared to depict every type of deformity imaginable. A caption under a mid-19th century photograph of Eng and Chang, the original "Siamese twins," said that they really were from Siam. The twins were pictured with their wives, a glum-looking pair of women in white bonnets. Marisa wondered what sort of marriages they could have had when they would never have had the chance to be alone with just their own spouses. The twins had been joined at the abdomen by a stretch of flesh.

Staring back at her from the next page was a group of naked African men with elephantiasis, their scrotums the size of basketballs. And facing that page, was a photograph captioned "dog-faced boy." With silky hair covering his entire face, the fellow did, somewhat, resemble a Pomeranian, or a cuddlier version of a character out of an old Wolfman movie.

Shelving the old book in her hand, she reached for another one. Cards and papers fluttered out, littering the floor. Marisa gathered them up, grateful the clerk hadn't seen them fall. Cracked and yellowed, most were souvenir picture postcards of early twentieth century sideshow performers.

The faded photographs showed fat ladies, strongmen, and more exotic attractions. Three postcards in a row, each of different couples, claimed similar titles. The topmost, "the world's oddest couple," pictured a hefty bearded woman, wearing a wedding dress, next to her husband, "the human skeleton," the scrawniest man Marisa had ever seen. The groom was dressed in nothing but boxer shorts and a top hat. The second postcard, "the world's most unusual couple," featured a ragged giant with a hang-dog face paired with a beautiful blond be-sequined midget woman. Something about this picture looked familiar. She held it for several seconds, trying to imagine where she might have seen it before but drew a blank and set it aside.

In the third of the postcard pairings, the "world's strangest married couple," were 660-pound George Corwood, bursting at the seams of his cowboy duds, and his tiny wife, Ursa, "the only living half-girl," whose body ended just below her torso. Small type in the left-hand corner on the opposite side offered a brief blurb about Mr. and Mrs. Corwood who, it said, had been photographed at their winter home in Gibsonton, Florida.

Marisa pulled a pad and pen from her purse and wrote down their names.

The postcard didn't appear to be as old as the others. Maybe the Corwoods were still alive. A long shot but it was worth a try, especially as they came from the same town as Dapper Dan Brogan.

*

Back at home, she set a pot of water on the stove and was about to check the answering machine when she heard a truck coming down the drive. Expecting FedEx with her editing assignment, she was puzzled by the big white van that pulled up instead. Blue lettering on its side read: John Guinness Construction & Development Corp. The van backed into a space next to the garage. A pro-wrestler-sized guy, with a long red ponytail and frizzy beard, jumped down from the driver's seat, strode to the rear of the van and rolled up the back door. His t-shirt bore the same logo as the truck. A similarly dressed skinny guy got out on the truck's passenger side. He was talking on a cell phone held next to his ear by a hand and arm heavily decorated by tattoos.

She opened the front door to ask what they were doing here. A black Porsche sped down the drive behind the van, spitting gravel backward from its tires. John Guinness stepped out, beaming a smile that deepened the lines of his face.

"Hey, Marisa. I had a crew with nothing to do for a couple of weeks. So I figured, why not send them over here to start on your repairs."

For a moment, she was too stunned to speak. When she regained her voice, it was angry. "Since when did I ask you to repair anything, beyond a toilet, that is?"

He pointed to the roof. "You've got a sag there. See? That means you've got one, maybe two bad beams. Nothing Steve and Jimmie here can't handle. They'll replace them along with the bad joists your termite man found under the house. After that, some new shingles, a coat of paint, and you won't recognize the old place."

"What kind of game is this?"

John laughed, oblivious to Marisa's ire.

"A technical glitch is holding up a job I had them on out near the Interstate. I can either pay my men to sit around and pick their noses or I can pay them to work. Either way, I've got to pay them, so here they are. At your service." He gave a mock-chivalrous bow from the waist.

Marisa knew the reason he kept dropping by and it wasn't to offer her free handyman services. She was about to say as much, but the phone was ringing. She raced inside and picked up the call on the fourth ring and heard a friendly male voice with a name she didn't quite catch and the words, "Third Bank of Sarasota."

Her mortgage application.

The banker got right to the point. "Did you know that there

were tax liens against the property you're trying to finance?"

"Yes, yes, that's why I need the mortgage," she answered. "Your earlier message said you had questions about my employment and I want to reassure you that I'll be making a lot more money once I get over this hump, so—"

"Ms. Delano, forgive me for interrupting, but the liens make any consideration of your application impossible. Your property is under threat of foreclosure."

"That won't be a problem," she jumped in before he could say more. "I'll pay off the liens the second I get the mortgage."

"No bank will lend money to someone who can't demonstrate that she has clear title to the property."

"But the house is worth many times more than the liens."

"I'm really sorry," said the bank officer, sounding like he meant it. "Have you considered private money? The rate of interest can be high but sometimes, private investors will take the sorts of risks that banks can't."

Before she could crash all the way, she thought of Harry. He arranged financing for developers all the time. If anyone could find her "private money," Harry Scanlon, could. She hung up with the banker and dialed the lawyer's number from memory.

The secretary who'd notarized the deed transfer papers answered on the second ring. "Mr. Scanlon is out of town. May I give him a message when he returns?"

Marisa said to have him call. "Tell him it's urgent."

*

She looked out the kitchen window. John Guinness was still there, leaning against his Porsche, chatting up his workmen who were squatting in the shade of a banyan tree.

Cocky bastard.

Did he really believe she'd let him bulldoze her home after repairing it?

Still, she thought, who said she had to let him play her? Why couldn't she play him, instead?

She was sinking in an ocean of debt and loss. And right now, John Guinness was paddling the only life raft.

"All right, little house," she said aloud. "We'll play his game. But he's not going to win."

She composed herself, forced a smile, and went out to bargain with the devil.

*

"Nothing's going to happen to this house," she told him, "not while I'm around."

"Hey, I'm just trying to be a good neighbor. I've got enough shingles left over from other jobs to re-roof a dozen houses, not to mention more wood than you'll find in your average forest. You want it to end up in a landfill? Or do you want it on your house?

"And you swear you won't hit with a huge bill when you're done?"

"Jeez, woman, can't you let someone do you a simple favor? There's no catch. They're witnesses." He jerked his thumb toward the workmen, who waved back. "Of course, I wouldn't turn down some payback on the deal."

"Such as?"

"Can you cook?"

"A little."

"Great. Make me dinner."

*

She left Guinness and his men and got set to put the kettle back on the burner when the blinking answering machine told her she'd missed another call. She hit play.

"Marisa Delano?" said a southern-accented baritone. "Dapper Dan Brogan, here. If you still need that interview, and you can get up to Gib'town this afternoon—"

She quickly wrote down the directions Brogan had left, relieved for the distraction. She scribbled a note, telling FedEx to leave the package on the porch, and taped it to the front door.

John's Porsche was already gone. Otto stood outside watching the workmen set up saw horses.

He glared at her as she got behind the wheel and lowered

154

the convertible top. She pretended not to notice.

"Hey, Otto," she said. "If you're not too busy, any chance you could mow the lawn this afternoon?"

He straightened his shoulders, turned his back on her and stomped back into his garage apartment, slamming the door.

"I'll take that as a 'no.'"

As she drove up toward the gate, she saw about half a dozen college-aged kids milling around near the entrance. They perked up at the sight of her. One of them, a lean red-haired guy in jeans and green t-shirt, held up a large sign: "SAVE THE GOPHER TORTOISES."

"From me? You've got to be kidding."

It wasn't worth arguing about. Staring past them, she steered the car north toward Gibsonton.

24. Lucinda

1923 — The Ten-in-One Show

We'd been with Casper's for a few years when, one afternoon, in a town where we had set up the ten-in-one on the grounds of a Wild West Show, a farm-boy of about 17 or 18 years old swept in and pushed past the crowd. He pulled in another, larger boy behind him by the suspenders. Bypassing Fannie, Drago, and even the curtain leading to the blow-off (where men only, for an extra four bits, could get a peek at the half-man, half-woman Jeraldine/Jeremia), he drew his friend over to the platform where Ivan and I stood.

"I tol' ya. I tol' ya they was fer real," he said, pointing as if we were hams hanging in a butcher's window.

"Holy, Hannah. Can you jes' pitcher 'em two together?" the larger boy shouted. "I still don't believe it. He'd split 'er wide open, like a stallion mounting a jackrabbit."

"Wouldn' that be somethin' to see?" the smaller boy said, giggling, as they both strode closer to the platform. He yelled to Ivan. "Hey, big fella, five dollars if you let us watch."

"Watch?" The larger boy interrupted. "I wouldn' mind a lil' piece o' that myse'f."

As the larger of the two boys tried to climb up onto the stage, Ivan bounded to the edge and grabbed the boy by his shirt. The farm boys, even though they were much smaller than

Ivan, were muscular and spry. The smaller boy ran around the back to the step leading onstage and jumped onto Ivan's back, pounding him, holding him around the throat. Ivan was pulled backward, and I heard him gasp for air as he clawed at the hands on his neck. The larger boy climbed onto the stage from the front and threw several punches to Ivan's rib cage and stomach.

"Stop! You're hurting him, " I said. I tried to pull the smaller boy off Ivan's back but he kicked at me with a filthy shoeless foot as if I was nothing more than a fly. I went sprawling backwards onto the stage, crumpling one of my fairy wings.

Somebody called out, "Hey Rube." Bud and the crowd he'd been leading around the sideshow top were two stages away, where Fannie sat. He ran to us, pulled the larger boy off Ivan and threw him to the ground. Perry ran in from outside and, together with two of the men from the audience, came right behind Bud and grabbed the boy as he jumped back up, ready to attack. They held him back while Bud climbed onto the stage, got his grips on the other, smaller boy, and yanked him off Ivan's back. Then Ivan and Bud tackled the small but sturdy farm boy down to the floor and held him there.

Casper must have heard the commotion from out on his bally platform. He stomped inside, and used the back steps to get up onto our stage where Ivan and Bud had the smaller of the boys pinned right in front of me. The stage shook with the landing of the big man's feet. Casper pretended he was just there to have a look, but I saw him "accidentally" kick the boy hard in the ribs with the steel toe of his boot as he stepped up to him. Still sounding his old jovial self, he said, "My, oh my, friends, what do we have here?"

By now, almost everyone, townie and freak, was gathered around our small stage. There must have been a hundred people in the audience: men, their wives, and children of every size. Casper jumped down from the front of the three-foot-high platform, not an easy feat for a person of his girth. Still smiling a calm, reassuring smile, he edged between the crowd and the three men who were holding on to the larger farm boy, and used his spread-wide arms to gently coax the onlookers back a few steps.

"Nothing to worry about here, folks," said Casper, "just a bit too much pepper in these fine young lads." He chuckled a bit, then put his beefy hand on the shoulder of the boy, nodding pleasantly to the audience members who had tackled this ruffian. The men loosened their hold on the boy and let Casper walk him toward the tent opening. Casper kept smiling, kept walking, kept making friendly comments to the people as he passed, and kept squeezing the boy's shoulder. If you listened only to Casper and watched only his face as he led the boy toward the outside, you'd think he was a benevolent and forgiving man. I knew he was squeezing that shoulder hard, so hard I could imagine tears coming to the farm boy's eyes. He wouldn't let up the pressure until the message he meant to deliver was acknowledged. He very quickly and very quietly let the boy know it would be dangerous to return.

Like everything else the man did, it was show business. Casper put the townies at ease so they wouldn't stampede out and demand their money back. He even made them feel like they had gotten a little extra for their four bits.

"I reckon we all know how young men can be," he called back to the crowd as he shoved the boy through the tent flap. "No harm done." He gave them one of his hearty laughs.

Meanwhile, Bud, who had just as firmly gripped the other troublemaker, quietly handed him off to Ivan, Perry, and Horace the snake boy. Then Bud coaxed the still murmuring and excited audience back to where Fannie stood smiling and posing sweetly. He resumed his spiel, with greater gusto, as the three men led the second boy outside.

I wanted to run to Ivan and ask if he was all right when he, Perry, and Horace came back inside after handing off the second troublemaker to Casper.

Ivan returned to the sideshow top in character, not as my gentle friend who had been attacked by a couple of hoodlums but as Ivan the fierce Gordian Giant who would destroy all who challenged him. He snarled and hunched his back as he walked in—not enough to scare the rubes away, just enough to convince them he was truly the savage Goliath that Casper built him up to be.

I took his cue and improvised. "My hero," I called as I ran to the front of the platform, batting my eyes like the rescued fairy princess I was supposed to be. He climbed the steps; I fake-swooned into his arms, projecting my lines to the crowd that was leaving Fannie's stage and making its way toward ours.

"You've saved my life once again, my brave warrior!"

He growled appreciatively. On with the show.

With everybody at our stage again, I twirled and smiled, and pattered on about Ivan's heroics. Ivan scowled and grunted, but played at letting me soothe him with a song into keeping to the back of the stage.

"Lullabye and good-night, go to sleep my sweet giant."

The rubes felt safe enough to come closer with the "ferocious" Ivan lulled into lying down. We sold at least fifty postcards of us that performance: "The world's most unusual couple."

*

The following morning, Perry hitched up his wagon and mules, threw his gear in the back and said good-bye to us all. He told Ivan he was weary of life on the road and besides, his pa needed his help back home.

Just like that, Perry was gone. Maybe he realized how dangerous the situation could have been if the farm boys had realized that Ivan and I weren't the real unusual couple. Or maybe, it was nothing more than what he said.

Ivan had to be crushed. They hadn't been apart for more than a few hours since that night I saw them together near the games of no-chance-at-all. But Ivan didn't talk about it. You'd never know his world had just been turned inside-out.

One rainy day, we were sitting under the ten-in-one top with plenty of time and no audience. I asked Ivan if he was feeling all right.

"My legs, always they give me ache," he answered.

"I was asking after your heart."

He looked down at me like I was speaking a foreign language. Then, a moment later, he nodded in recognition. "Is all right, Lucinda."

"I thought you cared for Perry."

Ivan shrugged. "And he is gone home, now. This is life we choose, Lucinda. It gives many good things. It gives us freedom like no other, but this life, it makes no room for regret. Peoples come and go. You cannot cry for them or you cry every day of your life."

I couldn't think what to say. Ivan did love Perry, I was sure of it, but he was sincere about what he'd just told me, too.

People come and go.

Don't some people stay with you, though, even after they're gone? How can you not cry for them?

I still dreamed of Cyrus Parker. I told myself I regretted that I never got to say good-bye. But, when I thought about it, all these years later, I couldn't say for sure what I wanted to tell him. I just knew that it wasn't good-bye.

In that moment, I felt so distant from Ivan. To my mind, love was 'til death do us part, with or without the wedding ring. I could understand longing for love, crying for love. Heck, I suppose I could understand fighting, screaming, and maybe even killing for love.

What I couldn't understand was just letting love go.

25. MARISA

Sarasota had long since bulldozed most of its derelict mobile home parks. You could still find communities of well-tended manufactured homes where retirees spent their time involved in volunteer work, golf and bingo. These residents were quick to scold any who made the error of calling their tidy little homesteads, "trailers."

Just forty-five miles north, Gibsonton reminded Marisa of what poor southwest Florida neighborhoods had looked like, pre-gentrification. Here, no beautification committee members argued over whether to landscape the main drag with queen palms or olive trees. No Gib'town resident would get insulted if somebody called his trailer a trailer, especially not when some of these live-in tin cans still traveled six months a year with their carnie owners, from mud show to rodeo, hitched to the backs of oversized pick-ups.

Marisa drove down Gibsonton Road, looking for the turn-off to Brogan's museum. There it was: Pelican Drive.

A young man wearing a Confederate flag-decorated baseball cap over his long mullet, loped diagonally across the road about 50 feet in front of her car. With one sinewy arm, he opened the door to the cab of a white concession trailer van that was parked half on, half off the curb, its unlit marquee sign advertising funnel cakes and cotton candy. He backed it into the road, oblivious to other traffic. Marisa waited, then turned.

Ramshackle house followed ramshackle house. It would take some doing to find one that had gotten a fresh coat of paint in the past decade. A mobile home to her right was dwarfed by the 18-wheeler in its driveway, a tilt-a-whirl ride loaded on its flatbed.

The narrow pot-holed street took her down a small hill and ended at a "T." A hand-painted sign said, "Museum," with an arrow pointing to the right.

Asphalt gave way to rutted dirt. Another sign, more professionally done, pointed ahead to "The Museum of the Macabre." Fifty yards down this unpaved section, in a big field, bordered by a chain link fence haphazardly strung, were scattered a half dozen old tractor-trailer cabs, three rusted carnival trailers, and a few food and game concession trucks that looked like they had been disintegrating in place for years. At the back of the field against the fence, was parked a newer rig, hauling a carnival ride folded for travel, its tracks bright yellow, its base electric blue. That and a white minivan were the only vehicles that looked operational in this elephant graveyard of old equipment.

The "Welcome to The Museum of the Macabre" sign, on the huge grey metal utility shed directly ahead, looked almost as sad as the abandoned vehicles. Still, a picky historian like Myrtle thought Dapper Dan Brogan was her best source for sideshow lore. She parked near the front door.

*

"You're writing this for —?" asked Dan Brogan, leaning back in his chair behind his pressed wood desk. They were in the tiny box office at the entrance of his museum.

"At this point, I'm just gathering research," said Marisa, hoping he wouldn't press.

Brogan overfilled the small space, and not just because of his hefty size. In his frayed, yellowing, white linen suit, which matched his thick wavy mane and long moustache, he would command attention wherever he was. His deep voice and careful enunciation suggested refinement despite the tendency to pepper the conversation with southern colloquialisms. There was a hint in the man's manner of bluer-than-thou bloodlines, of "old money" long gone. She might have bought it had the carnie not taken the act a tad far with wide-brimmed Panama hat, silver-tipped walking stick, and too-bright red bow-tie.

"You're not planning to do a muckraker job on me, are you?" he asked.

"Why, is there some muck that needs raking?" she joked. "No, I'm not looking for dirt, just colorful history, mostly about the old circus and carnival sideshows that traveled around in the roaring twenties."

Blue eyes, half-hidden under multiple folds of lid, probed her as closely as she studied him, broadcasting suspicion but also a deep humor. Their message: I know you lie, just like everyone lies, but I'll allow it as long as it amuses me.

Uneasy under that gaze, she felt compelled to justify her visit beyond the vague identification as a freelance journalist. She told him about the house, the legend that it had been built for sideshow midgets, and the strange events she'd experienced since moving in. She confided that she hoped that by unraveling its history, she might learn something that would help her to calm whatever was stirred up inside it and that seemed to want her gone. And maybe, she said, while she was looking into all this, she could sell a magazine story based on her research. Because what she needed most was money to pay the liens, to keep the house out of the hands of those who meant to destroy it.

She hadn't intended to reveal so much about herself but it all spilled out. When she looked up, something had replaced the suspicion in those blue eyes.

"What do you know so far about those old freak shows?"

"Nothing, really."

"Let me show you around," he said, getting up, with a bit of effort, from behind the desk. He opened the door, reached his hand through the doorway, and flipped several levers upward.

Spotlights blared on throughout the building, illuminating displays inset along the walls but leaving the center aisle dimly lit. Calliope music flowed from unseen speakers. He held out his arm to indicate she should walk out ahead of him.

The display to her left made her gasp. At least two dozen shrunken heads hung, seemingly suspended in mid-air. A closer look showed that each was dangling from nearly invisible clear filaments, probably fishing line.

Behind the heads, in the glass-covered display case set into the wall, were old black and white photographs, showing the naked South American natives who created such monstrous trophies. One photo of a stern looking Brazilian Indian showed him holding what looked like a freshly detached head by the hair. He was dipping it in a pot.

"Rather gruesome, I admit, but it's always fascinated me," said Brogan's voice behind her. "The photographs were taken by one of the few white men to mingle with the Jivaro tribe and come back alive. The Jivaro warriors would chop the heads off the bodies of the men they killed in battle, cook them up lightly in a broth until the flesh was just soft enough to remove from the skull, as you see here." He pointed to a photograph of a naked Indian man, scraping the skin off a skull. "Then," he pointed to the photograph next to it, "they sew the eye sockets and mouths closed and smoke them over a slow fire to preserve them. Not much different from the way you'd make beef jerky."

He said this all in a matter-of-fact manner, a chuckle in his voice. Marisa knew he had given the spiel hundreds of times, and it was well-rehearsed. It still unsettled her, making her unsure whether she wanted to avert her eyes or stare harder.

"I think you'll like this next one." He motioned her to a display window about eight feet past the shrunken heads. Set into the wall, behind the glass, were five enormous bottles, each filled with tea colored liquid. Inside each bottle, a human fetus floated.

Marisa cringed.

"Disturbing, are they? Did you notice the one with two

heads?"

One of the fetuses did, indeed, have two faces, if not exactly two distinct heads. Both faces had the same curious, alert expression, as if they were wondering what they were doing here. The face on the right almost seemed to be looking at her. Her stomach did a little twist. Next to each jar was an official looking document, with the medical details.

She walked to the next display window before Brogan suggested it. It seemed tame after the others. Just photographs of freaks from another time, and a poster inviting townspeople to "Come one, come all, to Casper's Cavalcade of Living Curiosities."

"That fellow in the photograph up toward the top, there, next to the sword swallower?"

She looked up where he pointed, at a photo of a teen boy, dressed only in briefs. His arms, legs and torso were covered by alligator-like scales, but he was otherwise not bad-looking.

"That's Horace Vanderee, the Snake Boy, in his prime. He's still around. Outlived three wives. He retired here in Gib'town. When his third wife passed on, his kids, old folks themselves, went and put him into one of those assisted living places. You'll want to talk to him, too. Horace can't recognize his own daughter's face, or tell you what he had for breakfast. On his good days though, he still remembers everything you'd ever want to know about life on the road with a traveling freak show, back when."

"Do you know which home he's in?" Marisa asked, her pen and pad out.

"Yeah, not too far from here. I'll get the name of it for you."

"And what did you say was Horace's last name?"

"Vanderee. Horace Vanderee."

"Great. And do you know how I might reach a freak show fat man called George Corwood?"

"Yeah, you can reach him through Sally. She's the one runs that psychic readers' place you passed on the way into town." He waited a beat. "You do know George has been dead for forty years."

Marisa, embarrassed, mumbled a reply.

"I'm happy to help you out, but what's in this for me? You say you want to write an article. So, okay, you plug my business here, I figure, one hand washes the other. If you're just here pumping me for information? Honey, you're taking my valuable time, and time's a commodity like everything else."

He motioned her toward the next display.

"How much?"

"Oh, heck. You seem like a nice young lady. I wouldn't mind asking around for, say, fifty bucks?"

"Fine." Marisa's cheeks burned. She couldn't afford it. But she needed to know.

"You won't be sorry, hon'," Brogan said. "I know everybody who's ever been in the business. Myrtle steered you right, sending you to me."

Inset into the next display case, a spotlight shone on a large, presumably mummified body — human on top but with fish scales, fins and tail.

"What the — it's a joke, right? You can't pretend that's a real mermaid."

Brogan chuckled again as he looked at her out of the corner of his eye. "When did you hear me say any of it was real?"

She thought back to the shrunken heads, the dead babies bobbing in jars.

He hadn't, had he?

"Show biz, hon'. I'll call you when I have more on Horace."

*

Before heading home, she stopped at the Cortez fish market and picked up two grouper filets for the dinner she'd promised to cook for Guinness tonight, then swung by the farmer's market and bought salad fixings.

The workmen had left and Otto was standing in the yard, kicking pebbles down the drive like a sullen overgrown child. She waved unenthusiastically as she pulled into the parking space.

The lawn looked like a hayfield. It was getting on her nerves more than Otto.

"I guess you didn't get a chance to gas up the lawn mower," she said, not hiding her annoyance.

Otto stared at her like she was a bug in a jar. "Exactly how did that become my problem?" he answered, kicking at another pile of gravel.

"Never mind," she muttered.

Picking up the FedEx envelope waiting by the door, she walked into her house. She considered trying to mow herself but she'd only have a couple of hours to work on the editing job before Guinness arrived. It could wait.

*

Sometime after the spinach salad but before she put water on for coffee, Marisa relaxed in John Guinness's company. He was different than she'd expected. Genuine and funny, he listened to her with what seemed like real interest and confided his own insecurities about the real estate market.

"What will you do if business doesn't pick up?" she asked.

"Well, I've been practicing a speech that served me well when I worked my way through school." He waited a beat, his expression turning more serious, before he continued, "Would you like fries with that?"

She laughed in spite of herself.

Could she have misjudged him? What if his offer to fix her house was exactly what he'd made it out to be, a peace offering?

She'd never considered that a Porsche-driving big-time developer might be facing his own struggles with the downturn. Yet, here was Guinness, telling her several of his projects had to be put on hold and a couple had fallen through. The only properties that were selling these days, he said, were at the extreme high-end, purchased by people so wealthy — they arrived in private jets and bought grand homes in each of the cities they flitted to around the world — they made him look like a pauper. Every builder in Sarasota wooed this crowd.

The ones whose courtships succeeded would ride out the hard times; the losers would be out of business.

To a certain degree, his candor was disarming her. She liked him, damn it.

Of course, she'd liked other men before, she reminded herself, and almost everyone of them had turned out to be a snake or a loser or both; her judgment in this area, not to mention her history, would earn her an F, even grading on a curve.

He carried their wine glasses in one hand and in the other, one of the bottles of French Bordeaux he had brought, as he followed her to the old carved settee.

"So, you've been married before?" he asked.

"Scars still show?"

He laughed. "All I see is a pretty lady, no trace of scar tissue."

"And you? Any ex-Mrs. Guinnesses out there?"

"Just one," he answered, "Two kids, Sean and Jennifer. I met Nancy while we were both students at U.S.F. We divorced about six years ago. She moved back to Austin, took the kids with her. So, I guess this is why you don't date. Not over the ex?"

"I don't want him back, if that's what you mean. I just haven't quite untangled all the knots yet. We had this strange connection. I'd be walking somewhere I'd never been before and there he'd be. We'd find each other without looking. Like magnets find metal. Sorry. Probably more than you wanted to know."

"Hey, no problem. Wish I could say I'd felt something like that for Nancy. I miss my kids though. I'm heading out to Austin tomorrow. The kids have a few days off while their teachers go to some conference." He reached out, put his hands on her waist, and gave a gentle tug. "Why don't you pack a bag and come with me?"

"We agreed, no strings," she said, running her hands over his in a way meant to restrain rather than encourage.

"Just thought you might want to get away," he said, with no more apparent disappointment than if she had recited a preference for decaf over regular. "I'm checking out some land in the hill country while I'm there. You'd love it. Green and open, close enough to the city yet it feels a million miles away. You see, even a greedy, land-grabbing developer like me can appreciate unspoiled nature."

Marisa recognized her cue to protest that he was neither greedy nor a land-grabber. But, charming as he was, the comment brought her back to earth, reminding her why he'd sought her out. She lifted her wine glass, and sipped instead of answering.

"You're real easy to talk to, you know?" he said, reaching across the old sofa again. He let his fingers trace their way down her arm and onto the top of her hand.

She only recognized her own vulnerability a few beats after he did. Her body responded to his touch even as her mind shouted alarms.

No, she could not do this. Not now, not with him.

"Any preference in music?" she asked getting up to change the CD.

"Whatever you like."

She replaced Miles Davis with Bonnie Raitt, and sat back down, not on the sofa beside him but in the chair next to it.

"I'm afraid I'm going to have to send you on your way, John," she said, glancing at her watch. "I've got to start work early tomorrow."

Settling for a chaste kiss at the front door, he said goodnight. Marisa wondered if she'd taken a bigger risk than she'd imagined in accepting John Guinness's help.

*

Vivid dreams filled her sleep, borrowing their themes from her long day. Midgets and freaks danced around a tiny stage as a colorfully dressed barker, a heftier, old-time version of Dan Brogan, called out to passersby with a rapid-fire spiel. Marisa could smell the stale sweat on the clothes of ragged onlookers pressing to get closer to the tent, waving money to buy tickets.

She was still immersed in this oddly realistic fantasy when a loud crash woke her. Disoriented, she jumped out of bed, her heart pumping so hard it pounded against her throat. Turning on the light, she realized where she was. In this time, in this house.

The dream faded. All that stayed with her as she strove to adjust to wakefulness was a name that didn't connect to anything: Lucinda.

Padding into the kitchen for a glass of water, she saw Murphy scooting down the stairs. Light glinted off the metal tag on the spiffy new collar she'd bought him. Sighing, she thought, the little guy has again knocked down something in the upstairs bedroom.

She walked up the staircase and flicked on the hall light. Nothing seemed out of place. The dolls in the playroom were lined up as she had left them. The second bedroom, too, appeared in order.

Construction materials that the workmen had left unsecured must have fallen somewhere outside. Must have, because nothing had fallen up here. In her sleep she simply assumed the noise came from within the house.

A flash of lightning lit up the playroom through the French doors leading to the balcony. She could swear something moved at the edge of her peripheral vision. The wind must have rustled the blue tarps the men had thrown over the roof to protect their repair work from rain. And the lightning threw a shadow. That's all. She reassured herself that even the crash could be accounted for by thunder from the storm headed this way that her sleeping self interpreted to fit her dream.

So why, she wondered, were the hairs on her forearms standing up again, as they did so often when she entered this room? Why did every part of her feel alert, yet dreamy at the same time?

There's an unmistakable, yet difficult to articulate feeling to a space shared with another. Marisa had that feeling now, as if the air were fuller or somehow compressed by the other, as opposed to the empty feeling of an area one inhabits alone. She felt the presence as a certainty, despite the evidence of her own eyes that nobody else was upstairs with her, not even Murphy.

She backed out and stood on the landing for several minutes, just listening. The only noises came from outside: crickets, the breeze whipping through the palms. She'd left the French doors cracked open a bit to clear the musty odors. Underneath the stale air drifted the scent of jasmine — night-blooming jasmine, she suspected, given the hour. The perfume, whatever its source, was so luscious and heavy, it seemed to exude from somewhere in the room itself. She remembered now that she'd noticed that scent before only at times when she felt the strange static electricity sensation.

Stop. Don't read something into every little smell and sound.

More than the scent, there lingered that sense of someone else present, definite and as tangible, in its way, as the walls and the floor.

"Who's there?" she said almost too softly to hear her own voice.

"WHO'S THERE?" she shouted.

The words seem to hang in the empty room.

Empty. Yes, now it was, of scent and sensation, as if she had broken a spell. The hairs on her arms lay flat. The charge in the air dissipated.

She shook the urge to try to coax it back, assuming there were any way to do that. It was still the middle of the night; she had to get some rest.

Marching back down the stairs to the kitchen, she poured a glass of water, walked to her room, tumbled into bed and turned off the light.

Fleeting images poked into her mind, bringing glimpses of the dream from which she had been roused. She stared into the shadows until her eyes were too heavy to resist closing. The wind blew harder up from the bay.

When the rain came, gently tapping on the roof, she was

half-asleep. She thought briefly that she should put out pots and pans to catch any leaks, but trusting in the workmen's tarps, she snuggled under the covers, instead. Soon, she found herself wandering the same strange disjointed carnival dreamscapes she'd left before being awakened by the crashing noise.

Oblivious to whatever storms might swirl around her real world, she clung to these images even after a brief jolt to wakefulness just after dawn caused by the squawks of birds outside the window.

She threw her hand across her eyes and tried to keep out the morning for a little while yet. In her mind, now long disconnected from whatever it might have meant, those three syllables danced around, a remnant from the dream. She grabbed the pen and pad on her night table, jotted it down — "Lucinda" — then closed her eyes again.

26. LUCINDA

1923 – ON THE ROAD TO NEW LILLIPUTIA

Two letters changed everything for me. The first came from Albert, and caught up with me at the Post Office General Delivery in a little town just south of Knoxville. He wrote to tell me he was getting married and wanted me to come to his wedding.

I hadn't been back to Hodgeson County since Albert helped me run away, six years past. I wasn't going to go back now, not even for this. I hoped Albert could understand and forgive me but, of all the places I'd been in my life, Hodgeson County was the one I least wanted to go to again. And my Daddy was the last person I wanted to see. That didn't mean I didn't love him, in the strange way that daughters love their fathers no matter what. That's what made it so plain to me why I couldn't ever go there again. It was the love that made it hurt so much.

I never stopped feeling close to Albert. Time and distance didn't change those feelings. It's just that the other feelings were stronger.

I'd seen Albert once since he said good-bye after leaving me at the circus. The summer before, he came to see me at the railroad station, when Casper's pulled in to a town about fifty miles from the farm.

I waited on the platform, looking for the Albert I still had pictured in my mind, a shoeless, freckled, bony boy, with dirty blonde hair and a crooked smile.

That wasn't the Albert who stepped out of the passenger car of the Atlantic Coast Railroad. The man with Albert's face had wide shoulders and wore a proper pin-striped suit, slightly wrinkled by the long ride but otherwise very respectable. His hair was tidily cut, parted and oiled. His black shoes were so shiny, they glinted in the sun. And he had a moustache. I nearly fell on my face at the change in him. I wouldn't have believed it really was him except that he still had that same sweet crooked smile, and freckles still salted his nose and cheeks.

"Albert?" I called out to the grown-up man with my big brother's face.

"Lucinda!" he yelled back, then ran and scooped me up into his arms and gave me a big kiss on the cheek. "You look beautiful, sis, just beautiful. Look at you, your dress, your hair, your shoes. You could be a movie star."

"Me? I'm the same as ever, but Lordy, knock me over with a feather, I'd have thought you were some business tycoon."

He blushed, the pinkness setting off his freckles. "Well, like I wrote you in my letters, I hardly work the farm any more. Mostly, I work for Mr. Miller. With the money I've been bringing home, Daddy told me to keep on at the store instead."

A few years earlier, Albert had taken a job at the big store in town to help Daddy make ends meet during the winter months. He started out sweeping, stocking the shelves, running deliveries, and doing other odd jobs. Mr. Miller, the store owner, found him so honest, reliable, and hardworking, he gave him a chance to work in the front of the store, with the customers. Now Albert was assistant manager.

"Tell me what it's like, Lucinda, to be in a show," Albert said. "Lord forgive me, but I do envy you, seeing so much that I'll never see."

"It's different than you might expect, Albert, not all fun and adventure."

"Well, sure, for you, it's natural as gravy on grits," Albert said, "but think of the people who wait all year to lay down their money to see what you see everyday. What I wouldn't give to talk to a real, what did you call, herma... you know, the man who's half a woman."

"Hermaphrodite," I said, remembering that I'd written Albert about Jeraldine/Jeremiah when I first joined Casper's. I guess I'd never written back to tell him that the hermaphrodite was a fake. He/she attached half a rubber ball to the right side of his chest with some spirit gum and covered it with stage make-up to create the illusion of half a bosom.

Nevermind his all grown-up appearance and spiffy clothes, Albert looked so wide-eyed, I decided not to let on.

He was supposed to return home later that same evening, on the last train.

"I asked Mr. Miller for tomorrow off, so I could stay overnight if you'll let me come watch you perform," said Albert.

"No, Albert," I said. "I love seeing you more than you can imagine, but I need to keep that separate from family."

"Good land of glory, sis', why? I'd clap louder than anybody."

I knew he meant it, but I couldn't let him to come to Casper's. This wasn't the circus. I wasn't gliding down a wire under a spotlight. Even with Casper's bally-hoo, nobody with any sense would mistake me for a fairy princess. I didn't want my big brother to leave with a picture in his head of me as a freak on display.

It didn't matter that the nickels and dimes I made selling pictures of Ivan and me added up to more money than I'd made in the circus and was probably more than what Mr. Miller paid Albert. The ten-in-one show left me feeling poor in other ways. In the circus, I moved quickly along from sideshow top to big top. I was the spec's fairy dancer, parading in front of a dazzled and adoring audience.

Here, I could only be an oddity, about as likely to inspire adoration as the two-headed chicken.

Albert didn't press to come to the show, and I was relieved when he switched the subject to the pretty girl who came into

Mr. Miller's store every Friday. He was trying to get up the courage to ask her to the harvest dance.

*

And now, he was marrying that girl.

As I re-read Albert's letter, I found myself trying to picture his bride, his wedding, his home, and his new life. I imagined her in her apron, waiting for Albert to come home, kissing him on the cheek, and taking his jacket to hang in the closet. After a while, it wasn't Albert and his wife I imagined any more, but me. I could see myself cooking supper as I hummed along with the radio, waiting for my husband to come home from work. At first, I couldn't quite picture him. Then the door opened and I saw it was Cyrus Parker. He came through the front door, smelled the stew I was cooking and the apple pie I was baking, and talked about how lucky he was to have me as his bride and how he was going to build us a big house so we could raise a big family. Traveling further along in this imaginary life, I could almost feel the warm weight of a baby in my arms, and detect the soft scent of milk on the little one's pink lips.

It was such an ordinary daydream, one that made me as sad as it made me happy, because I knew it couldn't come true. Albert was getting married. Not me.

*

It was as if my longing got so strong, it built itself a solid form, or so it seemed to me. Soon after the show reached Columbia, South Carolina, Casper handed me an envelope that was waiting for me there at the Post Office, General Delivery, from Mr. Samuel W. Gumpertz. He addressed it using my real name, Lucinda Lacey, not Lucinda Darling, the stage name Casper had given me.

I knew about Samuel Gumpertz. My circus midget friend, Nettie, had told me in her halting English about the village that Mr. Gumpertz had built for midgets in an amusement park in Brooklyn, New York. It reminded her of Germany, her home, as it was meant to. Mr. Gumpertz had recreated an old German village, except that it was smaller, built to a scale that was

178

comfortable for people our size. Nettie met Hans, her husband, there.

Wondering how the impresario had found me and what he might want, I tore open the envelope.

*

Dear Miss Lacey,

Between 1904 and 1911, an amusement sensation such as the world had never before seen thrilled visitors to Coney Island, New York. It was called a park only because no word had yet been conceived that could describe a place which so exceeded anything that had preceded it. The park was called Dreamland.

This place of Amusement on an Atlantic Ocean inlet was more than a circus, more than a theater. A visitor to Dreamland could view a replica of ancient Pompeii, witness the end of the world, and see demonstrations of the miracles of modern science, all in the span of an afternoon.

For all Dreamland's other wonders, Lilliputia, a miniature replica of 15th Century Nuremberg, that housed hundreds of midgets like yourself, was the attraction that most excited Dreamland's visitors. Lilliputia's inhabitants were more than acts and exhibits. They ran their own government and lived their lives as they chose with people just like themselves.

Dreamland, and with it, Lilliputia, was consumed by fire in 1911 but the dream did not die. I plan to recreate a smaller version of Lilliputia, one with perhaps a dozen inhabitants, in a new place. Like the original, the new midget village will rise at the edge of a sea. This one will be on a new frontier, a resort for the wealthy: Sarasota, Florida. It will be a replica of old Normandy, itself a seaside gem.

I am writing to invite you to join this unique community. All your needs will be met, your food, clothing and shelter provided. In addition, you will receive wages of seventy dollars per month during the winter season, October through March. The remainder of the year you are free to live on the premises, should you wish to do so, and your time will be your own.

Please let me know your decision soonest so that I may tell

my agents to make preparations for your arrival.
   I look forward to your prompt reply.

Yours very sincerely,
Samuel W. Gumpertz

One piece of information in Mister Gumpertz's letter jumped out at me: he was building his midget village in Sarasota, Florida. Cyrus Parker had left the circus so he could return to his family there.

I had found the way back to him — or the way back to him had found me.

*

I planned to leave for Sarasota in late October 1923, almost the end of the carnival season, and before Casper's Cavalcade of Living Curiosities headed northward again.

As we sat around the cook stove, listening to the crickets serenade each other, I pulled Casper aside and confided my plans. I left out any mention of Cyrus Parker.

Casper listened without interrupting, smiling like a kindly uncle, nodding patiently to show he was paying attention. When I was finished telling him everything I had to say, he did his best to talk me out of going.

"Why do you think we take Casper's Cavalcade from town to town, never spending more than a week in any one place? Why do you think all the carnivals, fairs and circuses do the same?" he asked. Without waiting for my reply, he answered. "Because once you play a town for a few days, maybe a week, even if it's a big one, you've played to everybody who's ever gonna come, Lucinda. You stay in one place and you starve."

This is Samuel Gumpertz, I told Casper, the impresario who created the midget village in Coney Island's Dreamland. If he believed it would work in Florida, he might know something we don't.

Casper's laugh came out like a snort. He leaned back, his fingers linked across his belly. He glanced at me sideways, shaking his head, the set of his mouth telling me that he figured I was being snookered.

"If Gumpertz knows so much, let him prove it," said Casper. "Let him build that midget village out there in a swamp somewhere and see if the rules don't apply to him like everyone else. What I'm saying, Lucinda, is wait a while. Stay with us for now. At least with Casper's you know you're gonna make money because you know that I know how to make money. This fellow, Gumpertz? You ask me, he ain't got the sense God gave a head a' lettuce. He makes a go of it for a year, maybe two, go with my blessing. I'll buy you the ticket. You go rushing out there now though, before they's even done building? Whatcha gonna do if this turkey don't fly?"

Casper made sense. What would I do in the middle of Florida if the midget village closed up? I had some money saved but that wouldn't last long. I couldn't be sure Cyrus Parker was even there any more or, if he was, if he'd feel the way I did.

Horace the snake boy called me over to the side after breakfast. He'd overheard me talking to Casper the night before and had a completely different point of view.

"If Mr. Gumpertz wanted to hire me, I'd be on the next train," said Horace. "That man only hires the best. Everything he touches turns to gold."

According to Horace, Mr. Gumpertz traveled the world to find attractions to bring to America. He'd brought back whole villages from Africa and the Orient. He said Samuel Gumpertz was famous for knowing what people wanted to see before they knew themselves. He never failed to pack the house, with people lined up waiting their turn to get tickets.

"Never mind what Casper says. He don't know," said Horace. "Sure, a guy like Casper has to keep on the road all the time. Mr. Gumpertz? He can set down wherever he likes and the crowds'll come to him like flies come to honey. That sideshow in Coney Island? The one he built after Dreamland burnt down? The rubes travel there to see it, not the other way 'round."

Horace told me that Mr. Gumpertz had been the manager for the Great Harry Houdini and even gave Flo Ziegfeld his start.

"You don't judge a man like that against Casper, no offense meant," insisted Horace. "You was very lucky to get this chance. I'd hate to see you go. I'll miss you something fierce if you do but, I wouldn't turn it down if I was you."

I told Casper what Horace said but he wasn't impressed. "Florida ain't Brooklyn," he warned. "Where does Gumpertz expect he's gonna find the crowds to keep coming for a show in a state that's mostly empty, 'cept for the alligators in the quags, 'specially when he's got nothing in it but midgets?"

Casper was a smart man but I wondered if maybe Samuel Gumpertz was smarter. Then Casper said something that made it easy to decide. He promised that I would always have a place in his ten-in-one. Knowing that I could come back again at any time, I decided that I had to take the risk. But I didn't want to go without the person who had been closest to me for so many years.

"Come with me, Ivan," I asked my friend. "Mr. Gumpertz will want giants for his midget village, too, if he's got any sense."

Ivan shook his head. "I cannot go, Lucinda. You must know this."

"Of course you can go," I insisted. "Mr. Gumpertz would be thrilled to have you, just like the circus and Casper."

"Is not good for me, to be forever in one place," Ivan answered. "I do not need roofs above my head and I will not trade freedom for feather bed. I am sorry. You must go. Find your happiness. I cannot go with you, my friend."

So that was that. If I left, I'd leave alone.

Would Cyrus Parker even remember me? Maybe he was already re-married. I knew I had about as much chance as the rubes playing rigged games on the midway.

I also knew though that sometimes, when one of those rubes just wouldn't give up, whatever it cost him, he got to go home with the top-shelf prize.

*

My final show with Casper's was in a small carnival about twenty or so miles east of Atlanta. After the tents came down, the old farmer who had rented his land to the carnival agreed to drive me to the railway station in his buggy. Ivan and I said little to each other on my last day but I hugged him for a good long time and cried when it was time to let go. I knew I might not see him again, this man who had been my closest friend for a half-dozen years. I watched his slightly hunched back turned to me, his long legs taking him in the opposite direction, and felt a wave of loneliness. I wasn't having second thoughts, though. I wanted a different life. It was the right choice.

The farmer who took me to the station seemed kind. He laid an old blanket on the seat for my comfort before Ivan lifted me up into it. After he got me settled in though, he didn't talk to me at all during the two-hour ride. His face was as rutted as the road that the buggy bumped along and his eyes seemed sunken into his profile as he stared straight ahead, never once looking at me directly. I sensed that his avoiding me wasn't meant to hurt my feelings but to protect them. It was almost like he thought I'd be embarrassed if he let on that he noticed I was different. It was his unwillingness to look that embarrassed me, more than all the stares in all the years of being an attraction in the freak show.

Until I got into that buggy, I didn't fully appreciate that I was leaving behind the safety of my world. I had lived these past several years among the people of carnivals, circuses and fairs, where being different was ordinary. I had forgotten how vulnerable I could feel when I wasn't surrounded by other extraordinary people.

The old farmer brought me to the railway station and laid my baggage by the ticket window. He tipped his straw hat, still not looking directly at me, then left.

"Sorry, ma'am," said the ticket seller who took my fare, "the last train's already left." He directed me across the road, to a frame rooming house with peeling white paint, where I could rent a room for the night.

I knocked at the front door and told the lady who answered I wanted a room. The pleasant-faced proprietress, her silver hair tucked in a prim bun, seemed to believe that I was a child playing a prank. I couldn't convince her that I was a grown woman, wanting to pay for a night's stay before continuing my travels.

The ticket seller, watching from his window across the way, must have overheard, and came by to help.

"Ain't you never been to the circus, Mrs. Cox? 'Cuz I have, and that there is a lady, fully growed, and in need of a room."

Accepting the ticket seller's word, Mrs. Cox showed me to a room. This confusion, after the long trip with the silent farmer, unsettled me. I decided not to take my dinner with the other guests. I didn't want to be forced again to explain what I was, or worse, to make others so uncomfortable that they needed to look away. I paid Mrs. Cox an extra thirty cents to bring that night's supper, and breakfast the following morning, to my room.

An hour after dawn, I boarded the first of the trains that would eventually bring me to Sarasota.

The glances of my fellow passengers were more polite than the stares I was used to on the bally platform or inside the freak show tent and they shouldn't have bothered me.

Somehow, this was different. The people who came to Casper's or to the circus wanted only a peek at my world. They paid their money to scare themselves silly with glimpses at "living curiosities" like me, their tickets allowing them to cringe in wonder and amazement, and then leave it behind. Now I had come to their world, uninvited, and they didn't have the option of leaving me behind. I suspect that they didn't quite know how to reckon with my intrusion. Neither did I.

There were fewer coughs, whispers and curious glances after the train had jostled along a while. I tried to ignore them the way the old farmer had ignored me, setting my gaze on the book I'd brought along for the ride.

Even this far into autumn, the air in the rail car hung as

thick and moist as Tennessee in July. I struggled to open the window next to my seat but had to give up. A minute later, I heard, "Excuse me, ma'am," from a gentlemanly southern-accented voice in the aisle. "Let me try that for you." I got out of my seat and the man leaned over, pushed hard on the window and it opened upward, allowing the breeze to blow through. He tipped his hat as I thanked him. He walked back to his seat a few aisles up, next to a pretty brown-haired lady, who looked back at me and smiled shyly. I smiled back. Such a small gesture, but I felt that I could breathe again, and not just because of the fresh air from the window.

I turned back to my book. Soon, the rocking of the rail car lulled me to sleep.

I woke up in time to switch trains in Tampa, and then boarded for the connection to Sarasota.

*

Mr. Gumpertz sent a shiny black motor car to the station. The driver looked familiar but I couldn't immediately place the face.

"Miss Lucinda," he said, tipping his cap as he reached for my bag. "Mr. Sam thought it'd be best for me to pick y'all up, seeing as how we used to know each other."

"Leroy?" I asked. He looked older and heavier but I recognized that twangy Georgia drawl. This was the Parker Circus razorback who had been smitten with the showgirl, Wanda.

He smiled, pleased, I think, that I remembered him. I saw that he was missing several of his teeth.

"I sure was glad to hear you agreed to come," he said. "If it wasn't for you and your friends way back when, those feds would've hauled my butt to jail, for sure. No offense, ma'am."

None taken, I told him. I felt a twinge of sadness, remembering that day Ivan hid Leroy in the hay bales. I missed my big friend.

At least now though, I figured I knew why Samuel Gumpertz had tracked me down and invited me to be in his midget village.

Leroy must have put in a good word.

He opened the back door and I settled into the softly upholstered seat. It was quite a change from the woven wicker of the railroad cars.

Leroy said he'd been with Mr. Gumpertz since soon after leaving the circus. They had been all over the country together but the midget village was the project that Mr. Gumpertz had poured his heart into like nothing before.

"'Course, it ain't a village yet," Leroy confided. "It's just a single house, so far."

Workmen were already constructing a stable and pouring the foundation for a city hall, said Leroy and Mr. Gumpertz was going to get some financiers to back him in building the rest of it. Soon, he said, it would be its own little city within the city.

"Mr. Sam is gonna do with his midget village what he done with everything else he touches," said Leroy, "make it the most exciting attraction for hundreds of miles in any direction."

With all the rich and famous people coming down for the winters, Leroy claimed that Mr. Gumpertz and his friends had already begun making Sarasota as important as Miami.

He could have been a ten-in-one talker, the way he rattled off his praise of everything about Sarasota, and Mr. Gumpertz, and what he had planned.

"How many of the other midgets are here already?" I asked.

"None," said Leroy, seeming surprised by my question. "Mr. Sam said he needed jes' one for now, to show them financiers what he has in mind."

Just one? I thought about Casper's warnings that Mr. Gumpertz' midget village would fail. Had Casper been right? If so, the sole inhabitant might just be the village idiot.

I forced the thoughts out of my head. I was here and it was too late to second guess.

"Mr. Sam, he's got connections with important people everywhere," Leroy boasted. "He got movie stars comin' down, got him some millionaires, heck, even the mayor of New York

City. That Mr. Sam, all by himself, he's putting this city on the map, Miss Lucinda."

Leroy's enthusiasm was sincere but I didn't see what he saw, nothing much that looked fine or glamorous. We drove past mostly scrub and brush on the outskirts of a town with few houses, and fewer of those that looked like they would impress movie stars and big city millionaires. The land was flat and had none of the natural beauty of so many other places I'd passed through. There were billboards all along the road, almost every one of them advertising land for sale.

"Only the deliberately blind will ignore this opportunity," read one that assured investors they would earn at least a 25 percent profit in the coming real estate boom.

Across the road, another big sign guaranteed all buyers in Baywood Estates at least double their money in less than a year, a profit that was, "unheard of in the annals of Sarasota history," it said. Down the road, another billboard warned people that, if they didn't get in on the ground floor of the fantastic land deal at Sapphire Shores, they would never forgive themselves.

The billboards reminded me of the sideshow banners that lured marks to Casper's Cavalcade of Living Curiosities. I figured their artists took the same kinds of liberties in order to turn the tip. Those who came to Casper's never seemed disappointed by the slightly less wondrous oddities beneath the ten-in-one canvas, not even the "living curiosity" of the two-headed chicken that was years past being alive.

Samuel W. Gumpertz knew better than me what this city could be. This was the man who had helped make Harry Houdini famous. If he believed that he could make Sarasota as important as Miami, so did I.

Leroy drove past Mr. Gumpertz's own house, the first one that looked grand enough for a movie star, at least by the little I could see from the street. "Mr. Sam even brung in some people from up north to put in central heating so he won't have to be near a fireplace to be warm in the wintertime. Hot air gets piped into every room. His's the only house in Sarasota that's got it."

The air in Florida didn't seem to need such fancy systems to warm it, but maybe that's what made Mr. Gumpertz's extravagance impressive. Samuel Gumpertz was, in this, as in all things, ahead of everybody else. He knows what he is doing, I told myself.

We arrived in the downtown, and things started to look more promising. It wasn't a large city but new buildings were going up all around. I had never seen so much construction in one place.

We turned onto Pineapple Avenue and, there it was. Its side faced the street so I couldn't take in the full effect but I knew right away. The dainty castle in front of me was the flagship building of the New Lilliputia Midget Village.

A wrought iron balcony, with an intricate lacey pattern like the ones I'd seen on houses in New Orleans, wrapped around French doors on the second story. Stained glass windows, in delicate swirls of purple, green and white, spiraled around a medieval-looking turret that towered over its main roof. The house had several gables, all different heights. The upstairs windows had carved shutters on each side, painted in dark purple, the same color as the swirls in the turret windows.

Leroy pulled open a metal gate, then drove the big black car into the circular driveway. A fountain with a carved lion's head, in the center of the circle, gushed water from the lion's mouth.

The upstairs looked closer than usual to the downstairs, which is how I could tell that it had been scaled down for people my size.

Leroy helped me out of the backseat then pulled my baggage from the trunk. He walked my belongings to the front door. The closer we got, the more magical it looked. It could have been straight out of one of my Mama's old fairy stories. I closed my eyes, not knowing why, maybe so I could hang onto that first moment of happiness before having it replaced by another.

Whatever misgivings I felt were charmed away. I was home.

27. Marisa

Cop

> "According to the findings by neuroscientists at the Brain Behavior Laboratory, men's "old" limbic systems, the region which controls aggressive behavior, are more active than the same regions in women's brains."

Marisa's own brain refused to absorb the meaning of the dense text she was editing. Clearly, she'd have to break up that first sentence and add —

Bang, bang, bang, bang.

The construction crew's noise derailed her train of thought.

Be grateful for the noise, she told herself. That racket outside was the sound of putting right what was wrong with the house. Okay, not all that was wrong, but at least the kinds of problems that could be fixed by workmen.

She picked up her red pen.

> "The brain regions governing speech and symbolic communications —"

"Whoo, oo, Kentucky Lou, I surely do need you," came blaring out of the workers' boom-box.

The twangy lament triggered a memory of that other name

that had followed her from her dreams: Lucinda.

She put down the manuscript and tried to fill in the blanks between the few fragments that had stayed with her. No good. It was gone, except for some fading images and that name.

She placed the manuscript pages on the big old wooden table in the dining room, put the water on for a pot of Cuban coffee, changed her mind, and pulled down a tin of herbal tea instead. The last thing she needed was a layer of caffeine jitters, on top of the construction noise, the job and the dream.

There was a blissful break in the power tool cacophony. She stood in the doorway, waved to the workers, and looked toward the bay.

Before she could fully appreciate the quiet, the ringing phone summoned her back inside.

"Hello. Ms. Delano?"

"Yes?"

"Detective Michael Ricci of the Sarasota Police. I'm calling about your break-in the other day."

"Detective, I'm embarrassed to admit this but it may be a case of simply neglecting to lock the door."

"The report here says both doors were wide open. You often leave the house like that?"

"I'd really be losing it if I did, but —."

"Ms. Delano, this could be related to another burglary in the neighborhood we're investigating. I'd like to come over and talk to you. How's noon?"

*

At five minutes past twelve, a car came down the drive. Figuring it was the detective, Marisa opened the front door and waited inside the doorway. The only clue that this four-door white sedan was a cop's car was its longer than usual antenna.

The man who stepped out had wavy brown hair and a generous moustache, which didn't look like regulation facial hair. His dark sport coat appeared just a bit too snug across his wide shoulders. He bent down to pick up something next to the car – a gopher tortoise that must have wandered in from the woods – and placed it further away, in a tangle of shrub and vines, before turning back toward the house.

"Ms. Delano?" the detective took out his wallet and flipped his badge. The electric saws screamed on in the background, momentarily drowning out the plaintive tune coming from the boom-box's tinny speakers.

"Hello, Detective Ricci. Sorry about the noise."

He filled the doorway as he walked through. "Nice place," he said. "They really build this for midgets?"

"Nobody knows for sure."

"And the stories about Cyrus Parker's treasure being hidden somewhere inside the walls —?"

"I think somebody would have found it by now, don't you?"

She led him into the living room and the mahogany settee with its slightly lumpy upholstery. She took a seat in the small rocking chair beside it.

He quickly got to the point.

"What time did you discover that your doors were open?"

"I was coming home from work, about six o'clock."

"And you called the police immediately?"

"A friend called. Detective, I don't think it was a break-in."

"Why? Does someone else have a key?"

"Maybe Otto Hinkle. He lives above the garage."

"This Hinkle, he have your permission to come in when you're not home?"

"I don't want to get him in trouble, just trying to answer your question. The more I think of it, the more sure I am it wasn't Otto."

He stared at his notepad for a moment. "So, who besides Hinkle do you suspect?"

She shrugged. She couldn't tell a cop that the culprit she had in mind wasn't currently alive.

"I'm guessing Hinkle parks his car across the drive next to yours. So, you could look out your kitchen window and tell when he's home, right?"

"I suppose. I haven't paid that much attention to Otto's

comings and goings."

Ricci flipped his notebook closed and held out a Sarasota Police business card. She took the card, thanked him, and walked him to the door.

As she watched through the kitchen window, Ricci stuck a business card in the door to Otto's apartment before getting in his car and driving toward the street.

28. Lucinda

I woke up to the sound of hammers and, just for a minute, thought it was the canvasmen, pounding tent pegs into the ground for the freak show. Then I remembered where I was. This was no one-night stand in a nameless town. Construction workers were building the barn for the village of New Lilliputia.

I'd settled into the bottom bunk of one of the child-sized bunk beds in the larger of the bedrooms upstairs. At the end of the circus and carnival season, if all went as planned, three other midget women would share this room with me. For now, it was mine alone.

Upstairs wasn't nearly as fancy as the floor below, but that made me think that Mr. Gumpertz planned to keep our bedrooms closed to the public. If so, I was happy to have a more humble room. It was still finer than any home I had lived in before.

I shook out my costumes and hung them in the closet near my bed, emptied the rest of my baggage into the two top drawers of one of the built-in dressers. then stowed my bag at the bottom of the closet.

I'd kept one of the little dolls that Ivan had rescued from the trash heap when the circus closed. It was dressed in chiffon with dainty wings and was supposed to look like the little fairy princess I'd played in the spec. I put it on the built-in dressing table. Just with that one little toy, already the place felt more like home.

I wandered into the men's bedroom, on the other side of the bath. It wasn't as big as the one for the women. Like the other room, it had two sets of child-sized bunk beds but no closets, and no other furniture. I guessed that the four midget men who'd be living here would have to share the small closet in the hallway.

The ceilings appeared lower than a normal-sized person's house but only by a little. Ivan would have to stoop to get around in here but Casper would do just fine.

The house smelled of fresh paint. A crystal chandelier hung from the high ceiling of the turret. I went downstairs, holding the lower section of the double banister.

The parlor, with its wood-paneled walls, glossy wood floors, and beamed gold-trimmed ceiling made me think of the grand ballroom in Savannah where Ivan and I had once performed in the off-season at a wealthy man's private party. I could imagine myself waltzing across this floor, just like those ladies in Savannah.

The carved chairs on either side of the small stone fireplace had been built for people my size but I sat on the floor, thinking how nice it would be to snuggle up with someone I loved with the fire lit.

On the walls were photographs of midgets, each with a small printed bronze plaque under its frame. The largest one was of Tom Thumb and Lavinia Warren on their wedding day. The bridesmaid and best man on either side of them were even smaller. Next to this was a portrait of the famous vaudeville troupe, the Singer Midgets, and several of not-so-famous midgets. Some photographs looked new while others, with browned edges and cracked surfaces were probably very old.

I found a picture of Ivan and me, and remembered the day the photographer shot it, with me standing on a chair, and Ivan dressed in a suit with sleeves and pant legs that were much too short. Ivan loved that suit because its poor fit made him look even bigger. Nettie and Hans Schmidt's picture was in the next frame. The plaque said they too would be citizens of New Lilliputia.

Sketches of other midget villages lined another wall. I'd just naturally figured that Mr. Gumpertz had come up with the idea at Coney Island's Dreamland but, long before then, there had been a Tiny Town in London and a Liliputstadt in Austria. A printed explanation on the wall said that midget cities had been around at least since Peter the Great of Russia, who'd had one made entirely out of ice and snow in the 1700s (that must have lasted only until the next spring thaw).

I lost myself in the pictures and midget history. I could have stared for hours more except for a rap on the front door.

Leroy stood there, smiling pleasantly at me.

"Miss Lucinda," he said, fingering his straw hat. "Mr. Sam sent me up with some groceries for y'all."

He turned to pick up the sack on the small porch, dropping his hat on the ground to get his hands free. "Here, let me take that, Leroy," I said, reaching for the hat and placing it on a hook by the front door.

"Mr. Sam is having a bunch of financiers" (he pronounced the word slowly and with some difficulty, as fee-nan-sayers) "up to his house for dinner tonight. These is the men he 'spects are gonna invest in New Lilliputia. He wants you to come by afterwards for a reception, sorta like a coming attraction."

I asked what time I should be ready and what I should wear.

"Mr. Sam said, nine-thirty. I could pick you up at nine o'clock? Best wear somethin' fancy."

I told him I'd be ready, then handed him his hat.

The groceries were welcome. Supper had been waiting on the kitchen table last evening but I had eaten nothing since.

Mr. Gumpertz had sent all the staples, including fresh soft bread, still warm from the oven, eggs, butter, milk, and potatoes.

The sink, stove, table and chairs were specially built to my size so I could easily reach whatever I needed.

Because of the life I had led, bedding down in tents and railroad cars during the circus and carnival season, and spending winters in hotels while playing vaudeville, I hadn't lived anywhere with a kitchen since I had left Daddy's farm in Tennessee. It felt strange, remembering how to do simple chores: lighting the stove, slicing the bread, breaking an egg in a bowl and mixing it up. Albert used to call them cackleberries. 'Scramble me up some cackleberries, 'sis.' I could almost hear him saying.

I'd have to write to let him know how being in this house made me feel that I hadn't traveled too far after all. I was again busy in a kitchen, one much more modern than ours at home, but a kitchen, all the same.

*

Leroy came for me at nine o'clock as promised. I wore my long beige lace dress, the best I had, topped with a fringed velvet shawl. At Mr. Gumpertz's house, a man in a fancy uniform took my shawl and led me into a sitting room. In a refined voice that sounded European, he told me that Mr. Gumpertz's dinner party was winding down, the men would be retiring to the cigar room shortly, and someone would come for me then. He gestured to a red velvet upholstered chair and I sat, nearly sinking in its overstuffed softness. He brought a silver tray with a crystal decanter and small sherry glass, poured a bit of the amber liquid into the glass for me, gave a slight bow, and left, closing the heavy carved doors behind him.

Darling as my new home was, it almost seemed plain compared to Mr. Gumpertz's mansion. Large white marble columns flanked the entry way. Thick oriental carpets cushioned each step I took across his floors. Under the carpet, the floor was made of marble slabs in different colors, from the white of the columns, to gray and black. The ceilings in this sitting room were as high as those in the lobbies of fine hotels and had the same kind of delicate, curved plaster designs I'd seen in the bigger ones. Statues of half-dressed women stood at each corner, and massive oil paintings of pastures dominated the walls.

I heard music, the hum of conversation, and bursts of laughter filtering in from another part of the house.

The door opened and a man walked in, spry, older, and dressed in a white tuxedo. His smile made me feel at ease and when he extended his hand, there was genuine warmth in the greeting.

"Miss Lacey, I am so glad you could come. I'm Samuel Gumpertz," he said as he led me from the sitting room through the hallway. Before he ushered me through the closed door, he asked, "You can sing, right?" I nodded.

"Can you do it without accompaniment?" I nodded again.

"Good! Think of a song to sing for my investors here, something happy. I'll cue you."

We walked through the door into another lavishly furnished room, this one filled with men in dinner jackets, some standing, some sitting in the well-stuffed chairs, puffing cigars. Nevermind prohibition. Each one had a big snifter of brandy.

"Gentlemen, I'd like to present Lucinda Darling, the first resident of New Lilliputia. Miss Darling stands less than four feet tall, yet is perfectly proportioned in every way, a true living doll. By January of next year, when the second residence at New Lilliputia is completed, the village will house from twelve to sixteen midgets, all perfectly proportioned living dolls, none of them taller than Miss Darling herself. In fact, Miss Darling here will be our tallest resident, nearly twice the height of the young man who is to be our smallest, Baron Herman Faust, a diminutive Austrian gentleman who, at twenty-five inches high, is as almost as small as a new-born babe."

Mr. Gumpertz used a long wooden pointer to call attention to a sketch, hanging on an easel, of what the finished village would look like. A manservant flipped the first sketch over. Under it were sketches of different features, then photographs of some of the other midgets Mr. Gumpertz planned to invite to New Lilliputia. As Mr. Gumpertz talked about what was on each sheet of paper, I heard the plans for the first time along with the men in the smoke-laden room.

He was going to ship in midget animals for the barn and stable, including Shetland ponies from England, pint-sized bantam chickens from the Orient, and miniature cows all the way from Australia. The New Lilliputia villagers would put on several shows a day for visitors such as a midget version of Keystone cops chasing a midget bank robber disguised as a baby.

"And now, Lucinda Darling will grace us with a song," he said to the gathered men. He started the applause and others joined in.

I sang the liveliest song that came to mind, no accompaniment, just my small voice in the large room:

"Yes, we have no bananas

"We have no bananas today..."

My eyes scanned those assembled as I sang. A couple of the men clapped along as I performed. Others watched politely with little interest. I spied a large man who, from photographs I had seen of him, looked like John Ringling. Mr. Ringling spent his winters in Sarasota, I knew, just as a number of other circus bosses did. It must be him. Next to him sat another man whose face I knew from the newspapers, John McGraw, the manager of the New York Giants baseball team. And a little to the right was a man whose face I had seen in the news, but whose name I couldn't remember. The paper said he was a big-time bootlegger. That explained the free-flowing sherry and brandy.

At the back of the room, to the left of a large curved window, stood a figure that I'd thought I'd seen many times over the years. All those other times, I'd been mistaken. Now, as I allowed my eyes to brush his, my throat nearly closed off mid-song.

Cyrus Parker. Although I turned away, his face imprinted itself on my mind. I looked everywhere else in the room but still saw him.

I sang the last note, the men clapped politely, and Mr. Gumpertz said a few more words before sitting down, but not before suggesting that I mingle with the crowd. He introduced me to three gentlemen nearby and we made small talk for a few minutes.

Always, my eyes returned to Cyrus Parker. And each time I looked his way I saw him looking at me. He'd changed little from when he was the circus boss and I was one of his performers. He'd lost weight and there were lines from the edges of his nose to his mouth that hadn't been there before. Everything else looked the same.

He stared at me openly with undisguised longing. It was also a sweet look though, warm and heartfelt.

I finally got up the courage to let my gaze linger on his face a moment. I smiled and so did he. Then, with my heart beating so hard that I couldn't hear what the gentleman to my left had said, I turned away again.

I knew he would come over. I'd seen it in his eyes. Yet I nearly stumbled when he found his way to me.

"Miss Lacey, so good to see you again," he said as he came up beside me.

"Mr. Parker. I'm happy to see you again as well."

Cyrus Parker then turned to the man I had been chatting with. "Laurence, remember when I owned that circus, several years back? Miss Lacey was one of my star performers—until the Ringlings closed me down, that is."

I'd hardly been a star but didn't see the point in correcting him. He and the man called Laurence spoke for a moment about Mr. Gumpertz's presentation. The man said something about "Gumpertz's Folly," and Cyrus nodded with a knowing look, then led me away by the elbow toward the back of the room, and through a door that led to a lighted garden walk.

"There isn't going to be a New Lilliputia, is there, Mr. Parker." I asked.

"In my opinion, I'm afraid not, Miss Lacey," he said this so gently, he might have been comforting a child. "Gumpertz will keep trying for a while to get investors but, in the end, it's the right idea in the wrong place. If this were Chicago or New York, he would have backers standing in line. Not here, though. These are businessmen," he said as he swept his arm out to encompass the people in the room we'd left a moment before. "They know that, in our small city, such an attraction simply won't draw the crowds. And the tin can tourists it might attract are not the ones that they want to bring to Sarasota. The men in that room are trying to develop Sarasota as an exclusive retreat for the wealthy, with golf courses and casinos, not roadside attractions. Some of them have taken to calling this venture, Gumpertz's Folly, as you heard. I'm sorry to be so blunt, Miss Lacey, but you asked. I believe you deserve an honest answer. I hope you aren't terribly disappointed."

I'd cut the few connections in my otherwise rootless life to move here. Still, I didn't feel all that disappointed. I think I would have given up just about anything to have Cyrus Parker look at me the way he was looking at me at that moment.

"What will you do now?" he asked.

I told him I didn't know. Carnival and circus season was all but over. A great many circus people spent their winters in the state. I was sure I could turn my time here to good use, I said, and make connections with a larger circus, maybe even Mr. Ringling's.

That wasn't what I wanted though. The real reason I'd come was standing beside me. I didn't want to go anywhere else.

As if reading my thoughts, Cyrus said, "You could stay here."

Before I could answer, he continued, "My daughter is going to need a governess. She's coming home from her boarding school at the end of the term. She doesn't want me to send her away again but I need someone to look after her when she's not at school. You'd be doing me a great favor if you'd consider taking the position."

Taking care of a child would be easy enough. I'd looked after my younger brothers, Jacob and Frank, back home on the farm. If I said yes, it would mean I'd be close to him. But I hadn't come all this way to be a nursemaid. I thanked him but told him I couldn't give him an answer just yet.

He let the subject drop. We stood there for a minute, finding nothing more to say. And then, he placed his hand gently on my back and guided me down the walk.

"Have you had a chance to see our lovely Indian Beach?" he asked. He let his hand travel across my shoulder and down my arm until he could grab hold of my hand. That small gesture startled me in its casual intimacy. And yet, it seemed so natural being there with him, smelling the salt of the bay, feeling the night air cool my skin, watching the shadows of the sea grass sway against the dunes.

We walked, still holding hands for several minutes, not talking, not looking at each other. Every part of my being felt as if it was expanding outward from where my fingers met his, making it difficult to sense exactly where he ended and I began.

What he had to say, when he finally said it, needed no preliminaries: "I want you, Lucinda."

Speaking it aloud seemed redundant. Still, some part of me couldn't leave it at that and allow what was happening between us to simply happen.

"Do you want me because I'm a freak or in spite of it?" I don't know why I felt I needed to ask the question so harshly.

I saw him flinch. He turned his head away, embarrassed. But after a moment, he looked at me with an openness I don't recall having seen before. And when he answered me, it was with as much candor as I'd asked.

"I don't know," he said, grasping my other hand, so that we faced each other. "Probably both."

"That makes no sense," I said, even as I realized that it did, in a way. It made the sort of sense that you feel rather than reason.

I'd packed up and traveled hundreds of miles because of the small chance I'd see Cyrus Parker. When I daydreamed about finding love, a home, permanence, Cyrus Parker was at the center of that dream. If I'd thought with my brain instead of my feelings, I never would have come this far. I would have seen how impossible it was.

Yet, here I was. And he did want me. He'd just said so.

Did that mean for this night only? No, I knew he felt at least some of what I did.

It didn't need saying that I wanted him more than I could imagine wanting anything.

Because he was a normal sized man or in spite of it?

I didn't know. Maybe both.

29. Marisa

"What the?"

A terrible pounding—so loud, not even the power saws of John Guinness' workmen drowned it out — came from near the staircase. It was as if a mob were battering down the door. Except the pounding originated from inside the walls.

Marisa ran to the staircase and stood on the landing halfway up the steps. The noise stopped. Her heart hammered, echoing the fading beat.

Above her head, she heard musical tinkling. The dainty crystals of the chandelier that hung from the top of the turret were lightly colliding with one another as if blown by the wind.

Seemingly of its own volition, the chandelier began to rise. Like a snake recoiling, the chain that attached the fixture to the ceiling bent up onto itself several inches. The fixture ascended until it touched the turret ceiling, several feet above.

Gravity made what she was watching impossible. She had to be imagining this.

As if an invisible hand released its grasp, the chandelier dropped, bouncing slightly on its chain as its weight pulled it taut. Marisa pressed her back against the wall and watched as the chandelier swayed dizzily above, its crystals clinking loudly.

She clung to the wall, her fingers seeking traction in the

pocked surface of the pecky cypress. She thought of Claude's uproarious chatter about miniature duppies. Not so funny now.

Boom, boom, boom.

She pulled her hands away from the wall as if they touched fire. The vibration resonated through the floor under her feet as she ran down the steps.

*

In the kitchen, Marisa grabbed the phone, walked out the front door, and punched in Kelly's cell number. The two workmen, Steve and Jimmie, taking a rest break under a banyan tree, waved to her. She waved back, trying not to let on how panicked she felt. Kelly answered on the fourth ring. Marisa moved out of the workmen's line of sight. Her words rushed out faster than her mind could process what she was saying.

Kelly's soothing voice came back through the receiver with assurances that Marisa barely comprehended. The odd events, large and small, replayed in her head: Murphy's reactions, her dreams, the open doors, Otto's warnings.

She could have dismissed all that, found a plausible explanation for everything. It was an old house and spooky stories had circulated the neighborhood for years.

None of it explained the chandelier. But it happened, damn it. She saw it. She wasn't going crazy.

*

The construction workers finished up for the day and steered their truck out the front gate just as Kelly's small caravan waited to steer its way in: Kelly in her Jeep, followed by Claude in his old canary yellow bug, with a taupe sedan trailing behind.

Kelly gave Marisa a hug. "Did you know you have demonstrators outside the gate? They're yelling something about tortoises."

"Well, they're the least of my worries."

"What I tell you about them duppies, mon?" Claude asked.

"Now you believe me?"

Marisa took the hand of the large woman in flowing blue caftan who stepped inside behind Claude. "I hate to impose on you like this, Rena. I owe you one."

"Kelly knows I'd do anything for her," Rena said. "Don't you darling girl?"

Blatant as Rena's flirtation was, Kelly seemed oblivious. One day, Marisa would have to explain Rena's devotion but for now, she had more pressing concerns.

Rena slowly paced the library, palms outward like antennae. She stopped at the bottom of the staircase.

"It's — she's — stronger than a few days ago," she announced. "What have you been up to, Marisa?"

"Nothing. Unless, the workmen upset her."

"You're pulling her house apart. Of course. That'll stir things up."

"Who's this 'her'?"

"I can't quite get a fix on her. Your aunt, she passed away, in this house, a couple of weeks ago, right? That's got to be it," Rena said, her expression changing to certitude.

"I'm not so sure it's Enid."

"Marisa, you're upset. Leave this to Rena. She knows what she's doing," said Kelly.

"The manifestations have occurred around the staircase?" Rena asked.

"Mostly."

"Claude, Kelly, move Marisa's table over here." She held her arms out to indicate an area halfway between the staircase and Marisa's computer desk, directly in line with the front door. "Do you have a picture of Enid?" Rena asked.

"There's one in the downstairs bedroom," said Marisa. "But it's old. She looks about twenty in it."

Rena told her to fetch the photo and some white candles, and at her instruction, they brought in chairs and arranged the furniture to give every chair at least a partial view of the stairway.

She next called for incense and a white tablecloth. "And let's have some music, Ravi Shankar or George Winston or whatever you have that's New Age-y will do."

Marisa lit a stick of Nag Champa, with a scent between spice and baby powder, while Kelly rummaged through her CDs. She chose an old Enya album.

Claude pulled a white sheet out of the linen closet, snapped it out a couple of times so it billowed above the table, and spread it on top. Rena positioned Enid's photograph at the table's center.

After instructing Claude to turn off the lights, Rena lit the candles and handed them around.

"Imagine the candles' flame spreading a protective golden glow over the group. Only those energies we invite into our circle may enter."

She led them in chanting, Ommm, then said, "Pass your candles to the center." They placed their candles around Enid's picture. "Now clasp the hand of the person on either side of you. Close your eyes. And, whatever happens, don't break the circle."

She waited for each to nod agreement, then continued.

"Beloved spirit of Enid Parker, you who have been waylaid in your journey to the next plane, your loving niece beseeches you, communicate with us."

They sat for a very long moment, holding hands.

Nothing happened.

Rena tried again.

"Enid Parker, your loving niece wants only to help you find your way to the light. Please give us a sign that you hear us."

Marisa's hands, linked with Kelly's on one side and Rena's on the other, felt uncomfortably warm. The Enya CD ended. She heard faint sounds of fidgeting from the others. Chirps from crickets outside announced the dusk. Somebody coughed. She opened one eye. Claude was looking all around, noticed Marisa, winked and flashed a smile.

Sounds she'd barely noticed before, like the faint whirring of her computer's hard drive a few feet away, seemed loud.

"Rena?" Marisa's voice sounded abrasive to her own ears, cutting through the silence. "Leave Enid aside for a moment. Try summoning Lucinda."

Rena shrugged, gathered her composure and spoke:

"Beloved Lucinda, you who are caught between this world and the next, we summon you to join with us."

A chilly burst of wind blew across the table in the closed room, extinguishing the candles. The sound it made was almost like a woman sighing. Another gust, louder and more powerful, swept over them with such force, it blew open the front door.

Marisa, Kelly and Claude jumped from their chairs, ran to the open door and out into the dark. The motion detector lights blared on, illuminating a female figure, walking toward them.

Marisa sucked in air, ready to scream.

The middle-aged woman approaching wore a round-necked flimsy white peasant blouse and a dark polyester a-line skirt. Clipboard in hand and cigarette dangling from the corner of her mouth, she reached out her other hand to shake. It was a very real hand, sweaty and square, not the sort that appears from the "other side."

"Marisa Delano?"

"That's me."

The woman detached something from her clipboard, and handed it to Marisa.

"You've been served. Sign here, please." She held out the clipboard and indicated the line with the X. Marisa, numb from confusion, did as she was told. The woman turned and walked back up the drive to a green SUV, parked just inside the gate.

Kelly peered over Marisa's shoulder, trying to read by the glow of the security lights.

"It's a subpoena," said Marisa, handing the papers to her friend. "Those demonstrators making the threatening noises about the gopher tortoises? They're suing me."

30. LUCINDA

OCTOBER 1923 – THE WRONG PROPOSAL

We made love throughout the night. Cyrus brought me back to the midget village just before dawn. I curled myself next to him on the car seat. He laid his arm over me, moved it to shift the car, and hugged me to him again.

We hardly spoke. It seemed unnecessary. I was too filled with emotion to allow room for words. He kissed me deeply at the entrance to my little house.

"We'll talk tomorrow," he said, and stroked my hair. He waited for me to lock the door behind me. I watched through the kitchen window as he drove off in his big Pierce-Arrow.

I woke up late in the morning and heard birds chirping but not much else. It took several minutes to figure out what was missing. Yesterday, the rhythmic scraping of the mason's shovel as he mixed concrete had been punctuated by the hammering and sawing of carpenters. Today, there was nothing.

I peered out my bedroom window and saw piles of lumber, brick and sand. Tools were placed in a way that suggested their users had taken a brief break and would be back to work momentarily. I suspected that dust would begin to gather before anyone took up the tools again. Cyrus had confirmed what Casper had warned me about. And it was even worse than Casper had said.

I looked around me at the beautiful house and felt a little sad that it wouldn't be mine for long.

*

Leroy stopped by at about noon to explain that, due to slow negotiations with financiers, there would be a delay in constructing the rest of the village. Mr. Gumpertz expected everything to go forward but the village wouldn't open this winter season, as planned.

"Don't worry, Miss Lucinda," he said. "Mr. Sam is gonna make this work. Jes' gonna take a little more time, is all."

I could tell by the way he cast his eyes down as he spoke that he didn't believe it any more than I did.

"Thank you for letting me know, Leroy. Should I move to a hotel?"

"Oh, no," Leroy said quickly. Then he seemed to think a bit and added, "Not jes' yet anyways. You stay in the house as long as you like. If Mr. Sam needs y'all to move, I'm sure he'll foot the hotel bill."

So that was that. I used the telephone in the kitchen to ask about hotels in the area. I found a furnished apartment in a bayside residence that John Ringling, the youngest of the circus king siblings, had built for winter visitors. It would be ready for me to move into after the weekend. I could enjoy this lovely house until then.

Late that afternoon, Cyrus called. Still in my dreamy state of the night before, I didn't pick up the cues, at first, that something had changed, until he asked if I'd considered his proposal.

"What proposal was that?" I asked, giggly and girlish.

"My proposal to hire you as my daughter's companion," he answered with odd formality.

"Cyrus, I don't know," I answered. "It seems awkward, considering what's happening between us."

"One matter need not intrude on the other," said Cyrus. "I promise that your position will be strictly professional. You will have your own private quarters. I'll make no demands on you, other than that you treat my daughter Enid well."

That wasn't what I'd hoped to hear.

"So, what happened between us last night won't happen again. Is that what you are saying, Cyrus?"

He sighed into the telephone. "I didn't say that. I care for you. I want you near me. It's just that I have a position in the community and well, it's complicated."

"It's not complicated at all," I answered. "I'm a free woman and you're a free man. There's nothing to stop us from being together except you and your 'position in the community.' I know what you're thinking. What would people say? Cyrus and his freak."

I was glad he couldn't see the tears dribbling down my cheeks.

"Lucinda, you don't understand, I —"

"I understand completely, Cyrus. Good-bye."

I placed the telephone receiver back in its cradle and crumpled onto the tile of the kitchen floor. My hands felt cold. My whole body did.

I could still feel his long slender fingers traveling lightly over my skin. I still felt his lips brushing my neck, my breasts, and my belly. I closed my eyes and all I could see was his face, blotting out everything else. What was I going to do?

He was a powerful, important man. What did I expect? How could a man like that think of me as anything but a temporary distraction? That's all anyone saw, looking at me, an amusing oddity. I knew that. I'd capitalized on it my whole life, ever since I ran away from home.

Step right up, folks—

31. MARISA

"I'm sorry. Mr. Scanlon's not back in town yet," said the secretary's voice on the phone line.

"Does he know I called?" asked Marisa.

"I told him."

"Does he know it's urgent? I'm being sued."

"All I can do is take another message," the secretary answered.

The phone began ringing as soon as she hung up. Marisa grabbed it, hoping it was Harry Scanlon.

"Hey, hon'," Dapper Dan Brogan's mellifluous baritone drawled over the phone line. "I got you the name of that home where Horace is at. Told them to put you on the approved list of visitors. Write this down."

Marisa scribbled the information on a pad next to the phone. She called the home for their visiting hours. She could make it there in time to spend about a half hour with the old man if she hurried. There was no sense hanging around, waiting for the lawyer to call back. He knew she needed him.

Opening a can of cat food for Murphy, she dumped it in his dish, and dashed out the door.

*

"I don't think he even knows who he is half the time, so it don't matter if he don't know you," said the large nurse at the reception desk. "Ol' Mr. Vanderee's always happy to see a friendly face. Just don't go getting him all excited. That man's on the north side of a hundred. He need to take it slow, you know?"

Marisa promised not to upset him, and went in search of room 206. Despite the long, wide white hall, and the open doors that gave glimpses of wheelchair-bound residents, the place looked cheerier than a hospital. Small tables held arrangements of artificial flowers every twenty feet or so, and the night tables in the rooms were of painted wood instead of the typical institutional laminate. It could almost be mistaken for an old hotel, except for the mingled odors of antiseptic and urine.

Marisa found the room and tapped on the half-open door. A soft grunt answered her knock. She waited another moment, decided that the sound must have been an invitation to enter, and walked in.

The two hospital beds in the room had metal rails on their sides, but neither was occupied. An impossibly old man, with a clear plastic cannula wrapped around his ears and under his nostrils to deliver oxygen, sat at the end of the room in a wheelchair. Patches of cotton candy-textured hair sprouted randomly on his red-blotched scalp — no competition for his luxuriant white eyebrows. His eyes stared blankly. His mouth gaped open.

Marisa recognized him as the same teenaged boy in the photograph in Dapper Dan Brogan's exhibit, only by his skin. Dry from age, it looked more scaly than in the picture.

"Mr. Vanderee? I'm Marisa Delano, a friend of Mr. Brogan's. I was hoping I could ask you about the old sideshows, or freak shows, or whatever they called them back in the 1920s."

Horace Vanderee's mouth made a chewing motion, then hung open again. He continued to stare at nothing through cataract-clouded eyes. Marisa realized he might be hard of hearing. She tried again, speaking more loudly this time.

"Mr. Vanderee, I would like to ask you some questions about the old traveling freak shows." He gave no indication he'd heard. Was he even conscious? "I wondered if you'd ever run across a midget named Lucinda?"

Like Rip Van Winkle awakening, the old face brightened. The gaping mouth re-arranged into an almost wistful smile. The pale ancient eyes appeared to soften and become more alert. He looked at Marisa, reaching one gnarled hand from the arm of his wheelchair, as if trying to touch her face.

"Lucinda," he said, sweetness underlying the raspiness. "You came back."

*

Marisa pulled off I-75 at the exit for Sarasota, still feeling annoyed at Birdie, although she wasn't sure she had the right. She'd met the woman only once. It wasn't as if Alberta Lacey-Pruitt had an obligation to tell Marisa everything. But, damn it, she'd asked Birdie, point blank, about sideshows. And Birdie had played dumb.

Poor old Horace Vanderee, with his addled brain and failing sight, mistook Marisa for Lucinda Lacey. Unable to convince him otherwise, she played along while Horace reminisced. Little of what he said had made much sense. Marisa pieced together that the teenaged Horace Vanderee had had a crush on the midget, that Lucinda had left the freak show — Horace called it a ten-in-one — and joined up with a midgets-only show in Sarasota. How Lucinda had ended up in the midget house, and why the house was on Cyrus Parker's estate, were still anybody's guess.

The most valuable information Horace Vanderee, erstwhile Snake Boy, had given her was Lucinda's last name: Lacey, as in Alberta Lacey-Pruitt. That couldn't be a coincidence. No, this was the aunt that Birdie had coyly referred to, Marisa was certain of it.

She turned up the street where she'd seen Birdie pedal her trike. Driving slowly, she scanned each of the mailboxes that lined the curb in front of the houses. Most just displayed numbers. A grey one to the left in front of a typical Florida bungalow showed the name, Smith. She kept on at a turtle's pace. Halfway up the block, in front of a robin's egg blue frame cottage with a wraparound white porch, she spotted what she was looking for. Stenciled under the number 639 on a plain white mailbox was the name, Lacey-Pruitt. She pulled over, parked, and knocked at the door.

*

"So, Birdie," said Marisa, putting the now-empty lemonade glass on the kitchen counter, "that aunt of yours who lived on the Parker estate, what was her name?"

"Lucinda. Lucinda Lacey. Why?"

"She didn't just live on the estate, did she?" asked Marisa "She lived in my house."

Setting her mouth in a thin line, Birdie answered with a single word: "Yes."

"And she was a midget, like you?"

"Correct."

"Why didn't you tell me before?"

"I did tell you," she protested. "What more was there to tell? Lucinda Lacey, my aunt, my father's younger sister, is the reason why they call your place the midget house."

"So, the rumors are true."

Birdie's face contorted. "I can state to a fair degree of certainty that the rumors were not true. Ignorant people spread vicious lies."

"Birdie, you just said —"

"I said it wasn't true," Birdie slammed her hand on the counter, startling Marisa. "She's been dead for decades. Why won't you let her rest in peace?"

"Because something in my house is trying to scare the living daylights out of me — and doing a pretty decent job. And like it or not, that 'something' seems to be your aunt who apparently isn't resting very peacefully."

"You're just like everyone else," said Birdie, frustration spilling with her words. "Why did I think you'd be different? I can see now what my poor father must have endured. He gave up everything to come here. Everything! He dug through the records when no one else could be bothered. And when he figured out who was really to blame, he spent years trying to clear my aunt's name. But would anyone listen? No. They condemned her without a shred of evidence. They must have thought my father was quite the fool, expecting the good decent people of Sarasota to give a circus freak the benefit of the doubt. Better that such monsters were never born — right?"

"My God, no, Birdie, I never—"

"Please, just leave," Birdie said. Tears reddened her eyes. She turned her head away. "Please."

"I never meant to upset you," said Marisa, walking awkwardly toward the door. "I'm so sorry, Birdie, really I am." The apology sounded hollow to her own ears. She had hurt the older woman; nothing would undo that. It didn't seem an adequate excuse that she had no idea what Birdie was talking about.

32. Marisa

Family ties

Otto held out the cardboard box and smiled warmly as she opened the door to his knock. "I've been sorting through my things and there's just so much I've collected over the years that I don't have a need for anymore."

He walked into the kitchen without waiting for an invitation and set his carton on the table. "Before I haul it to Goodwill, I thought I'd give you first dibs."

"Spring cleaning?" asked Marisa.

"Peace offering," said Otto. "It's painfully clear that other people are pulling the strings while we're here squabbling with each other. It's not worth it. Truce?" he held out his hand to shake.

She was skeptical but shook it.

"Now, this was my mother's," Otto said, pulling out a chipped old turkey platter with a dainty flower pattern. "It's still serviceable and, since you're more likely to entertain large parties than I am, I thought it might come in handy. Mother would have wanted to keep it in the family." He presented the platter with a celebratory air.

"Oh, and here's something else you might enjoy," he said, rummaging through the old newspapers that cushioned the carton's contents. He held out an iridescent orange pressed glass vase. "Another of Mother's treasures that I'm told is quite old, but simply not my taste. I thought it might look better in your little house."

He stood with his hands clasped in front of him, gazing at Marisa as if with great affection. "There's an old toaster in the box too, probably antique, maybe even worth something if you can get it repaired, plus a few other odds and ends. Anything you don't want, feel free to toss out. You won't hurt my feelings. I just hope some of it can be put to good use."

"Thank you, Otto, that's kind of you."

"Enjoy," Otto said as he turned to leave. Then, as if another thought had just occurred to him, he turned. Pulling Ricci's business card from the pocket of his short-sleeved shirt, he looked at it quizzically then held it out to her.

"Marisa, I found this stuck in the doorway last evening. Do you have any idea what this is about?"

"That's the detective who came after I reported my front door was open. I thought somebody might have broken in but it was probably just the wind."

"They sent a detective because the wind blew your door open? Goodness me. Your tax dollars at work, as they say."

"Yes, well, the detective wanted to talk to you about it."

Otto blanched. "You didn't tell him that I'd had anything to do with your door incident, did you Marisa?"

"He just wanted to know if you'd seen anything suspicious."

"Not a thing. You know I'd help in any way I could if I had. By the way, Marisa, as long as we're chatting, I wanted to tell you that I feel terrible about our spat the other day."

"Otto, if you're trying to get me to reconsider—"

He waved his hands to shush her. "I wasn't dropping hints. Goodness, no. I will never understand what you see in this house but it's clear that you love it and I respect that. I'm simply trying to make amends. You're all the family I have now that Enid's gone and, well, I guess you could say the same about me."

"I suppose."

"So, we can just put all that unpleasantness behind us?"

"It's as good as forgotten."

"What a relief. Oh, I left the gas cans by your car. If you fill them, I'll give the lawn a good mowing. Consider that part two of my peace offering. I'd take them to the gas station myself but I'm looking at a few condos on Longboat Key this morning and the real estate agent is picking me up in her car."

"You're moving out?"

"Since you won't sell your house, my inheritance goes back to being worthless, doesn't it?" he said. "It seems pointless to stay. Of course, now that you've told me about your break-in, I feel guilty leaving you alone here."

"It was nothing. Good luck with the real estate hunt."

33. LUCINDA

DECEMBER 1923

It surely wasn't how I planned it, but the move from the midget house to John Ringling's Bayside Apartment Hotel was the best thing I could have done for my career. Ringling's equestrian director, Fred Bradna, and his wife, the star bareback rider, Ella Bradna, were spending the winter there. The Bradnas befriended me, seeking me out at meals and inviting me to get-togethers with other members of the Ringling organization. Fred reminded Mr. Ringling that he'd heard me sing at Mr. Gumpertz's home. Before long, I had an offer to perform during the next season with the Ringling Bros. and Barnum and Bailey Circus, opening at Madison Square Garden in New York City in early March.

Meanwhile, Mr. Gumpertz sold the midget village's land to a real estate speculator. The speculator turned around and sold it to someone else the same week for almost double the money. The darling little house was already gone. The speculator sold it off separately to someone who had it lifted off its foundations and carted away on a huge flatbed by truck.

I learned all this from the concierge at the Bayside. He said it was nothing unusual. Sarasota was in the frenzy of a land boom. Real estate was gold. And prospectors roamed everywhere, looking to strike it rich.

With the money he got from the property sale in his pocket

and probably a little bit of guilt, besides, for luring me to Sarasota on a flimsy promise, Mr. Gumpertz offered me a generous contract with his Coney Island sideshow in Brooklyn, New York. He said he'd give me star billing, if I chose his show over Ringling's.

Each of the offers had good things and bad things about it. With Gumpertz, I would be nothing more than a featured oddity, but I could stay in one place. With the Ringling Circus, even as a lower-level performer, I'd be more than a freak on display. Mr. Ringling wanted me to sing and dance in the opening spectacular. But it would mean living in a rail car with a couple dozen other performers, never spending more than a few days in any one town.

I hired a lawyer to look over the two contracts and negotiate with Mr. Ringling and Mr. Gumpertz for me. Casper had also asked me to come back in the spring. I should have been thrilled to have so many choices but none of it mattered much. I left it to the lawyer to decide where I should end up.

The lawyer, a suave man with brilliantined black hair, treated me like a child who didn't know what she wanted. I suppose that's what I looked like to him, not just because of my size but also because I just didn't care about the money or any of the other terms he thought were important for me to think about.

What difference did any of it make? What I wanted was an ordinary life, the kind my brother Albert was building with his new wife. I wanted that with Cyrus Parker. It was exactly what I couldn't ever have. This must be what it felt like on the carnival midway when you knocked over a couple of bottles at the game of chance, but not enough to win the prize. Maybe you didn't walk away empty-handed but whatever they gave you instead, you still felt like you lost.

For that one night we spent together, I believed I had a chance, and that made me want it so much more that it hurt.

I walked inside a heavy gray cloud, even when I sat in the sun on the sugary white sand of the beach and stared at the endless turquoise water.

Cyrus tried to call a number of times. I knew this only because the concierge told me so each time. I refused all his telephone calls and asked the concierge to tell him to stop trying. What was there to say? He'd made his position clear. At best, he would make me his dirty little secret, with him under false pretenses. He probably thought that he could sneak into the servants' quarters after his daughter was tucked in, and then disappear before anyone knew he'd been there.

Or maybe he didn't want me any more at all. The job offer was something his conscience told him he owed me. Well, thank you very much, Mr. Parker, but I'll do just fine without you.

I didn't mind taking advantage of whatever guilt Mr. Samuel Gumpertz might feel if it meant my lawyer could squeeze a few more dollars out of the impresario. Cyrus's guilt, if that was what it was? I wanted no part of it.

A few weeks before Christmas, a delivery man came to my door with a vase filled with dozens of pink roses. The card attached said, "Please have dinner with me on Tuesday. I will send a car at seven o'clock. Sincerely yours, Cyrus Parker."

I paced around my small suite like a tiger in a cage. I wouldn't go. I'd send his driver away with instructions that Cyrus was never to contact me again. Then, I decided, why not? I'll have dinner with him, if for no other reason than to get one last look at the man. But no, I couldn't. It would be too painful.

Back and forth, yes and no, I changed my mind, not even sure when I woke up on Tuesday morning and began to dress what I planned to do.

What harm was there in getting ready, just in case? I pulled on the deep green silk dress and matching hat I'd had made by Ella Bradna's seamstress, new silk stockings with my prettiest garters, and black pumps. I sat with my hands folded, looking at the clock tick past noon, then one o'clock. I worried that I would wrinkle my dress and look a mess by the time Cyrus's driver called.

This was crazy. Why was I making a fuss over something that would end up a big disappointment? I couldn't go.

Unbuttoning my dress, I hung it in the closet. I took off my pumps, got back into bed, pulled the covers up to my chin, and closed my eyes.

A bell chimed, over and over, insistently. After a moment, I realized it was the ringing of the telephone. I'd fallen asleep. I picked up the receiver.

"Mademoiselle Lucinda, your driver is here," said the voice of the concierge.

"I'll be down in ten minutes," I answered without thinking.

*

Cyrus's driver tipped his hat when I came downstairs, held the door of the Pierce-Arrow automobile, helped me into the back seat, then said nothing to me on the drive to the estate. It was just as well. I kept my hand on the door, thinking I might want to jump out before reaching Cyrus's driveway. The thought of seeing Cyrus made me almost forget to keep breathing.

The wrought iron gate into the Parker estate was closed; the driver stopped the car and stepped out to unlock it. Brass and frosted glass street lamps illuminated lines of chubby cherub statues along the private road. They almost seemed to dance in the flickering yellow light.

Before we got to Cyrus's mansion, on the right side of the road, I saw something that shouldn't have been there.

It was my house, the midget house that Mr. Gumpertz had had built for his village.

Cyrus must have been the one who bought it and had it lifted from its foundations and carted away. Lordy me, why?

"It isn't many men who would buy a governess her own house, 'specially one who hasn't accepted the job yet," said the driver. "Mr. Cyrus must think you're real special."

We pulled up to the front of Cyrus's big house on the waterfront. The driver opened the car's back door and held out his hand for me. I took it and stepped onto the gravel drive.

Above the wide marble steps that led to the house's entrance, Cyrus stood stiffly in the open doorway. He half-smiled at me, looking almost shy.

The heavy scent of jasmine filled the night air. I looked around and found its source on a hedge to the side of the steps. Without thinking, I plucked a sprig and breathed in the perfume.

And, just like that, I knew that every step I'd taken in my life had been leading me here, to him.

If I'd grown normally instead of being a sickly small child, if Mama hadn't died, if Daddy hadn't beaten me, if my brother Albert hadn't taken me by the hand and run away with me, or even if all that had happened but we'd left too early or too late to run into the circus train, I wouldn't be standing on the bottom of Cyrus Parker's marble steps.

Yet, I was here. So I believed, rightly or wrongly, that fate had attached me to this man.

Up I walked toward Cyrus, holding the small white flower.

He loves me; he loves me not.

34. LUCINDA

I think I could have died in those first weeks we spent together and been content that I'd gotten enough out of life to make it worth living. I felt so lucky to be with him. I couldn't think of anything more I wanted.

We spent almost every moment together, with no one else around while Cyrus's daughter was still away at school. His cook prepared our meals and we served ourselves. He gave his other servants a paid vacation, not wanting to be interrupted by maids or butlers or the rest of the world. Through days that blended into night and back into day again, we drank each other in, mingling our bodies, resting in each other's arms.

It took time to get accustomed to my lover's house. It was unlike anything I had seen since I'd been in Florida, or anywhere else, really. Its exterior was stone, maybe marble or granite, and there were sculptures carved right into the walls. Taken by themselves, the sharp-taloned birds and crouching gargoyles would have been frightening except that the full effect was so beautiful. The house looked like pictures I'd seen in books of the palaces of France.

One morning, he shook me awake early, as the sun was just rising and, instead of making love to me, he tickled my waist, jumped out of bed, and tossed me one of his white sailing caps.

"Put that on," he said. "I'm taking you out on the boat."

I placed it on my head, which must have made me look

ridiculous, as it was twice the size I needed and it sunk over the top of my ears. Cyrus laughed at the sight of me, then plopped himself back on the bed, pulling off the hat, then my night clothes, and covering every inch of me with kisses as we both giggled like children. We didn't get out to his dock for another hour.

*

Anywhere else I could have been at this moment, it would be snowy winter. Here in Florida, the air barely held a chill even on the wind that swept up from the water.

The palms near the dock made a rustling sound and the bay sent an occasional spray across my face as I waited. Cyrus wedged a picnic basket between the seats inside the smaller of his two sailboats, then unhitched its ropes and loosened the sails. He offered me his hand and I stepped into the boat, a little nervous at the way it rocked until I sat.

"Here, take the tiller," he told me when we were out in the open water. I said I couldn't. I'd never so much as been on a sailboat before and would surely sink us if I tried to steer.

"Don't worry, you can't do any damage. Just keep it steady."

I held on where he showed me. He placed his hand over mine. A blast of wind undid my ribbon and, as my hair whipped around my face and his, together we steered toward a small island covered with low-lying brush. It had a sliver of sandy beach but no houses and no other people.

Cyrus pulled the boat part way onto the beach and tied it to a post while I stepped barefoot onto the soft sand and picked up pretty shells to put in my pocket.

We found a hollow in the dunes and laid out our blanket. The cook had packed the basket with fruit, cheeses, deviled eggs and sandwiches.

I rested my head on his lap. Cyrus peeled an orange, fed me a piece, then tossed the next section into the air, catching it in his own mouth.

"Hey, big fellow," I teased him, "Is that a trick you learned in the circus? And how did a fine upstanding citizen like you fall into such a disreputable business, anyway?"

"It pays to have a disreputable neighbor," said Cyrus.

Even before the Ringlings began buying up banks, land and railroads in Sarasota, he said, other circus kings had come to Florida to sit out the long winters.

"When I was away at school, Charles Thompson bought the estate next door to my parents' home," said Cyrus, "He spent his winters at his bayfront compound but, the rest of the year, he traveled the country with a small circus he owned."

Cyrus met Mr. Thompson when he traveled home from Princeton for the holidays. Mr. Thompson, closer in age to Cyrus's father than himself, saw Cyrus maneuver his skiff around the bay and asked if he would teach him how to sail.

"And I said, absolutely, if you teach me how to juggle."

They struck a deal to teach each other the skills the other lacked.

Cyrus said that he became an adept juggler but, more than that, he became intrigued by Mr. Thompson's tales of life on the rails in the circus. So, when he graduated, over the objections of his father, he joined the Thompson Circus for a season as a performer, picking up other circus skills while he was there.

"You wouldn't think it to look at me now, but I learned to do a respectable loop-de-loop in the trapeze act."

With his head for business, Cyrus said he soon focused his attention on helping Mr. Thompson increase the show's profits. Charles Thompson had been taking the circus in more or less a straight line, from one railroad stop to the next.

"He thought it was the cheapest, most efficient way to go," said Cyrus, "because the circus had to pay the railroad, which supplied the locomotive and the track, so much per mile traveled for each car in its train. But I had a hunch he'd do better focusing on where the money was coming from, not where it was going."

Cyrus said he convinced Mr. Thompson to zigzag around the eastern seaboard instead, chasing this county's harvest and that factory's payday so the circus would show up when folks had the most cash in their wallets. Cyrus's scheme increased Mr. Thompson's profits more than enough to cover the extra railroad fees, even when the circus had to double back to play the places it skipped past.

"And then, the season was over and my father reminded me that I had responsibilities," said Cyrus. "So, I gave up my disreputable ways and went back to work at the bank."

He set that institution on a more profitable path, he said, then followed his parents' wishes and married a young woman whose father owned another smaller bank. The banks merged soon after. But he wasn't content.

"I was living the life my father wanted for me," said Cyrus, "not the life I would have chosen for myself. When Charles told me he wanted to retire, I saw my chance. I bought him out."

Cyrus changed the name from the Thompson Circus to the Parker Circus, and took over the management. It gave him an excuse to travel the country again, free of the constraints of a banker's life.

"And what about now?" I asked him. "Are you content?"

"I have everything I need," he said. He picked up my hand, kissed my palm, then pulled me toward him.

*

A Charlie Chaplain movie was playing downtown and I wanted to go see it when we got back but Cyrus said he was too tired.

"If you're that keen on going, I'll have my driver take you there and back."

"Go to the picture show alone?" I said. "That's no fun. Maybe I'll just go up to my house and fill the tub with warm water and bubbles."

Cyrus offered to scrub my back and teach me backgammon afterwards.

"I thought you were tired."

"I want you to myself. Can you blame me?" he said. "Besides, I don't enjoy sitting for hours in the dark, staring at a screen."

I chose to believe there was nothing more to it.

35. Marisa

Looking For Lucinda

Marisa puzzled briefly over Otto's box of Goodwill rejects. Maybe this really was Otto's way of making peace. She hoped he found a condo soon. His presence made her claustrophobic.

With a cup of coffee at her elbow, she picked up her red pen, determined to get through her editing assignment for the Brain Behavior Laboratory. She needed that check more than ever. But first, she had to earn it.

Her mind wandered to the séance, then to Horace Vanderee. And then, to Birdie.

At least, now, the ghost had a name: Lucinda Lacey. She had a history, as a freak show midget. But how did she get to the midget house?

Birdie knew, but no way was Marisa going to get the details from her. And she didn't even know what she'd said that offended the woman so.

The phone rang.

She checked the caller ID. Brogan. She picked up.

"Hello."

"Hey, hon', what did you do to old Horace?"

"I went to see him yesterday."

"Yeah, well, he up and died in his sleep. Least, he died happy. Told the nurse something about Lucinda coming back, laid himself down for a nap. And that was that."

"Oh, no, I'm so sorry."

"It was his time. Anyway, if it's this Lucinda you're trying to find out about, I might have something for you. Can you get up here by noon? Carnival season starts in a couple of days and I've gotta pack up and head to the panhandle."

She glanced guiltily at the pages and red pen. Promising herself she'd stay up all night, if necessary, to finish the job, she said, "I'm on my way."

She grabbed her car keys and briefcase, hopped into her aging convertible, and started to go, almost forgetting the gas cans. Might as well take advantage of Otto's offer to mow, she thought, sticking the big red containers in the trunk.

36. Lucinda

Meeting Enid

We had been together four weeks to the day when Cyrus sent his driver to the train station to pick up his daughter, Enid, who was coming home from boarding school.

I realized our situation would change now. We couldn't be as open with each other. He hadn't yet told her — or anyone else — about us. I understood that, or thought I did.

The servants came back from their vacations and I spent the night in my own little house.

I returned to the main house on the premise that I was there only as Enid's companion and we would have lunch as a way of getting to know each other.

*

The sun glinting through the Venetian glass windowpanes in the enormous parlor-like room that Cyrus called the salon reflected soft colors across the floor and walls. Painted on the ceiling, small plump cupids peeked out from behind puffy clouds in a blue sky, looking like they were set to shoot their arrows into the salon below. Cyrus sat in one of the antique chairs, which were covered in gold velvet and brocade.

I concentrated on the room's beautiful details because they took me away, for an instant, from the harshness of a scene where I was at the center, but had no say.

"Tell her to get out of here," the blond-haired child said to her father, tears streaking her face. Enid was, at ten years old, slightly taller than me. I was the "her" she wanted out.

Why had I let Cyrus talk me into playing this role? I shouldn't have gone along but I did want the child to like me. I loved her father and hoped that, one day, I might be Enid's stepmother.

Cyrus hadn't thought this through. That was plain. His rationale for the deception seemed to make sense when we talked about it. I couldn't have predicted anything like this.

"You can't make me mind her, Papa," said Enid. "All my friends will laugh at me. She's a circus freak. You have to get rid of her. If you don't, I'll simply die of embarrassment."

Her. She. Why not call me "it," since that was how she saw me. The little girl didn't care that I was right there and felt the slap of each word.

I tried to look poised with my hand lightly resting on a sofa. Truth be known, I needed the furniture to steady the knees that threatened to collapse under me.

Cyrus didn't have any idea how to handle his daughter. How could he let her go on like that?

At last, he spoke. "Enid, you're being extremely rude. There's no question that Miss Lacey is staying. She's cancelled her other arrangements. I've already bought her a house to live in and have had it moved to the grounds."

"Why does she get the pretty little house?" Enid countered. "I'm your daughter. I should get it. Send her back to the hotel in town, Papa. Agatha can be my companion."

"Miss Lacey is staying," said Cyrus. "And what's this about Agatha? If that maid's been filling your head with nonsense, she does so at peril of the position she holds. For heaven's sake, Enid, Agatha's barely literate. It's Miss Lacey or back to boarding school with you."

"They threw me out."

"I'll find you another," said Cyrus. "If you wish to stay in Sarasota, with me, you'll be kind and polite to Miss Lacey and you'll obey her as you would me. Do you understand, Enid?"

"I'm your daughter," she yelled. "I'm supposed to be the important one. Not her. I'm supposed to be the one you buy presents for. How can you choose her over me?"

Her face bright red, the child turned and stomped out of the room.

"Enid!"

He stood there for the longest time, staring at the spot where Enid had been. I could see how angry he was but I also could tell that he had no idea what he should do next. It shocked me that a ten-year-old child could boss her father that way, and that her father would give in. My own Daddy would've whipped a child who so much as raised her voice and that would've been the end of it. For a moment, I felt a wave of disappointment about Cyrus's weakness.

Quickly enough, I realized how crazy that was. Cyrus was nothing like my Daddy and that's one reason why I loved him. He let his little girl push him around. Who was I to say this was so terrible? What would life have been like if my Daddy cared so much for me that he allowed me to stomp my feet, make demands and walk out? What kind of woman would I be now if I hadn't run from my Daddy's violence? I could take care of myself in ways most women couldn't. But, I could never risk standing up to my father as Enid had.

Seeing Cyrus at a loss, and realizing what it said about his gentle heart, I loved the man even more.

The maid, Agatha, stood right there on the other side of the high arched doorway. She pretended not to be interested as she dusted a credenza. I didn't believe it was any accident that she was in a convenient position to hear the argument. She turned and glanced at me, then turned away again, looking scared as a jackrabbit coming nose-to-snout with a hound. What brought that on? She grabbed at a cross she wore on a ribbon around her neck, muttering something while squeezing her eyes shut.

Lordy, it was me she was scared of. No wonder Enid pitched

such a fit. Who knew what crazy talk Agatha was filling the child's head with?

Would Cyrus fire the maid? I didn't think he'd have the heart, not if his daughter felt attached to the woman.

"My apologies, Miss Lacey," Cyrus addressed me formally as he did whenever someone was around. "She'll come around but I believe it would be best to postpone lunch. My driver will take you back up to your house in the meanwhile."

"No need, Mr. Parker. The walk is short." My legs wobbled just a bit as I scooted past the maid with what was left of my pride.

*

Flowering vines rambled along the ground and crowded out the lawn. Where trees stood in their path, the trailing greens pulled themselves upward by tendrils and climbed, sprouting orange, purple and yellow flowers along boughs already dripping with Spanish moss, this tangle making it impossible to distinguish one plant from the other.

As I got nearer my house, I saw that Cyrus had sent the gardener to plant some bushes out front.

"Good afternoon," I said to the old man who was stooped over a shovel by my doorway. "Are you putting in a garden?"

He straightened up, pushing his hand at the small of his back, then tipped the wide brim of a tattered straw hat. His wide smile deepened the crevices in his brown face. "Afternoon, ma'am," he answered. "Mr. Cyrus asked me to make the place look pretty. Got y'all some red hibiscus here for along the walkway, and flowering ginger for under the kitchen windows." He walked a bit and I followed.

"The most special plant, ma'am, is this one. That goes in the back, un'er the bedroom window." He picked up and held for my inspection what looked like a straggly twig with a cluster of stingy white flower buds.

He must have seen my disappointment.

"It don't look like much now but you jes' wait 'til it blooms. Mr. Cyrus said y'all was partial to the smell of night-blooming jasmine. I cain't blame you. There ain't another scent like it." He gave me a half wink as he set the plant back on the ground again.

The tiny white flowers by Cyrus's steps. Now I remembered. The blooms were no prettier in themselves than a field weed, but their perfume had to be the sweetest in the world.

I felt touched that Cyrus had asked the gardener to plant the bush where I'd be able to smell its flowers when they bloomed, at night. I thanked the man and walked inside.

My house. It really was mine now. No gamble of a sideshow impresario, no whim of his investors could take it from me. I had an appointment with an interior decorator the following Tuesday. I sat in the window seat in my bedroom, leafing through catalogs that the decorator had sent. I knew what I wanted. Nothing fancy or rich like the main house but cozy, with lots of lace. A rocking chair. A canopied bed. A carved settee for the parlor.

And, out in the garden, I'd ask Cyrus to have his workers build me a potting shed, with a tile roof to match the one on my house, a place where I could coax cuttings to grow into new life. And in the middle of my plantings, in view of the bay, I'd place a pretty wicker chair.

*

I fell asleep and woke up with a catalog open on my lap. The house was very dark. I heard creaking stairs. The door to my bedroom opened and I saw the silhouette of a man.

"Lucinda?" he whispered.

"Yes, Cyrus," I answered. "By the window."

He clicked on the overhead electric light and came to the window seat, kneeling beside me.

"I don't know how to apologize for my daughter's behavior," he said. "She lost her mother when she was hardly more than a baby. I'm all she has."

I ran my hand across his face and over his hair. "Don't ask me to come back to your house again, Cyrus. She hates me. It won't do any good to pretend I'm here as her companion."

"Lucinda, you must return to the house. I've told everyone you're Enid's governess. I—"

"Cyrus," I interrupted, more forcefully than I planned. "You've asked me to stay and I've said yes. We have a right to be together. Please don't ask me to help you justify your decision to others."

He covered my mouth with his, lifted me from the window seat and carried me to the bed. I didn't know if he was overcome by desire for me or the desire to not discuss this any more.

Later, when the first hint of dawn turned the sky from near-black to deep blue, I felt him rise from bed, and heard him walk down the stairs and out the front door.

From then on, that's how we spent our time together. He'd arrive in the dark after Enid was asleep, and leave before the servants arrived or his child, in the big house down the drive, awakened.

I didn't know how he thought he was going to work things out with Enid. The scene in the salon had me convinced that it couldn't be done. For as long as Enid lived under his roof, Cyrus and I would be living in our separate houses. She'd never accept me.

He must have known it, otherwise, why have my house moved to his estate? It wasn't, as I'd first thought, an extravagant impulse. He was being practical.

Enid wouldn't be a child forever though. One day, she'd be grown, she'd marry and begin a life of her own. Cyrus and I had our entire lives. I'd waited this long for happiness. Here it was, doled out in small bits but with the promise for more to come. I could wait a while longer for it to be complete.

37. MARISA

Brogan wore the same shabby white suit and red tie as when Marisa met him last. The Panama hat still lay on the desk. A well-chewed cigar smoldered in a square glass ashtray and perfumed the tiny space.

But it was what he held in his hands that Marisa focused on: a worn manila file folder, the corners of yellowed newspaper clips poking out through its sides.

"Horace's son asked me if I'd go to the home, pick up the boxes old Snake Boy had in his closet, send the family any letters or photographs, and throw away the rest. I saw these old clippings, I said, man oh man, I know who's gonna want to get her hands on this."

"May I see the file, Mr. Brogan?"

"Hold on hon'. You're gonna be pleased, I promise." He opened the folder just enough so that he could peek inside but not enough to reveal anything. One beefy hand clamping it closed, he laid it flat against his belly.

With his free hand, the showman grabbed his cigar and puffed. He leaned back in his chair, his expression wistful.

"They're all gone now. All the freaks, 'cept for Hugo the fat man, and he don't hardly count, what with half of America gone super-sized. Now it's the Snake Boy, may he rest in peace. Gib'town may not look like much to you now, but we used to have us a tight-knit little community here, the freak capital of the world. Did you know that? I mean, we had a giant for our fire chief, a constable who was a dwarf, and the Monkey Girl called out the Bingo numbers on Tuesday nights. That girl, I tell you, fur all up and down her face and body but, damn, she had the prettiest voice. I'd go to Bingo just for the pleasure of hearing her call out 'B 5.' She was something. They're not making any more like them, either. It's the end of an era, hon'."

"I wish I could have seen it, Mr. Brogan. I gather your file has something to do with my house?"

"Oh, right, the file," Brogan casually placed it back on the desk. "Seems ol' Horace had a thing for this Lucinda. Kept every article ever written about her, it looks like. Who'd've thought the old guy was such a romantic?"

"May I take a look?" she asked again, holding out her hand.

Brogan ignored the gesture. "Like I say, the son asked me to handle the odds and ends. He don't have any use for this stuff. Didn't even ask for a cut when I told him I had a buyer."

"You want me to pay you for a bunch of old newspaper clippings?"

"They ain't just any clippings, hon'. It's what the clippings say that makes 'em worth the money," he said as he coyly shuffled through the contents again.

She leaned in, hoping to get a glimpse, but all she could read was the name at the edge of a fragile yellowed page that poked out the side, The Sarasota Times, and the year, 1924. Brogan, noticing where her gaze had landed, tidied the folder contents so all pages were tucked neatly inside. He wasn't going to reveal so much as a headline for free.

"How much are you asking?"

The man chewed his stogie, leaned back in his chair, and blew three smoke rings in succession before answering. "How's five hundred sound?"

Marisa could have kicked herself for letting him see how eager she was. She reached for her briefcase, and got up from the chair.

"Thank you for your time, Mr. Brogan."

"You'll be back," said Brogan, pausing to puff on the cigar, "or you'll be sorry. Trust me, you're gonna want what I got here." He tapped a fat finger on the file.

*

Marisa drove to the historical society in Sarasota, parked, and marched to the back office. Myrtle was sitting at her desk, talking into her phone. She waved to Marisa, pointed to the phone receiver and made a jabbering motion with her fingers and thumb.

"Yes, I hear you," Myrtle said into the receiver, rolling her eyes for Marisa's benefit. "Yes, yes, so true. My, look at the time. Must dash off to a meeting. Yes, you, too. Good-bye." She feigned exhaustion as she hung up.

"Myrtle," Marisa said. "I need your help."

"Why, of course, dear, anything."

"Was there a paper called The Sarasota Times?"

"Long ago. They stopped publishing in the 1920s. I believe we have all the editions on microfilm but I'm afraid there's no alphabetized index. Is there something specific?"

"Yes but I don't know what." Seeing the confusion on Myrtle's face, Marisa said. "It might have something to do with my house. Just point me."

*

Advancing the wheel of the microfilm machine through about the 2oth edition of The Sarasota Times, Marisa stopped and scrolled back slowly. There, on a page from a 1923 article, was an artist's rendering of a sideshow-like attraction that the paper claimed would draw tourists from other cities on the peninsula. All the inhabitants — human and animal — were to be midget-sized. One of the buildings looked very much like her house. As it was just a sketch, not a photograph, it was hard to tell whether it was supposed to be her house.

She pulled some change out of her briefcase, fed it into the microfilm reader, and made a copy. This couldn't be what Brogan thought was worth $500.

An hour later, she had read so many old issues that her

eyes stung. She got glimpses of what day-to-day life must have been like in that time in the tales of raids on bootleggers' operations and the housewife-centric advice in something called the "Ladies Day" column but nothing that came close to what Brogan hinted was in Horace's folder. What made those clips so important?

Myrtle popped her head into the room. "Just checking whether you need me before I dash off to my meeting."

"You go ahead," said Marisa as she forwarded the microfilm to another page.

Myrtle peeked over Marisa's shoulder at her notebook. "Lucinda?"

"Lucinda Lacey," answered Marisa. "She lived in my house at one time."

"Wasn't that the name you gave your imaginary friend?"

"I don't remember her having a name."

"You were tiny. Your mother and I tried to figure out where a three-year-old would pick up such a moniker. We figured you heard it on Sesame Street."

Marisa just smiled in response as the historian wandered off, but her mind filled with static, like a radio tuned between stations. She grabbed the edge of the desk, feeling faint under the pressure of the words so casually spoken.

Memories flooded in, pushing back against the inchoate noise, yet these were too disjointed and vague for Marisa to make sense of them. She'd been little more than a toddler, a time when reality and magic hadn't yet been neatly sorted into their separate categories. She'd giggled as she skipped along behind another child in the upstairs hall of Aunt Enid's house, and cried when the child disappeared. Her mother, checking to see what had upset her, forbade further trips upstairs, seeming more distressed than Marisa at her daughter's story. She had insisted that Marisa imagined it all. And although Marisa had later sneaked back up the turret when her mom was busy with Aunt Enid, she hadn't been able to find the girl again. That, plus her mother's rebuke, eventually convinced the young

Marisa that her playmate had been a whimsy, fashioned in a lonely little girl's imagination.

But she couldn't process this now. It would only lead her down blind alleys. She had to stay focused.

Giving the wheel of the microfilm reader another turn, she forced herself to concentrate on the pages scrolling past.

She saw the photograph before the headline, the same one that was on one of the old postcards at the Ringling Circus Museum. The newspaper had cropped out the hang-dog-faced giant, the other half of the "world's most unusual couple," but Marisa knew, with as much certainty as she knew anything: This was Lucinda Lacey. She could have sketched that same dainty heart-shaped face from memory, those large sad eyes, and the high cheekbones. This was the face that coalesced out of a cloud as Marisa dozed. This was the woman who shared her home.

The caption identified her as Lucinda Darling. Obviously a stage name. Scrolling back up from the photo, she read the headline and subhead:

FIRE DESTROYS PARKER MANSION
Cyrus Parker and Employee Found Dead After Blaze; Investigators Ask, Was it Arson? Murder?

The story focused on the sole survivor of the fire, Enid Parker, Cyrus Parker's then-11-year-old daughter.

In the more florid style of the day, the reporter wrote of the sweet young child who lost her father and her home to the blaze. None of the servants was in the house that night, a fact that only an employee like Miss Darling would have known. Miss Darling, the reporter pointed out, had her own residence on the property, but it did not sustain any damage. Enid had confided some damning information to the reporter: her father planned to discharge Miss Darling from her position as Enid's governess. The child claimed that the former carnival and circus sideshow performer was suspected of theft and that her father, Cyrus Parker, agreed to allow her to stay on only until she could find other quarters. Based on statements by the child, and a long-time Parker employee, authorities believed the disgruntled ex-governess retaliated for her dismissal by setting the house ablaze, causing not only Cyrus Parker's death but her own.

Miss Darling apparently slipped and fell while trying to run from the burning mansion. She suffered a fractured skull, which killed her.

The employee giving the corroborating statement, a maid, Agatha Simpson, recounted that she had seen Lucinda Darling exhibit animosity toward the child in her care, little Enid, on more than one occasion. She told authorities that she had wanted to warn Mr. Cyrus but it wasn't her place to do so. While she wondered why Mr. Cyrus kept Miss Darling on as long as he did, she pointed out, by way of possible explanation, that Mr. Cyrus was a very kind man.

Marisa couldn't read more. She'd been spooked by the presence that inhabited the midget house and wanted it gone. The spirit of Lucinda Lacey apparently was just as intent on getting Marisa to leave what she still considered her house. But Marisa had never before considered the possibility that Lucinda's ghost might do more than attempt to scare her away.

All that changed now. By all accounts, Lucinda had killed out of spite when she hadn't gotten her way. If the risks of arrest and punishment hadn't deterred her when she was alive, what, Marisa wondered, could deter Lucinda in her present state? Rena had said it, and Marisa noticed it too: Lucinda was getting stronger.

*

Despite all that had happened, her mood lifted slightly when she pulled through the gate and saw John's Porsche parked next to the construction truck. His workmen, Steve and Jimmie, were standing on the flat part of the roof over the great room. John Guinness, in red golf shirt and black jeans, stood on the ground yelling up to them. "Torch down the edges of that patched area," he said. "Don't just caulk it. That sucker has to last."

She opened her trunk, pulled out the two red gas cans she'd filled at the Citgo station, left them by the lawn mower on the side of the garage, and walked over to John.

She couldn't remember when she'd been more relieved to see another human being. Could she really have hustled him out the door just the night before? All she wanted now was for him to put his arms around her and tell her he'd keep her safe.

John Guinness had done more to help her hang onto her house than anyone else. Who would have guessed it?

But he'd be leaving for Austin soon and she'd be completely alone. She couldn't ask him to stay and wasn't quite sure what she wanted from this man she barely knew, beyond the immediate comfort of his presence.

The one certainty was her uneasiness about being alone in the house after what she'd read.

"Hey, Marisa, the guys are almost done up there," John said, a big grin lighting up his face. "They patched things up so tightly, you should make it through the next dozen hurricanes. What do you say we celebrate tonight, after this job is officially done?"

She wanted to tell him what she'd discovered about Lucinda but she couldn't, not in front of his men.

Looking up at him with forced cheeriness, she answered, "Sure, let's celebrate. My treat — to thank you for all this. I'll take you to the best restaurant in Sarasota and nightcaps at Beachbum's. That is, if you haven't torn it down yet."

John laughed. "You're on. But I warn you, I can eat an awful lot when it's on the tab of a pretty lady."

"The sky's the limit. Wait. Revise that: the Mastercard limit's the limit."

She heard a car behind her, turned around and saw Detective Michael Ricci driving toward them.

With the other cars and the truck lined up next to the garage, Detective Ricci pulled his unmarked car to the side of the drive halfway onto a patch of grass.

Ricci stared at John Guinness as he walked over.

"Miss Delano," he said as he nodded. "Guinness, what are you doing here?"

"Me? I'm a friend of Marisa's," he answered. "What about you? Chasing criminals or you just like the view?"

"The view's pretty nice," Ricci said, letting his gaze linger on Marisa. "I'm following up on something," Ricci continued. "Why? You have some sort of interest here?"

John mockingly held up his hands as if to show he was unarmed.

Ricci nodded and looked down at the ground for a moment then, squinting at the sun in his eyes, looked toward the ladder Jimmie and Steve were climbing down.

He stared at John as if he meant to bore right through him. "I was at the city commission meeting when you went over there with your proposal."

John looked down at his own shoes. "Forget about that," said John. "It's off the table."

"You're not going to tell her?"

Marisa was still reeling from her discoveries about Lucinda. She couldn't get a fix on what was happening between these two men other than that they seemed hostile to each other.

John shook his head. "Go to hell, Ricci."

When Ricci spoke next, it was to Marisa, not John. "You know what eminent domain means?"

Marisa shrugged.

"Eminent domain," Ricci continued, "is when the government forces you to sell your property so it can be used for something else."

"Like for a highway?"

"Yeah, right," said Ricci. "Only sometimes, it's for another reason. Like when some developer convinces them your property is blighted. And, if they'd just let him tear down the quirky little house that's standing between him and the deep water dock he wants for his development they're looking at a big jump in tax revenue from the thirty, forty shiny new

McMansions he'll build once it's gone."

"Marisa" interrupted John. "I wouldn't do anything to hurt you."

Like hell. What an idiot she'd been. Nothing she believed was so. Nothing was safe.

Her pride forced her to hold herself together despite her body wanting to fold in on itself.

"Tell me the truth, John. What about eminent domain?"

"I talked to the city commissioners," said John, "but they turned me down. I don't see why Ricci's bringing it up now, except to make me look bad."

"Don't try to lay this off on the detective."

"You always knew I needed this parcel, Marisa. I went along with your fantasies but now it's time to get real."

"You bastard."

"Don't force me to foreclose. You'll end up with crumbs."

"Force you to foreclose? You don't have any rights, here, John. A guy named Nicholas Young holds the tax certificates. Harry convinced him to give me more time."

John shook his head. "Nicholas Young didn't want to wait. I bought him out. You're dealing with me, now, Marisa. Lord knows, I've been patient, but—"

"Leave," she said.

He didn't move and didn't answer.

"Get the hell off my property," she said, louder now.

"If that's the way you want it," said John, not looking at her.

Shaken but unwilling to let John Guinness see the effect he'd had on her, she rummaged in her purse, pulled out her key, unlocked the house, and pushed the door closed behind her without looking back.

38 . LUCINDA

I sat at the edge of the water, watching pelicans and seagulls glide on the wind. The birds seemed so carefree, diving for a quick bite when something silvery within the rippling green-gray water distracted them from their lazy flight. Then, they sailed upward again, letting the breeze carry them, with only an occasional flap of their wings to show that they had opinions on which direction they might want to steer next. The sun, low on the horizon, turned the sky lavender nearest the bay, then pink, the colors reflected against the sage of the wavelets. Above that, a mountain range-like array of plump clouds settled, fading from peach-glow bottoms to soft white tops.

Glancing behind me, I spied Agatha peering at me through a window in Cyrus's mansion. Anger flashed over her expression before she dropped her head and made the sign of the cross. I could see her muttering. Whether she was praying or saying a charm against the evil eye, it felt almost like an assault.

Ignorant woman. She treated my very existence like a curse. But, I reminded myself, she wasn't the first fool I'd ever encountered. Casper's Cavalcade had lured more than its share of the superstitious and we'd willingly taken their money. Agatha wasn't my problem. I turned away and walked back up toward my own house.

Once home, I changed into an old dress and apron, and

pulled on a pair of gardening gloves, determined to distract my mind from the only thing it wanted to focus on: the baby.

Tugging out the uninvited weeds did little to switch my attention from the struggle going on inside me.

How would I tell Cyrus?

Would he be happy? Ashamed? What about the chance that our child might be a midget, like me?

It could be years before we'd know for sure. I'd looked like an ordinary enough little girl until I was about four or five years old. Even after I stopped growing, nobody figured out for another few years that I would never have a growth spurt and catch up with other children my age.

Every man wants to have a tall, strapping son.

Could Cyrus love a son who might be no taller than me?

I figured I knew the answer but didn't want to look it full in the face. If Cyrus couldn't or wouldn't let on that we were lovers, it was foolish to expect him to admit he was the father of my child.

I was only two months along. Before I started to show, I had to make arrangements. And then, I'd tell Cyrus.

I'd write to Albert and ask to come back to the farm. He and his wife had been living there since Daddy passed away some months before. I was sure they would let me stay until the baby was born and weaned. After that? I couldn't guess. Could I re-join Casper's, travel the mud shows with a baby on my hip? My head hurt just thinking of it.

I pulled at a stubborn vine that had wound itself around the base of a ginger plant, not noticing the thorns until I felt the pinch and a red droplet puddled on my index finger. I stuck it in my mouth to soothe it. I was about to get the clippers out of my new potting shed when I looked up, and saw Enid strolling down the drive from the gate.

She was wearing a white and blue checked gingham dress with ruffles at the sleeves and collar, and shiny black buckled shoes. Her blonde hair was pulled back with a blue ribbon. She looked so innocent, a picture of the model child.

She stopped to pick up one of the large land tortoises I often saw ambling around the estate. She looked at it from the front, frowned and poked at its face with her finger so it pulled itself back into its shell. Then she carelessly dropped it on the ground and walked to me.

"What are you doing?" she asked.

"Weeding, Enid."

"We have people to do that," said Enid. "It's rather filthy work for someone who imagines herself to be good enough to socialize with my father."

I brushed my gloved hands against each other to shake off the dirt. "I like working in the garden, Enid. It helps me to think. I don't believe your father would look down on good honest work."

"What do you know about what my father approves of?" asked the child.

"You're right," I answered. "I can only speak for myself."

Enid seemed more agitated after I agreed with her than I imagine she'd be if I said she was wrong.

"Agatha says that freaks are of the devil," said Enid, looking through the bay window into my kitchen. "She says you put a spell on Papa. That's the only reason you're still here. I told her I'm not afraid of you. I'll make Papa fire you and give me the house, for me and my dolls."

I didn't answer her. Sooner or later she'd get bored and move along.

"Show me the inside," said Enid. "I want to see it. Now, please."

"Enid, I'll invite you in some day if you behave, but I'm busy in the garden now."

Her eyes squinted into slits in a face reddened with anger. How could I have thought she was pretty? Just then, she was the ugliest child I'd ever seen.

"You don't get to decide," yelled Enid. "My father owns this house and I'll walk right in any time I want."

I got up from weeding faster than I think I'd moved since

I last slid down the wire in the circus. I stood in front of the door, blocking her way.

"This is my home, young lady," I said. "Your father owns it, but only those I invite are welcome inside. You can't bully your way in through my door. Now you'd better go before I decide to tell him about all this."

She stared hard at me, then turned down the walk and onto the drive, stopping to shove the tortoise she'd passed earlier out of her way with her foot. The animal flipped onto its back, its paws grasping at the air.

Turning the animal right-side up, I set it in a grassy area, and watched it hustle away as quickly as its small green feet would carry it. Enid never slowed her pace.

"Don't even think of telling on me," she called over her shoulder in a sing-songy taunt as she walked down the drive toward the big house. "My father will never believe you. Besides, I'll tell him you slapped me, and then he'll have to send you away."

*

That night, as Cyrus came upstairs in the dark, I had bigger things on my mind than Enid. I had written of my delicate condition to Albert. Now there was no reason not to let Cyrus know. No reason except that I dreaded his reaction.

I hardened myself for the confrontation. When I saw him though, my heart melted. He kissed me all over my face: my nose, my eyes, my mouth, then ran his fingers up and down my arms and back. I felt so good, so safe in his arms, I didn't want to imagine being without him. Just let me have this night and then, I'll tell him, I thought. I knew though that if I said nothing tonight, it would be more difficult the next night and the next.

"Cyrus," I said. "There's something important I need to say."

"You look so serious, Lucinda," he answered, gently brushing a wisp of hair away from my eyes. "Can it wait just a moment? I have a little surprise that might coax a smile from your lips."

He reached his hand into the inside pocket of his jacket and pulled out a pale blue jewelry box tied with white ribbon.

"Open it."

I untied the bow and folded back the tissue paper. The necklace and earrings inside were the most beautiful I had ever seen. A large red oval cabochon, surrounded by at least a dozen sparkling clear-as-glass jewels, dangled from a gold chain.

"That jewel in the middle of the diamonds is a five-carat ruby and the ones on the earrings are two carats each. Do you like them?"

I was too stunned to speak. He placed the necklace around my neck and clasped it.

I found my voice but all I could say was, "Why?"

"First, tell me that you're pleased."

"Cyrus, I'm overcome. These are too extravagant."

"They're meant to be," said Cyrus, "in case anything ever happens to me. These pieces are very valuable. If you ever need to sell them—"

"Sell them? Cyrus, you've only just given them to me."

"These are a practical gift, Lucinda. If it ever becomes necessary, they'll bring enough to keep you comfortably for life, I should think. Now," he said, getting up and walking to the dressing table, "Let me show you the little hiding place I had the carpenters add to this room to store your valuables.

"You push under the vanity here," he said, getting down on his knees and pushing the wood panel under the right side of the built-in dressing table, "and it opens like a spring latched-door."

The boards were painted wood, no different from the rest of the wall. It was only when he pushed down at the bottom of the second to last wood strip where it met the corner, that its secret was exposed. The whole bottom of the panel flipped open on a hinge. I would never have guessed it was there.

"These are yours. No one can take them from you. There's also a bill of sale here in your name, to prove ownership." From the same inside pocket where he'd kept the jewelry box, he pulled out a piece of lined paper to show me before placing it in the hiding place in the wall.

Then he pushed the hinged panel closed again, and it looked as solid as the left side.

"Where will I wear such jewels?"

"You'll wear them for me," he said, grabbing me around my waist and pulling me toward him, "so I can watch the sparkle of diamonds reflected in your beautiful eyes."

For a moment, I'd hoped he meant to take me out to some grand ball, all aglitter in a floor-length silk gown and new jewels. But it was clear he planned to keep me and the jewels hidden.

*

It wasn't until after we made love that I had both the courage and the opportunity to say it. With my head next to his on the pillow in the dark, I whispered: "Cyrus, I am going to have a baby."

Whatever I expected, I didn't count on his silence. I wondered if he'd heard me.

"I'm going to have a baby, Cyrus."

He rolled over on his back, pulled the covers over himself and looked up at the ceiling. And I knew he had heard.

Feeling suddenly alone in this bed, I listened to the night sounds, the crickets' chirping punctuated every so often by the hoot of an owl and the soft rustle of wind-blown branches.

At last, Cyrus answered, his voice soft but clear.

"This changes everything."

Yes, there was no arguing about that.

"I have to do some thinking about this, Lucinda."

He got out of bed and began to dress.

"I have an early meeting with the board of trustees tomorrow. I'd better get back so I can catch a few hours sleep beforehand."

A sob tried to push its way out of my throat but I shoved it back down. It wouldn't do either of us any good for me to get all weepy in front of him.

"Cyrus?"

"Give me a little time," he said, kissing me on the forehead. "I promise you, no matter what, I'll always take care of you and the baby."

He'd take care of me and the baby. I knew what that meant.

He wouldn't marry me. He'd never bring himself to love our child. He was probably already considering how to hide us away, like the diamonds and rubies.

39. MARISA

Marisa had almost forgotten about Ricci when she heard a quiet knock on the front door.

"Hey, sorry to be the bearer of bad news," said the cop.

She took a deep breath to compose herself. "I needed to know and nobody else was going to tell me," she said. "That isn't the reason you're here though, Detective Ricci, is it?"

"I wanted to catch your tenant, Hinkle, so I could close out the file on your break-in. His car's parked by the garage, but he doesn't answer his door. For a guy with no job and no friends, he's a hard man to track down."

"He's out looking for a new place."

They stood in the doorway, neither one speaking for a long moment until Ricci broke the silence.

"Between Guinness and the Green Coalition, you're getting squeezed from both ends," he said.

"You seem to know more about my situation than I do."

"Yeah, well — cop, you know?"

Responding to the sympathy in his voice, she felt the tension in her shoulders begin to release.

"What I can't fathom is, why the charade?" she said. "Why did he pretend to help me? I mean, it wasn't even pretending. He did help. So why do all that if he planned to seize my house and tear it down?"

"You're over-thinking."

"What do you mean?"

"Guys like that, it's all about the head games, feeling like they're smarter than anybody else. That's their idea of fun. But look, I think you can reason with the Greens. If they're suing, it's because they figure you're working with Guinness."

"I dropped the papers off with Harry Scanlon. Maybe he can convince them to leave me alone."

"Scanlon's your lawyer?" Ricci again looked like a tough inquisitive cop.

"That's him. Why?"

He pulled the notebook from his inside pocket, scribbled something, tore out the page and handed it to her. "This is my home number," he said. "Call if you need a friend."

*

Alone now, Marisa took the path down to the bay, past the ruins of Cyrus Parker's marble steps. The tide was low, exposing a good six inches of razor-sharp barnacles that clung to what was left of a sea wall.

Sitting on a bench, listening to the gentle lapping, her pent-up emotions broke through the dam of her self-control. With nobody around but the pelicans, she didn't hold back. Quiet tears gave way to sobs.

After a few minutes, she'd poured off much of the frustration and sadness, enough to turn her mind to the options she had left. Why had she been so certain that fate wanted her to save the house? She'd ignored anything that contradicted that belief. But reality refused to be ignored.

Well, at least the house was fixed. And if Lucinda got to her before Guinness and the Green Coalition, all her worries were over.

It was all so impossible, she almost laughed.

Reaching into her jeans pocket, Marisa looked at the paper with Michael Ricci's phone number. Despite her usually lousy instincts about men, even she could tell he was different. She didn't have to wonder whether she should trust him. She knew it, just as she knew she could trust Kelly or Myrtle. Not that it mattered. He couldn't help with her predicament. Maybe nobody could.

*

Birdie had parked her big old tricycle next to the porch in front of her cottage. The small woman was on her knees, pulling weeds out of her little front yard garden, her long skirt gathered up in front to keep it off the dirt.

"I really ought to hire someone to tidy up this vegetation," said Birdie, dusting her hands against each other before offering her right one to Marisa in greeting. "I'm getting too old for bending and digging."

Marisa squeezed her hand and helped her to her feet. "Birdie, I wanted to apologize for yesterday. I think we misunderstood each other."

Birdie nodded. "Let's go inside. I can cook us up some cheese omelettes if you're free."

*

Birdie assembled the ingredients for the impromptu meal. Marisa took the whisk and whipped up the eggs while Birdie grated cheese. "More wine?"

She poured before Marisa could answer.

"I went to the historical center today," said Marisa, "and looked up some old newspaper clippings about my house."

Birdie said nothing. The only way Marisa could be sure she'd heard her was the change in the older woman's expression; it seemed to convey disapproval. She decided to push on anyway.

"Did you know that Cyrus Parker planned to fire Lucinda?" Marisa asked.

Birdie broke off a chunk from the block of cheese, popped it in her mouth, and chewed.

"What did you suppose that meant, 'Cyrus Parker planned to fire her'?" asked Birdie. "Fire her from what?"

"From her job. As Enid's governess."

Birdie took the egg mixture from Marisa and poured it into a pan on the stove. "Marisa, no offense, but do you believe everything you read in the paper? I mean, you of all people. You know how often reporters get it wrong."

Marisa knew. "People make mistakes. Reporters have to run with whatever they have at press time and make corrections later."

"Or never. Some mistakes never get corrected, right?"

"What about the story do you think is wrong?" Marisa asked.

Birdie placed the food on the table and motioned to Marisa to sit. "How about everything?" she said. "Oh, they probably spelled her name right. They got just about everything else so utterly wrong, it would be funny if it weren't tragic."

"Sorry I brought it up."

"No, I'm happy you did. I'll tell you what I can."

"I'm listening."

"All right. First off, Lucinda was never Enid's governess," said Birdie. "Oh, they used that as a cover story. Back in those days, and probably in these days too, respectable bankers didn't take up with circus midgets. Cyrus Parker did, indeed, however, take up with this one. They were lovers."

Marisa almost dropped her fork. It all made sense now. Harry had repeated the rumor about how the house burned down, but he hadn't known the most important detail. Lucinda was the jilted lover. Cyrus decided to end it and, out of spite, Lucinda set the fire.

Birdie shook her head. "Whatever you're thinking, Marisa, you're wrong," said Birdie. "She didn't kill him."

"Birdie, there are too many coincidences for it to have been accidental. It wasn't just Cyrus who died. Lucinda did too, when she tried to run away."

"Oh, I never said it was an accident," said Birdie. "Somebody set the fire. Lucinda got the blame. My father suspected the maid, Agatha Simpson. Back then, it was common for people to fear circus freaks. This Agatha seemed to believe Lucinda was giving her the evil eye."

"Enid told the police that nobody else was there. Just Enid, her father and Lucinda."

"Enid was eleven years old, Marisa. The maid had half-raised her since she was a toddler and she'd just lost her father. Who would she blame?"

"If the maid hated Lucinda, why didn't she set the midget house on fire? What possible reason would the maid have for burning down the main house and killing her employer?"

Birdie shrugged. "You want everything to fit neatly with your preconceptions, Marisa. People don't always behave so rationally."

"It's too pat. Like saying, the butler did it."

"Think what you like. Lucinda didn't kill him."

"How can you be so sure?"

"Because she was pregnant. Cyrus sent my father two train tickets and a letter asking for my aunt's hand in marriage. At the wedding, which Cyrus planned as a surprise for Lucinda, Albert Lacey was going to give the bride away."

Marisa kept her thoughts to herself. Cyrus may have planned all that but, like Birdie said, nobody told Lucinda. Lucinda was a soon-to-be mother, unwed at a time when that held greater stigma. She must have heard the rumors that everyone else had: Cyrus meant to throw her out. Tragic. Birdie gave it the right label but had formed the wrong conclusion. Birdie's story provided the last piece of the puzzle: Lucinda's motive.

40. Lucinda

We didn't talk about the baby again, except in vague ways, although it was all I could think about and, I imagine, what was on Cyrus's mind most when he saw me.

Cyrus began coming to my house later in the night, and there was liquor on his breath when he got here, brandy, I think, though I couldn't be sure.

I decided I would leave in a month. I didn't tell him what I planned. I wanted my last few moments of happiness. Maybe I was being selfish but I knew, once I was gone, I wouldn't see him again. These last weeks would have to last me forever.

I changed my mind several times about what to do with the jewelry. I'd take it, I thought. I'd be practical, just like Cyrus said he wanted me to be when he gave it to me. I'd sell it and use the money to raise our child. And then, the next instant, I decided I couldn't. Those rubies were his, not mine, and if he couldn't acknowledge us, his lover and his child, well, then we wanted nothing from him.

Except, I couldn't ask Albert and his wife to support me and the baby. They were family but they weren't wealthy. Cyrus was. So, I would take the jewelry.

Or leave it.

I didn't want to have to choose. I wanted Cyrus to tell me how happy he was, how he was planning for us to have a fancy wedding and inviting all of Sarasota and half of Tennessee, how he'd treasure our baby no matter what.

But I knew I couldn't expect any of that.

So, I tended my garden and walked by the water in the daytime, and waited for his steps on the stairs at night.

A few days later, still avoiding the only topic that mattered, he told me about an argument he'd had with Enid. He planned to send her back to boarding school, but farther away, to Switzerland this time. It was called a finishing school. They taught young ladies the refined manners they would need to be accepted into society. She didn't want to go.

That's all he said about it, and I didn't ask him for details.

I sensed that this decision was as much about me as about her. He hadn't yet found a way to tell his daughter what was between us. He'd rather send her half a world away than face her reaction when I began to show.

*

He didn't come the following night. I watched out my window as the sky grew darker and filled with stars. It seemed he'd abandoned me already.

"Damn you to hell, Cyrus," I yelled, knowing that the main house was too far away for anyone to hear me. "Damn you, damn you, damn you. How can you leave me like this? I hate you."

Love you.

I punched his pillow, held it, wept into it, exhausted my fury and sadness into it, and curled my body around it.

Hate you.

I wasn't aware of falling asleep and I can't say what woke me, maybe the yellow-orange glow that flooded through my windows, masquerading as the dawn.

Sitting up, I saw sparks, like 4th of July rockets, trace arcs across the sky. The top of a tall palm caught a cinder and flared like a giant matchstick.

I got up and looked out the French doors to see where the fire was coming from. Oh, Lordy me, it was Cyrus's house.

I ran down the stairs, out my front door, and down the trail toward the main house by the waterfront.

Fumes scratched my throat, threatening to close it. My eyes stung but I could see my way by moonlight and the fire.

Like something solid and alive, smoke wrapped itself around the south side of the house and pounded against its outer walls. Fingers of fire reached through the shattered windows, throwing shadows that made the palm trees seem to shimmy and jump.

Waves of heat blew across my hands and face. Tears poured down my cheeks, not just from my fear for Cyrus and his daughter, but from the bitter air that pushed back at me.

"Cyrus," I yelled, but nobody answered. Gravel dug into my feet.

I held one arm in front of my mouth and nose, trying to breathe through my nightdress's thin cotton sleeve. The closer I got, the more the fire and smoke slowed me down.

The big house's front door hung open, like a mouth gaping at the violence being done to it.

Something like an explosion hit the back of my skull. Bright blue light filled my sight. I couldn't feel myself any more.

I floated above.

Yet when I looked down, I could see myself, still as the gravel on the ground.

Hands took hold of my ankles. I watched without emotion as my attacker heaved the empty body that once was mine down the path.

I felt lighter than a soap bubble, bouncing on the air. Colors appeared sharper than I remembered them being on the sunniest day.

Almost as if I had a motor inside me, I got tugged upward into a spinning tunnel. I was heading into a light, whiter than I would have thought possible. I knew, without knowing how, that I was at the border of death. I wasn't scared. I wanted to cross into that peaceful place.

And then I thought: Cyrus. I couldn't leave him. He was

still in the house. I had to get to him before the flames did. I struggled against the pull of the light and the tunnel let me go, disintegrating into nothing, while I tumbled in freefall.

41. Marisa

Marisa walked into Harry's office. "Is Mr. Scanlon back in town?" she asked the receptionist.

"He got back late yesterday. But he has meetings all day."

"Ask him if he can squeeze me in for five minutes. I'll wait right over there." Marisa pointed to a sofa in the reception area.

Marisa had no money to retain Harry but she counted on his past relationship with her mother to give her some leverage. He had to understand that her financial situation, although dire, was temporary, and she'd make it up to him. It wasn't her style to pressure acquaintances for favors but, damn it, she didn't have a choice. If Harry could just hold off the Green Coalition lawsuit, and arrange a short-term loan with one of his "private money" sources, maybe it could all still work out. She'd pay the liens with private money. That would get Guinness off her back. Then she could apply for a mortgage once she found a real job, and pay off the private lender.

She paced the office's small reception area as she went over her plan, point by point. She saw no serious gaps in logic. With luck and a bit of help from Harry, it would work.

That still left one major problem: Lucinda Lacey. Would it be safe for her to stay in her home? She shook the notion from her mind. Deal with what it's possible to deal with. As disturbing as the revelations about Lucinda were, they were irrelevant if she couldn't save the house.

Several people came through the front door, sat on the other chairs and sofas near her, got announced by the receptionist, went into the office and came out again. She watched the last of these exit, a stocky man in yellow Hawaiian floral shirt and beige Bermuda shorts. The waiting room was empty. She approached the receptionist again.

"Does he know I'm here?"

"I'll remind him," said the young woman, picking up the phone.

*

"Marisa," Harry greeted her with a hearty smile as he came through the door into the reception area. "Sorry you had to wait."

Just seeing him relieved some of the tension she'd been feeling. It was all going to work out, she told herself. It had to.

Instead of ushering her into the conference room, he led her to his office to a seat facing his desk, walked in behind her, and shut the door.

"Did you get a chance to read the subpoena I dropped off from the Sarasota Green Coalition?"

Harry nodded as he sat behind his desk.

"They can't sue me for something I didn't do, can they?"

"Anyone can sue for anything."

"Harry, I'm going to need your help with this."

"You've got it. But, first you have to agree to follow my advice," he said, pushing a document from his side of the desk to hers. He placed an elegant gold Cross ball point pen on top of it. "Sell."

She looked at the heading of the document: "Contract for Sale of Real Estate."

Buyer and seller were clearly typed out on the page. "You're representing Guinness? Against me?"

"I work for a lot of people, Marisa," said Harry. "I can assure you, though, I have only your best interests at heart."

"But I trusted you."

"Then, trust me now," Harry said. "It took all my negotiating

270

skills to convince Guinness to offer you that," he pointed to the contract, "instead of filing this." He pulled another document off the top of a pile on his desk, and slid it to her side of the desk. The second document started off with the same heading, "CIRCUIT COURT OF SARASOTA," as the subpoena she'd been served in the Green Coalition lawsuit. Underneath that, it read, "Application for Tax Deed Sale."

Marisa scanned the court document. It listed John Guinness as the petitioner and Marisa Delano as the delinquent party to be foreclosed upon for defaulting on tax payments.

"The men involved here have money and influence. If a girl like you tries to get in their way, they'll bulldoze right over you. Take the money. You won't be sorry, Marisa, I promise you." He tried to hand her the pen again.

She pulled away, the noise in her head layering a track of static over Harry's words so that none of it made sense.

"I need time to think," she said and got up to leave.

"Here, take the contract with you." Harry pulled a large brown envelope from a desk drawer, and placed the document inside before handing it to her. "Guinness and his partners would only agree to seventy-two hours. After that, I'll be forced to file this." He picked up the "Application for Tax Deed Sale," gave her a sad smile, the sincerity of which she couldn't gauge, and dropped it back on his desk.

*

Marisa drove to Gaia to see the one friend who was always there for her. Not that Kelly could offer more than a shoulder but she needed to talk to someone she trusted.

"He's helping Guinness steal your house?"

"Guinness and his partners. And that," Marisa said, reaching into her briefcase and pulling out a handful of pages, "may not even be the worst of it."

"My 'invisible house-guest' isn't just prone to rattling chandeliers and spooking cats. At one time, at least, she was capable of violence. For all I know, she still is." She showed Kelly the printout of one of the 1924 articles about Lucinda

Lacey.

Kelly skimmed it, handed it back, and reached out to squeeze Marisa's hand. "Are you sure you want to stay out there, knowing this?"

Marisa slumped. "Doesn't matter what I want, does it? It's not my decision any more."

"Guinness will tear down the house."

"Maybe it was always meant to be this way. Maybe this is fate's way of waking me from my illusions," Marisa said, fingering the article. "What if it isn't safe for anyone to live in the house?"

*

Leaving Kelly at Gaia, Marisa headed back to the midget house. She shouldn't have been so quick to unpack, she thought to herself. At least she still had all her cartons. All she'd have to do is pile everything back into boxes and — what? She wasn't sure where she'd go now. She'd given up her apartment. There had to be a hotel in town that allowed cats. Her bank account was nearly empty but she still had her Mastercard and, if she signed the contract to sell to Guinness, she'd have money to pay the bill by the time it came due. She'd have more than enough, come to think of it, for that and who knew what else? She could start over.

Still, it seemed so wrong to give in. Never mind that she had no choice. She was beaten. She knew it. More than beaten, she felt shell-shocked.

All the hope, the excitement, the belief that she was meant to save something precious and what had she accomplished? Nothing.

She turned through the gateway and headed down the drive.

There was her house, awaiting her arrival. She felt something like a rebuke from the cosmos, although she knew it came from within. She again felt with a strange certainty that this was more than a compilation of timber, concrete and glass. This was a friend — a friend she'd let down.

I'm sorry, little house. I did my best.

It just wasn't enough.

Otto's Camry was parked in front of the garage. She thought she should stop to tell him. At least then, he could go to Guinness and cash in his squatting rights to the garage apartment. But it would mean explaining what had happened and she couldn't do that. Not right now. Guinness would be in touch. Let him break the news. She turned to walk to her own house instead.

The front door was ajar.

She pushed it, feeling dread but unable to stop herself from walking inside. The back door, too, was open.

She looked around for Murphy. Surely he would again forego adventure for the safety of the indoors. In a fog, she walked from room to room, calling his name.

"Murphy," she tried to keep the panic out of her voice. If he sensed she was afraid of something, he'd never show himself. "Murphy, please. I'm in no mood for this."

Where was he? She wasn't willing to believe he could be gone. It would be too much to bear.

"Murphy?" she called one more time and then it all hit her like a mountain collapsing on her head and she crumpled to the floor of the great room, the pent-up sobs forcing their way up from her gut as if determined to turn her inside-out.

At the edge of her vision through the open back door, she saw movement. Her tears distorted the view. She couldn't be certain but it might have been a small animal, flashing across the path to the ruins of the main house. She wiped her eyes and ran to the door.

"Murphy?"

She hesitated at the threshold.

"Murphy, here sweetie." She saw no trace of whatever it might have been. She wasn't going to take chances though.

Opening the fridge, she grabbed a few slices of turkey cold cuts, and raced out the back toward the ruins.

"Murphy, goodies. Goodies, Murphy."

*

The sun hung lower in the sky. She hadn't found the kitty in the fifteen minutes she'd spent searching. She laid a few bits of turkey on the ground just off the path on either side of the drive, then walked a few feet away and laid a few more.

Behind her, footsteps crunched down the path. Otto was half running, half-walking toward her.

Talk about making matters worse. If Murphy was out here, he'd never show with Otto around.

"Marisa," Otto called, out of breath. "Come quickly."

"Otto, this isn't a good time."

He melodramatically pointed with his left hand back toward the house, his right hand pulled awkwardly behind his back.

"The garage," he said, lower lip trembling, "it's on fire."

"Holy mother—" She looked up the path and saw smoke seeping from the windows of his apartment. "Did you call 911?"

"How could I?" he whined. "The phone's in the apartment."

"For chrissakes, Otto, why didn't you go get my phone?"

A cascade of thoughts bumped into one another as they flooded her consciousness. Was the building insured? Yes, it had to be, Harry would have seen to that. What would the insurance pay if it was destroyed? Enough to pay the liens? Maybe. So, maybe it wasn't the worst that could happen. Otto's life estate was going up in smoke. And the insurance money might be enough hold off the wolves.

She shook all that from her head. First, she had to call 911; then, she'd see whether this was an answer to her prayers or an even bigger disaster.

She passed Otto and kept on going. It struck her as strange that he hadn't moved but she was too preoccupied to focus on why. In that same instant, Marisa got a whiff of something stronger than the smoke, a chemical odor. She glanced back at Otto. Why was he just standing there?

Sensing something deserved her attention, maybe even more than the fire, but not registering what or why, she kept going.

She felt shock more than fear when he grabbed her from

behind. Otto's large moist hands. That odor. Awful. She tried to wrestle away but his grip on her neck and face were surprisingly strong. She gulped for air. And weakened. The chemical simultaneously chilled and warmed her throat, clouding her mind, and dimming her vision. Otto, what are you doing? She wanted to say. The words wouldn't come. Her brain and mouth had somehow come disconnected.

This is it, she thought, surprise her last emotion. This is how I'm going to die. She fell forward in what seemed like slow motion and hit the ground.

He followed her down, still covering her mouth and nose with the chemical-soaked handkerchief, forcing it on her: breathe this or nothing.

She gasped for life, aware that it was probably death.

42. Marisa

Don't let go

Marisa's arms felt like they were being yanked out of their sockets. Something dug into her wrists. Fingers. Nails. It took a moment for her to rouse enough from the chemical-induced stupor to comprehend: He was dragging her.

She squinted her eyes opened for a second. Sticky red blood poured in under her eyelids. The pounding in her head competed with Otto's voice. Her mind wanted to let go again, drift back to where the hurt wasn't. Dream images flitted into her mind, competing with consciousness.

Focus, she told herself. If she let the weariness win she was dead.

"... would have been best for both of us. I didn't want to have to do this."

She concentrated on his voice, for clues to what might be her chances for survival, assuming survival were still possible.

"You only got Enid's house because of that tricky lawyer. He got to Enid after her mind started going."

The gravel scraped her waist and back through the shreds of her shirt. She could feel blood trickle down under the waistband of her jeans. Her raw skin felt like it was being etched with acid.

Focus on the pain. Pain was good. Pain was consciousness.

Hope. Focus.

His monologue flowed on like a river, "...a trick I learned from Enid. That's how she got the property. Everyone blamed the midget. Who would suspect a sweet little girl?"

Birdie ... was ... right? Half right. Not Lucinda. But not the maid, either. Enid.

She spiraled back down into a chemically induced daze. Disjointed dream images galloped through her mind. Lucinda swinging on a trapeze, leaping off to fly through the air. Rena, red-lipped, plunging knives into the ground, cackling like a lunatic. Birdie, pumping away on her tricycle's pedals, beckoning Marisa to hop onboard, flying half off the ground, a gust of wind sweeping them up into the sky, faster, higher, then dropping them. Tumbling, circling down.

A wave of nausea jolted her back to awareness.

Heat. The crackle of fire fast devouring dry old joists and timbers. A familiar, vaguely chemical smell. Not like on the handkerchief.

Gasoline.

He used it to set the fire. Marisa had filled those gas cans for him. They'd say she set the fire to collect the insurance. Died by accident. She'd take the blame. Just like Lucinda.

Lucinda. Sorry, I believed — Am I going to die like you?

He dropped her on the drive. She heard his shoes walk a short distance. The old garage door screeched a complaint, resisted his attempt to open it along every inch of its track.

If only she could resist like that. With the rough ground no longer tearing at her skin, it seemed that it would be so easy to fall asleep, just let go and let it happen, no more pain, no more worry.

No. She bit the inside of her cheek. *Have to stay alert.*

And then what? Couldn't run. Could barely move. All she wanted was... a ... little ... rest...

She bit down hard again, on her cheek, on her tongue. Tasted blood. *Good. Stay awake.*

Heat washed over her body like a wave. Marisa squinted

open her eyes, lifted her head slightly and willed away the vertigo that small act caused. His back was toward her; he still struggled with the garage door.

Just inches from her left arm by the side of the drive was the handle of a hammer. It must have been left behind by John Guinness's workmen. Reaching her hand toward it without moving the rest of her body, she just touched it. She couldn't grab hold. Millimeter by millimeter, she tugged at it with a single finger, then two. Would he hear it scrape on the ground? See her arm move? He seemed preoccupied. She had to try. Grasping it now with all the fingers of her left hand, she slowly shoved it under her left forearm. Didn't completely hide it. It would have to do.

Her eyes on Otto, she creeped her right arm across her body, felt for the hammer's handle, and let her fingers rest there.

Flames licked out of the apartment windows; yellow-orange cinders rained on the ground. The wind blew from the south, threatening to sweep the fire across the drive and into the house.

She squinted quickly in that direction, thought she saw something in the shadows: the movement of a long skirt on a tiny feminine frame, in the open doorway of the house.

Birdie! Was she crazy? If she tried to stop him, Otto would kill her too.

He started to turn. She closed her eyes, feigning unconsciousness.

Wait, she told herself. Unable to see, she couldn't be sure of her timing. Otto's footsteps came closer. She felt his presence before he reached her, almost as if his rage had a form of its own, preceding his physical body.

Marisa sensed him stooping down to grasp her arms, ready to drag her into the fire. She gripped the hammer and swung backwards blindly, as hard as she could. She felt the impact vibrate through her own body as it hit him across both shins. He fell backward, shrieking his fury and pain.

Vertigo forced her head back to the ground but, in that

second, she saw a blur of movement at the door of the house. Using every speck of energy she had left, she screamed, "Run Birdie or he'll kill us both. Run and get help."

Run and get help. Run and... run... run...

She couldn't be certain any more whether she was saying it out loud. She could no longer hear herself, no longer feel herself. It was as if she were engulfed by a black cloud.

All that had been light around her got crowded out by blackness. Blackness poured in on the periphery of her consciousness, crowded out the fire, crowded out the smells, the sounds, crowded out the fear, the pain.

43. MARISA

STILL HERE?

How long Marisa was swept up into the blackness, she couldn't guess. It was as if she had left this plane of existence and hadn't yet entered another.

Then, she saw a white light.

And a red light. And a white light. Quickly alternating, flashing, abrasively bright lights, powerful enough to pierce her awareness even through closed eyelids.

Opening her eyes, she looked around. The lights were spinning on top of red trucks, white trucks, black and white cars. Police. Firefighters. She heard a whooping noise — a quick blast from a siren.

Somebody yelled orders into the crowd that had gathered. "Get that ambulance over here. Pull it in next to the fire marshal's truck."

She thought she recognized the voice, but couldn't place it. The world seemed to spin, a three-quarters clockwise turn.

Marisa closed her eyes again. Her head hurt. Slowly, she noticed that other parts of her hurt: her arms, her back, her face, her legs. She had never before felt so grateful to ache all over. If she was still alive, that meant that Birdie was too. She had gotten away, called for help. Marisa felt a serenity that seemed at odds with the manic scene that surrounded her.

She let her hands explore the space beneath her. She was prone on a padded board. Men in dark uniforms prodded her. One poked a needle into the crook of her right arm. She tried to sit up but only managed to get one side an elbow's height off the stretcher. A mask covered her nose and mouth. She pulled it off with her free hand.

"Hey, what do you think you're doing?"

That voice — now she recognized it: Detective Michael Ricci.

"Lie back now and rest," he said. "The EMTs here are going to take you to the hospital."

"I don't want to go to the hospital. I want to lie down in my own bed."

"Let them check you out," he insisted. "If you're all right, I'll come down myself, pick you up and bring you back home, okay?"

*

She half-swooned on her way to the bathroom in her hospital room but held herself steady along the wall. Bandaged and stitched in a half dozen places, the image that looked back at Marisa from the mirror resembled something out of a bad horror movie. The young doctor who checked her in the morning wanted her to stay another night but she said no. He told her she had a mild concussion, which wasn't surprising after getting her head banged around as Otto dragged her. Her skin was scraped raw across much of her back. But nothing was broken. Nothing that required 'round the clock care, from what she could determine.

Detective Ricci came to visit and found her dressed and demanding that the nurse call her a cab. He, too, tried to persuade her to stay, but failing that, insisted on driving her home himself. He kept asking how she felt during the drive home. She answered on automatic pilot, "I'm fine," not quite focused and certainly not fine, but feeling stronger, in a way, thanks to his presence. By the time they came to the gateway to her house, she really did feel almost as well as she'd claimed she was.

The house, too, had survived another day. Seeing it again was almost like getting a jolt of caffeine.

Cinders from the garage fire had landed on her convertible, burned through its top and sizzled right on into the car's interior. Somehow, seeing the wreck of her car didn't dampen Marisa's mood. Coming so close to death, and beating it, made the usual concerns feel trivial. She felt surprisingly free.

Ricci offered his arm and led her to the door. Her friends waited inside. Claude hugged her as she entered. Birdie offered a cup of tea.

"Tea?" said Kelly, walking toward Marisa with Murphy in her arms. "I think she's probably ready for something with a tad more kick."

"No, tea sounds perfect," said Marisa. "Thanks. And Birdie, I can never thank you enough. You saved my life."

Birdie looked at Marisa oddly. "I did no such thing."

"But I saw you. When Otto was dragging me to the fire."

"The concussion has you a little confused," insisted Birdie. "I came when I heard the sirens. The EMTs were already working on you."

Some guy driving down Bay Shore saw smoke and called 911," said Ricci. "We found you and Hinkle lying on the ground. He was dead, and you were out cold."

"Otto's dead?"

"As a door knob. We figure, when the fire got out of control, he panicked, and his heart just stopped. It happens like that sometimes."

No, that had to be wrong. Birdie had been there. Marisa had seen her. She'd begged her to get help.

Her memory replayed the event: what had she seen? A small figure in the shadows, just inside the door.

Her exhausted mind wasn't yet willing to consider the alternative. Instead, Marisa reached for Murphy before he could wiggle out of Kelly's arms. "Where did you find him?"

"In the play room," said Kelly. "This was stuck on his new collar." She dangled an earring from her thumb and index finger. It was a large red stone, set off with a few white stones.

"That a garnet?" asked Marisa.

"Marisa, I carry garnets at Gaia. This is no garnet," said Kelly, dropping the earring in her palm. A red as intense as that of last night's emergency lights caught the sunlight pouring through the bay window. The star pattern at its center seemed almost to glow.

"What you have here is a perfect star ruby, I'd guess at least two carats, surrounded by diamonds," said Kelly. "And there's more where that came from, upstairs, in a secret panel under the vanity. Wait until you see the necklace. You're rich."

Epilogue

Two weeks later

Marisa

Marisa slid carefully off the bed. She still ached all over. She looked in her mirror, turning her face left and right. The scratches had healed without scarring. The swelling was gone but remnants of bruises still blotched her face in shades from blue-black to yellow-green.

Kelly looked through the closet for the clothes Marisa asked her to find, a soft white gauze skirt and lavender scoop-necked shirt.

"Jeez. Michael's coming over and I still look like bride of Frankenstein." She stared at the image in the mirror and patted more foundation on her skin.

"It's Michael now? Not Detective Ricci?"

"He's talking to the leader of that environmental group. He thinks he can get them to drop the lawsuit."

The Sarasota Green Coalition's lawsuit was one of the last hindrances left to Marisa's peaceful enjoyment of her home. Kelly had arranged for Sotheby's to sell the jewelry in an upcoming auction. Meanwhile, the bank had loaned Marisa enough money against its value to pay off Guinness with interest and cover the current year's taxes to Sarasota. The auction house estimated the value of "Cyrus Parker's treasure" — which, according to the receipt they discovered in the hiding place under the vanity was actually Lucinda Lacey's treasure — at more than a million dollars. The midget house was finally hers, free and clear. And she'd have enough left over to live comfortably for the foreseeable future.

"So, what's with the detective?" asked Kelly. "He got a thing for gopher tortoises?"

Marisa smiled. "I think he likes me," she said and patted more make-up over the bruises.

"Here, give me that concealer," said Kelly. "You're doing it all wrong." Kelly dabbed the beige cream gently over Marisa's black-and-blues and smoothed it with her index finger.

*

Michael Ricci held out a sheaf of legal-sized pages. "Just sign this agreement, giving the environmental group right of first refusal if you ever want to sell, and they'll dismiss the lawsuit."

"You realize, I'm never going to sell."

"Doesn't matter. They're buying up Guinness's stake in the rest of the estate."

"After what he put me through, he's selling? Just like that?"

Ricci explained that the rest of the property wasn't worth as much without the piece that Marisa owned. "Cyrus Parker built his house on the one part of the north Sarasota bayfront with water deep enough for big sailboats." Without access to the deep water, Guinness couldn't develop a marina. And without a marina, he couldn't sell the houses he built at the prices he'd planned. His partners backed out. Guinness was lucky the Greens were willing to take the land off his hands, even for half what he'd paid.

"So the scrub jays and tortoises are safe?"

"As long as they stay in the neighborhood, their home is as secure as yours."

A car came down the drive. Kelly looked out the window.

"Rena's here."

"Not again, Marisa," said Ricci. "Haven't you had enough of this spirit stuff?"

"Lucinda's still around, Michael. She saved me and I'm grateful. Doesn't mean I want to share my house with her. Rena thinks she can help her cross over."

"This," said Ricci, "is more weirdness than I can handle. Catch you later." He leaned down to kiss Marisa and passed Rena as she walked in through the front door.

*

LUCINDA

All night long, they've been calling me, telling me to go into the light.

Lordy me, where would they have me go? There isn't any light; nothing at all since the night that Cyrus died. The night that I—

They say my loved ones wait on the other side.

If only that were so.

Cyrus crossed over without me long ago.

Mama is with Daddy.

No one waits for me.

I would have had a child, if I'd survived a little longer. All I had, in the end, was this house. Others held the deed, but the house and I know it's mine.

When it's gone, I don't know what will become of whatever I am. For now though —

"Lucinda. We know you're confused, but it's time to find peace. Step into the light."

Wait. I think I see something. A pinprick of white?

"Let go, Lucinda. There's nothing keeping you here."

It looks like a tunnel.

"Nothing more you have to do."

Something's in there but the light is too bright.

"Albert's waiting on the other side."

Albert? It is you. I can see you. I hear you inside my head. And Mama?

Mama. You waited for me. If only Cyrus— Must I miss him forever?

"Just a little farther, Lucinda. Don't stop now. Keep going, over the threshold, all the way into the light."

No, it's too bright. Blinding. Mama, can you make out what that is at the end? Oh, Lordy me.

Cyrus!

ACKNOWLEDGMENTS

More people helped with this book than I probably can ever thank. Gary Sledge, my editor at Reader's Digest, planted the seed for the story. My fellow writers, Sarah Wernick, Kathryn Lance, and Claire Tristram, critiqued the work at various stages and offered helpful insights. Murphy, my darling kitty, opened my eyes to things that went bump around the house that I couldn't see but that he could. Thanks, too, to Lauren Silver, my wonderful friend, who convinced me to move forward with the book's publication. And to Oscar Trugler, whose artistry in creating the cover design perfectly captures the mood of the tale.

The house I live in, known locally as "the midget house," although not a living, breathing being, inspired me as I sought its origins.

Circus historian Bob Horne, past president of Showfolks of Sarasota, a society that exists to benefit circus people, was incredibly generous with his time and documents. Bob supplied much of the detail about traveling shows of the early twentieth century as well as some of the interesting insights about behind-the-scenes quirks of circus life.

Circus performers Margie Geiger (Wallenda), Giovanni Zoppe (Nino), Arthur Grotefent (Wallenda), Aaron Garcia, Marco Lorenzo Robles, Kelsey DelMonte, Trevan DelMonte, and others patiently explained their acts to me. Some graciously put up with my nosing around and peppering them with questions as they set up their gear and rehearsed for their circus performances.

I also have to acknowledge the assistance of several organizations including Showfolks of Sarasota, the Ringling Circus Museum, and the Sarasota Historical Society.

Thank you all. This book couldn't have been written without you.

ABOUT THE AUTHOR…AND THE HOUSE:

Anita Bartholomew is a former long-time contributing editor to Reader's Digest and the co-author of Dr. Yvonne Thornton's award-winning memoir, Something To Prove (Kaplan 2010).

In 1999, Anita bought a house in Sarasota, Florida, one of two near-identical structures standing side-by-side that, according to an unverified local legend, were built for midgets who performed in the Ringling Bros. Barnum & Bailey Circus. Neighbors hinted that her new house might be haunted, a notion Anita shrugged off. After a few odd occurrences—the doors she locked upon leaving were hanging wide open on her return; and her cat seemed to interact with someone who wasn't there—she began to dig for answers about the house's history. She questioned historians, circus experts and local circus people, and searched rare old books about midget villages, sideshows, and carnivals for clues to the house's origins. Although still a mystery, her imaginings of what the house's history could have been form the basis of this, her first novel.